Maggie's Secret
By Beryl Lowe

Maggie's Secret

Copyright © 2016 Beryl Lowe

All rights reserved. This book or any portion thereof may not be reproduced or used in any manner whatsoever without the express written permission of the publisher except for the use of brief quotations in a book review or scholarly journal.

The views, content and descriptions in this book do not represent the views of Anixe Publishing. Some of the content may be offensive to some readers and they are to be advised.

Objections to the content in this book should be directed towards the author and owner of the intellectual property rights as registered with their local government.

All characters portrayed in this book are fictitious and any resemblance to persons living or dead is purely coincidental.

First Printing: 2016

ISBN 978-0-9574523-9-8

Published by

Anixe Publishing Ltd
77 Ridgeway Avenue
Gravesend, Kent DA12

www.anixepublishing.co.uk

Ordering Information:
Special discounts are available on quantity purchases by corporations, associations, educators, and others. For details, contact the publisher at the above listed address.

All trade bookstores and wholesalers: Please contact Anixe Publishing Ltd

Tel: 00357 26622279; or email anixe@jgoodwin.info

This book is dedicated to all my friends and family.

Acknowledgements

Thank you to my friends John Goodwin, Linda Palmer and Sharon Whitehouse. Without their patience, time and enthusiasm these pages would "still be in the cupboard".

With special thanks to Sharon Whitehouse who also designed the cover.

Contents

PROLOGUE..3
Chapter 1 FIRST LETTER 5
Chapter 2 Who Am I 7
Chapter 3 SECOND LETTER 23
Chapter 4 England 1966...........................25
Chapter 5 Wilf...41
Chapter 6 Australia 1966 85
Chapter 7 Ruth 113
Chapter 8 Alex 129
Chapter 9 THIRD LETTER....................137
Chapter 10 Honeymead 1966.................141
Chapter 11 Stephen 157
Chapter 12 New Zealand 1972...............177
Chapter 13 Life on the Farm 193
Chapter 14 New Year 1980....................205
Chapter 15 The Gallery 215
Chapter 16 Cancer..................................229
Chapter 17 New Zealand 1985...............243
Chapter 18 New Zealand 1988...............275
Chapter 19 Laura and Janet....................289
Chapter 20 Relationships 301
Chapter 21 New Zealand 1993...............313
Chapter 22 Asha.....................................323
About The Author 359

PROLOGUE

I am being blackmailed

The first letter arrived four days ago

> I KNOW WHO YOU ARE,
> YOU KEEP QUIET
> – SO SHALL I

The SECOND letter arrived TWO days ago

> I KNOW YOUR SECRET,
> 10th OCTOBER 1966
> YOU KEEP QUIET –
> SO SHALL I

The THIRD letter arrived THIS MORNING

> I KNOW YOUR SECRET,
> 10th OCTOBER 1966
> WHO WILL PAY – YOU
> OR THE NEWSPAPERS?
> BE ALONE – BY THE
> PHONE TOMORROW 6.30PM
> FOR INSTRUCTIONS

Chapter 1 FIRST LETTER

Honey Mead Farm New Zealand June 1993

I turned from my easel and went out on to the veranda as the plane flew low overhead. Ralph tilted the wing, a sign he would be home for lunch. It was a beautiful clear day just wisps of cloud in the sky, everything green and fresh after a shower in the early hours of the morning. I looked at the clock, time to put on the jug, I thought. Jack will be here soon with the mail.

Over the years it had become a habit for the current postman to make his morning coffee break at the farm. I enjoyed the exchange of conversation, I will not call it gossip, but it did keep me in touch with what was happening in the area and people had taken to sending messages to one another, a kind of inner communication system. Also having the post delivered to the kitchen table saved a long walk down the drive to the mail box by the main road.

I never looked at my post until Jack left. I liked to think it good manners on my part but must admit I got a thrill from anticipating the contents of the pile of mail, there may have been a letter from England or America. I had learnt at an early age that to enjoy receiving letters, as I do, one has to also write them and I enjoy doing that, relating the happenings of life on the farm.

After Jack had finished his coffee and gone on his way I sat down to look through the post before Liza came to fetch it or I took it through into the office.

The letter was in a very ordinary white envelope postmarked in the city. The content was one piece of white paper on to which had been pasted words and letters of different sizes cut from magazines.

I KNOW WHO YOU ARE.
YOU KEEP QUIET – SO SHALL I.

A cold shiver went down my spine. It was the realisation that I was holding something to do with someone who was sick – mentally sick. I dropped the paper and stood up aware that I was holding my breath and my heart was pounding. A sort of premonition, like watching something from a film or television series, I sat down once more and picked up the piece of paper again.

I KNOW WHO YOU ARE.

WHO AM I? – I closed my eyes and let my mind drift back to my early memories. I became a child again.

Chapter 2 Who Am I

England Revisited

My name was Margaret – Margaret Davies back then – I was born in a small market town in North Yorkshire, England in 1946. One of my first memories is of my father singing to me, singing as he bathed and dried me before the open fire, wrapping me in a big soft towel. As I snuggled on his lap my mother handed us mugs of hot chocolate.

'That will make you sleep my dears and give you sweet dreams too' she said.

The lilt in her voice was like the songs Daddy sang - they had both been born in Wales.

My father was an auctioneer at the cattle market; he sold other things too but mainly farm animals and equipment. He was very handsome, his hair thick, black and curly. He only had one arm, the other one he lost in the war when his ship was blown up. He didn't like to talk about it. I never thought of his artificial arm as creepy, I was used to it, but Mary Roberts, my best friend didn't like it at all. My fault really.

One day after school we were at my house, I was helping my mother by putting the ironing away in the drawers in the bedroom. Mary was with me and I asked her to put some things into a drawer. When she opened the drawer she let out a scream, there was my father's artificial arm.

I picked it up and said 'Silly, it won't hurt you' and I chased her around the room with it.

Mary threw herself into the corner in fear, pulling the curtains over her head. 'I hate you, I hate you' she cried. Hearing those words I stopped in my tracks.

'I'm sorry Mary,' I said, 'I don't want you to hate me,' I want you to like me, we are friends aren't we. I put the arm back into the drawer and held out my hand.

Mary took the curtain from her head as I spoke and peered at me through the material. She came forward and took my hand; we went down the stairs together.

'Would you like some milk and cake?' my mother asked.

'Yes please,' we both sat down at the kitchen table.

'What was all that noise?' my mother asked as she poured the milk into the glasses. 'Oh, nothing' I replied, looking at Mary.

'Nothing' she agreed. We smiled at each other and took a bite of cake.

My mother was gentle, her hair fair and fine, with a natural wave. I remember her telling me that when she was younger she wanted to have black straight hair, but she realised as she grew older how lucky she was, she didn't need a perm as was the fashion and perms were very expensive. I felt happy to be like my mother, my sister Jenny looked more like my father.

We had a big black car, a Humber was the name. My mother used to drive it and looked so small behind the wheel. There was a sort of door knob on the steering wheel that my father used to turn the wheel with when he was driving. I had to sit on a cushion to see out of the windows.

When we went on holiday to Morecambe Mary was allowed to come with me. Her grandmother gave her some pocket money. I liked Mary's grandmother; her eyes twinkled as though she knew lots of secrets. Mary and I used to sit on the rug in front of the fire while her grandmother rocked in her chair. She would tell us stories of when she was a girl and the things that happened then. Things like, the sinking of the Titanic, the ship that couldn't sink, until it hit an iceberg, and women wanting the vote.

We asked about the "vote." What did it mean? She told us about women's rights and how important it was to vote, especially when women had died to get it. One had thrown herself in front of a horse at a race track, she told us, others had chained themselves to railings and had refused to eat. They were taken to prison and 'force fed.' We couldn't imagine that, - we were eating chunks of warm bread just out of the oven, spread with strawberry jam. Mary had a moustache of jam on her face.

While on holiday we learnt a lot about life or so we thought. There was a young couple staying at the hotel, we heard someone say that they were on their honeymoon. Mary and I watched them; they held hands and whispered to each other all the time as though they had a secret. We even followed them around the town, we stopped when they stopped, hiding in the doorways just like we had seen on the films. One cold day they went down on to the beach and walked along until they disappeared under the pier. No one else was on the beach. We watched them from the promenade. They didn't come out from under the pier.

'Let's go and see where they are' I said to Mary.

'Let's get our ice cream first' she replied.

We bought our ice creams then stole silently down the steps from the promenade on to the beach; we crept slowly along, keeping to the wall until we saw them. They were lying on the sand; he was on top of her holding her hands outstretched.

'Is he hurting her?' I whispered to Mary, 'No silly, they are making a baby' she replied knowingly.

'Oh yes' I answered. We stood peeping from behind the big supports holding up the pier and watched as we licked our ice creams.

My sister Jenny was born in 1939 at the start of the war, so is six years older than me. I remember always wanting to be able to do the things she could do. I was told I was clever and shouldn't waste my chance to go to grammar school and university if I was lucky.

Jenny worked in a new department store in the city. She went there on the train each morning and some evenings didn't return until late. She was able to go to the new entertainment centre and somehow always managed to be able to buy the latest fashions to wear. I know she received a discount at the store. I suppose I was just plain jealous of my older sister.

As the years went on we became very good friends. Once I had established an identity of my own, I realised that we were very different and didn't envy her anymore.

I had my own friends and way of life and she had hers. I remember how she always had boyfriends galore; it was her easy going personality. Life was fun; she certainly was a city girl whereas I loved the country and life in our small town.

Jenny had long legs, dark silky hair, eyelashes that looked artificial they were so thick and long, big brown eyes and soft full lips. I heard some boys talking at the bus stop one day.

'Jenny has come to bed eyes' one boy said, all the others agreed laughing.

I was very young at the time but remember discussing it with Mary. We thought it was very funny and I used to watch Jenny as we ate at the table, absorbed in looking at her eyes trying to work it out, "come to bed eyes?" – I would report back to Mary what I thought – in fact Mary became a frequent visitor to my house, especially at tea time if Jenny was home. We would do our homework together and time would pass until father and Jenny came home from work and Mary would be invited to stay for tea. It worked well really as we could both watch Jenny and discuss it later in my bedroom. Other days I would go to

Mary's house for tea and I would watch Mary's brother, Gary. He was older than Mary but not as old as Jenny – I found it fascinating, not having a brother of my own. Boys my age are so boring, they do silly things like soaking conkers in vinegar then baking them in the oven to go hard, then making a hole in the middle to put string through and smashing them against each other to break them again, - stupid boys. But I liked Gary, I think mainly because he seemed to like me, or at least he was kind to me. He mended my bicycle chain when it broke and he also taught me to mend a puncture. I sometimes wished he was my brother and Mary could have Jenny as her sister.

In 1961 when I was fifteen years old Jenny married Mark Powell. He had been in the R.A.F. until recently and looked very good in his uniform, tall dark and handsome. I was a bridesmaid in a rose pink dress; we had short dresses which was Jenny's choice of course. She wore the usual white dress, a short veil on her head and carried a prayer book and posy of flowers.

I remember the occasion well. It's not because of the wedding as such, but that was the day I met Martin, Marks younger brother. Martin was an usher looking very smart in his dark suit. Tall like his brother but with fair hair and complexion, like me I suppose in comparison to Jenny. Martin was eighteen years old and hoping to go into the Police Force. I don't think he noticed me really, as a girl I mean – although afterwards at the reception he teased me about being a beautiful bridesmaid. I couldn't imagine Martin could care about me, especially when I saw him talking to Jenny's friend the other bridesmaid, who was twenty years old. Oh at that moment how I wished my life away to be older. Little did I know what life had in store!

Mark and Jenny came back from their honey moon and moved into a cottage across the park from our home. The cottage needed doing up quite a lot.

One day my mother asked if I would take some new curtains she had been sewing across to Jenny's house. Oh lovely fate, I thought as I went into the kitchen. There, on a ladder doing something with the electrics, was Martin. My heart pounded, my stomach churned, my voice squeaked then gave up so that, when Martin was asking me ordinary questions, I was acting like a robot and felt a complete idiot.

Yes! I was in love, well and truly "smitten" as the saying goes in the north of England. Jenny asked me what I would like for my birthday.

Martin asked if I was having a party. I said I didn't know and he replied, 'well if you do then don't forget to invite me.'

Those words sounded like music to my ears. There had to be a party, that's all I want for my birthday, so I told Jenny what I would like.

Weeks went by living on cloud nine or being in the darkest depths. When things were good I feared they would end, and I lived on a perpetual roundabout of emotions, each day depending on my being with or speaking to Martin on the telephone.

My mother told me that Jenny was pregnant but two weeks later she had a miscarriage. For some time Jenny was upset and people told her "there's plenty of time". I don't know if Mark and Jenny were really happy. I know she had wanted the baby but I had to admit that I was too enthralled with my own life at that time.

There was an incident once when it was someone's anniversary and we were all at a village pub by the river. Jenny was sat on the wall and I noticed Mark go over to her and pull her skirt down over her knees, she asked him what was wrong and he mumbled about showing all she had to every man around. It was the first time I was aware of this attitude but remembered, when I thought about it, that Jenny had to change her dress before she went out. "It was too low at the front," he told her.

I asked Martin what was the matter with Mark and he said, 'Oh, he's jealous of other men looking at Jenny.'

A few months later Jenny and Mark came round to our house for tea. Jenny was pregnant again and after the baby was born they were going to live in Australia. Mark was hoping to join the R.A.A.F. over there. My mother's face brightened then dropped at each piece of news and the thought of not seeing much of the baby and Jenny too of course. But it was a new start and Mark had not been happy in his job, in fact he had not been happy since he left the R.A.F. which he had done, so he said, because Jenny had wanted him to. She didn't want to go on postings abroad and leave the area. Strange that they would be leaving the area altogether and he would be getting another uniform.

I must have been growing up to have this realisation. Was he trying to upset Jenny? Was he jealous of our close family and taking Jenny and the baby away from other people's attention and caring? Perhaps Australia will be the making of them I can hear someone saying, plenty of opportunity to get on there.

They had a beautiful baby boy and named him Michael John. He had thick dark hair and long limbs obviously going to be tall like his mother and father. He was the apple of my mother's eye and she must have suffered agonies knowing he was going to be taken away in just a few short weeks. How could Jenny do this to mother I thought. Mark can work in this country, go back to the R.A.F. if he misses it so much or join the police force like Martin. But no! Mark was set on Australia. We all went to the station to see them off. Five weeks at sea like a cruise holiday. What a wonderful time, what marvels they would see.

Jenny going to Australia made me start thinking about living in another place. I had never been the kind of person to desire the city. I had visited London, been abroad to France with the school, done Scotland and the Edinburgh Tattoo and usual holiday places.

And so, as each day passed, I followed the route on the map of where Jenny, Mark and Michael were. I really looked at Australia and how it was made up of different states, like America. I then thought about New Zealand, made up of two islands, north and south. I wondered if I would ever go there, would I ever see Jenny again.

It was these ponderings that cast my mind back to many years earlier. I had been with my mother in town; she had left her shopping bag with me while trying on some shoes. As I put the bag down on the floor a letter had fallen out, a letter to be posted. It had an airmail sticker on it and an address in New Zealand. I put it back in the bag, thinking I must ask my mother about it but had then been distracted with buying shoes and had totally forgotten the incident.

By the time they arrived in Australia I was well into my second year of A' Levels with a plan to go to college and become a teacher – Art, History and English were my favourite subjects.

Martin was happy in the Police Force; he fancied becoming a detective. He didn't like road patrol but accepted that all these things had to be done to be able to get advancement. Of course he looked gorgeous in his uniform, in my eyes better than Mark in his. I was glad that Martin was not in the services, I don't think I could have borne him going away to war; at least in the Police Force he would only have to move about in this country and I would go anywhere with him if he asked me. I now understand Jenny.

I know common sense said, at seventeen, I was too young to get married but I didn't feel like that. When my eighteenth birthday came round, luckily it was a Saturday, Martin and I officially announced our engagement. We had decided on a ring and spent a beautiful day in the city buying it. I walked around holding my left hand out in front of me looking at it.

My mother and father were taking us out to dinner to celebrate then Martin [MARTIN] and I were joining friends later to go dancing. It was a magical time; everything seemed to be in tune. The band played our favourite song and we danced. I really felt as though I was on a cloud, my feet not quite touching the floor. My heart felt as though it would burst with happiness as I looked up at Martin and thought how lucky I was and I realised the meaning of the words "love hurts". I was so happy.

I felt someone at my elbow, I turned and there was John Hunter, Martin's friend from work, I had a flash of thought – why is he in his uniform at the dance?

There had been a crash, a lorry and trailer had jack-knifed across the road. My mother had died instantly as the saying goes, but we wondered what that meant later. My father had died on the way to the hospital.

Jenny flew back for the funeral, so yes, I did see her again, but oh, what terrible circumstances. She only stayed a week as she had to get back to Mark and the baby. She shared my room, I don't really know why except we felt we wanted to be close together in the short time we had. She had some terrible bruises on her lower back. She said she had fallen the day before she came over to the funeral. We talked about what to do with the house, as our parents had left it to both of us equally along with everything else they had. One side of me didn't want to sell it and the things it held; I felt disloyal to my parents but on the other hand wanted to run away from the pain of memories. Jenny couldn't take anything with her so obviously the best thing for her was to have the money in Australia.

We decided to sell the house. Martin and I would have a new start, we were getting married. There was a teachers training college only ten miles away and I had been accepted. With a car I could attend college each day and would be able to have a Police house with Martin now being a married man. We would have a June wedding – a June bride is always a bride, I thought. I had grown up quickly in those first few months of 1964.

By the end of June 1964, I had run the gamut of emotions. My parents had died and I had married the love of my life – surely one end of the scale to the other.

We had a 'small private wedding,' that's the wording a magazine would use. It was lovely, such a beautiful day. The sun shone. Everyone was able to wear summer clothes, the women in lovely hats; it was a truly picturesque day. Photographs were taken inside the church as well as outside on the steps and in the garden of the hotel where we had the reception with blossoms and flowers everywhere. I wore a very simple cream lace dress and my bridesmaid – yes – Mary Roberts wore a pale turquoise blue one. As the photographs were taken I realised how few we were in the family, not only on my side – with the death of my mother and father – but because Martin only had his grandmother, as his parents had died in the war. His father in the R.A.F. didn't return from a mission over Germany and his mother died in London. She was nursing there and a V2 bomb hit the hospital. The two boys lived with their grandparents, but grandfather had also died some years earlier.

Martin's grandmother was not a well woman, tired out with the life she had had, and what living had done to her. She had once been young I thought.

I missed my mother and father dreadfully; I was glad that at least they had had Jenny's wedding day.

We only had thirty guests at the wedding, but more came to the evening "get together" as we chose to call it.

A very dear kind man came to the wedding. It was funny the way we met. I had been to the cemetery two weeks earlier. I had gone, although it sounds stupid, to talk to my mother. How silly, but I wanted to tell her about my dress as though she didn't know already. It was quiet and peaceful in the churchyard and I felt nearer to her somehow, well it was my last contact with her I suppose.

Anyway, there was this man standing by my parent's grave. He had once been very handsome, I could tell, being of medium height with hair that, when younger, would have been quite red. I bet he had taken a lot of teasing when he was at school. As I walked up to him his stance was quite bowed and, although he was there in front of me, I know that he was really many miles away in some other distant place in his mind.

He came out of his reverie on hearing my footsteps on the gravel pathway. He looked quite lost as he turned to me then I saw brightness on his face and his eyes seemed to light up as though he recognised me. I had never seen this man before but felt a rapport with him, perhaps it was this place. He spoke my name

'I'm sorry, should I know you?'

He told me that his name was Wilfred Franklin. He had known my mother many years ago in the war-time. He had also known my mother's father. Way back, my family and his were connected, his great grandfather had gone to New Zealand, and the ties went back to the borders of Scotland and the mountains of Wales.

Whenever he had leave he tried to find out about his ancestry, and at the end of the war had worked with my grandfather at the bank. Apparently, married men were sent home first from Europe through Britain and being single and having worked in a bank in New Zealand, people like him were given the chance to work their last month's here; it would do them some good in their future careers. Having already met my grandfather while researching in the north of England and knowing he was a bank manager, he had written to ask if he could work there instead of a bank in London.

He had kept in contact with my mother, so knew of her life and family and my grandfather's death. He had always intended to return to England again but life had been very busy when he got back to New Zealand after the war. He had left the bank after a couple of years; his father had become ill and could no longer manage the farm on his own. Wilf had gone into banking to please his father as it seemed the right thing to do after the struggle to give him a good education. But he had always preferred the land, so it was no hardship for him to leave banking and join his father on the farm.

The years had been good to them and his banking experience had helped him with the business side and so they had increased their land and stock. His father had died quite young really but his mother had lived until last year. He had wonderful help on the farm so, when he had received a letter from a friend of my mother's, he realised it was too late, but still needed to come over.

My mother had given a friend a letter to post to him if she should die. He was only in the north for a few days, then to London but he came back to Yorkshire for our wedding.

He invited Martin and me to visit him at any time and we were really impressed with the talk of life in New Zealand. We laughed and said how funny if we were to go to New Zealand while Jenny and Mark were in Australia. Jenny is my only family now, as Mark is Martins, except for his grandmother: But how could we leave her alone after all she had done for him, but who knows one day maybe.

I wrote to Jenny and told her about Wilfred Franklin, she replied saying she remembered a man from the other side of the world when she was a child. He used to stay at Grandpa's house and he had red hair.

Chapter 3 SECOND LETTER

Back in New Zealand 1993

After a second cup of coffee and a good talking to myself, I put the first letter away in my drawer. There was work to be done. I was preparing lunch today; Emily was away visiting her sister and wouldn't be back until late afternoon.

It was two days later when the second letter arrived. As usual Jack brought the post, had his coffee and scone then went off on his rounds. I had looked at the post with trepidation the day after the first letter arrived but there was the usual stuff and a letter for me from a friend in America, I forgot my fears and enjoyed the news from the states.

The second letter was once more in a plain white envelope, posted in the city, again one sheet of white paper. This time the uneven eerie letters spelt – 10TH OCTOBER 1966. I felt sick, my throat constricted. I knew I was touching paper which had been held by someone with a sick mind. I dropped it as though it was contagious and dirty. What should I do – should I tell someone, the Police? – But what could I really say? The frightening part of this being, is it someone I know, and if not then is it someone who is watching me? I felt fear, fear for what? Fear for whom? I poured myself another cup of coffee hoping to steady my nerves and sat at the table and picked up the corner of the paper.

10TH OCTOBER 1966

I KNOW YOUR SECRET

YOU KEEP QUIET – SO SHALL I

Chapter 4 England 1966

Dare I remember 1966, were there any good moments? I suppose if I start at the beginning of the year I have to admit that there were some very happy months.

We celebrated New Year's Eve with friends and all said we wondered what will have happened by next year at this time. Mary Roberts, now Mary Greenwood, was heavily pregnant and complained of not being able to have a 'real' drink as she called it, but never mind she would make up for it next year. Twins were expected in a few weeks, perhaps on my birthday. We're going to be godparents, Martin and I.

I looked forward to the time when we would start our own family but that time must be a few years away yet. I didn't mind as I enjoyed being at college, my two years finished in the summer. Also Martin would have to move on if he wanted promotion, which he did. He was quite ambitious and enjoyed his work so to start in a new place would suit us. I could work in a school in the same area and hopefully in about three years we would be in a position to have a family.

Beginning of June, Michael's birthday soon, I must not forget to send off his card and present. Three years old, how three years can fly by. I must enclose a photograph too. Jenny likes to show Michael photographs of his family, being so far away. She always shows him where letters and presents come from on the map. I am Maggie and Martin is Marty. Jenny called me Maggie when I was a baby; no one else called me that although I quite like it. I like nick-names. I recall my mother correcting Jenny. 'It's Margaret dear' she would say 'that's the name she was christened with. That started a discussion about being christened and I listened intently about babies having water put on their heads.

How could I forget the wonderful holiday Martin and I had, the first time we had been to Spain, the first time I had flown in an aeroplane. It was a second honeymoon, our first being spent touring in Devon and Cornwall. Spain was magical. Clear blue sky and green sea, silver beaches to walk along for miles. Swimming in the sea then lying on the sand to dry in the sun then into the sea again. There is something about swimming in the sea that is special compared to a pool, the buoyancy and being lifted up and down by the swell of the waves. One day, when we are old, I thought, we could live here. To be able to spend the evenings sitting outside in the sunlight and not being cold when the sun goes down, to need only light clothing, a sweater around ones shoulders. It was sheer heaven to me, a person that feels the cold badly. It was being in Spain, lying on the beach one day that started us talking about Jenny and Mark and their life in Australia.

They took the beaches and warm weather for granted now, living close to the sea. Mark had a friend, Alan, who owned a boat so they spent many weekends either at sea or helping Alan do 'things' with his boat. It was a lovely time to be in Spain, June. The mid-summer being too busy for our choice, but school teachers are governed by school holidays and that's how things would be from now on, or so I thought.

We had only been home for one week when fate repeated itself. I had been shopping and arrived home with the usual bags of food from the supermarket and fresh vegetables from the open market in the town centre. John Hunter, Martin's police friend, came towards me, I felt a shiver, and I flashed back to the time he brought the news of my parent's accident at the dance. I thought he didn't look well, quite grey in fact. He didn't speak, he just looked at me. I handed him a bag of shopping to hold while I put the key in the door. He took the bag but still didn't speak, perhaps at that stage there was no need for words as the silence spoke volumes. I was aware that the cold shiver that I had felt was nothing to do with the past experiences but the present time.

I didn't know what to do; I acted automatically, pushed open the door and went in. John followed me. I went straight to the kettle and switched it on, a sort of putting off the inevitable. There was still silence between us. I knew the answer but not the details 'what has happened?' I heard my voice saying as though it came from somewhere in the distance. The kettle shrilled and I poured the water into the teapot. Standing behind me John started to relate the afternoon's happenings. We sat at the table, each holding a beaker of hot tea in our hands as though the warmth would give us comfort. There was so much I needed to ask but so little I wanted to know. Let it go away, let it never have happened; let me return to this morning as we planned our day. We had sat, Martin and I, at this same table, drinking from the same beakers, tasting the same tea, from the same teapot, from the same kettle. Oh! To be able to go back to that same moment to capture and save it forever, never to step out of it again.

He should never have been there I was told. It was a change of plan and he happened to be passing near the weir when someone shouted out that there was a child in the water. I know Martin wouldn't have given a second thought about going into the water. He was an excellent swimmer; quite proud of his achievements in the water. He had won medals at school.

It was not the first time someone had drowned in that weir; there are notices all along both sides of the bank warning of the danger. But children will not see danger, in fact they had known the danger and that's why they used the crossing of the stones along the top of the weir as a dare, a dare to prove how brave they were. One boy had gone too far and become frightened, the other one had tried to help. The smaller one trying to pull the older one back had slipped and slid down the slope into the rapidly churning water.

Martin had not wasted a second, after taking off his shoes and jacket he went in. He had somehow managed to get a footing under the water and, with just his head above water, had literally (with an unknown strength) thrown the boy out of the water, breaking the boys arm in the process. The effort and recoil of throwing the child must have sent him off his foothold onto the rocks and he was swept into the torrent of water. Maybe he was knocked unconscious but I am told it is like being in a washing machine going round and round, twisting over and over, the pressure keeping the body under the water.

Mark came home for the funeral; his grandmother was in a bad way.

'Why am I here?' she said to me, 'it's all the wrong way round, I want to go, I've had my life and now this – Oh, Margaret what are we to do?'

I put my arms around the thin, shaking shoulders and we wept together. She brightened up when Mark arrived, fussing in the kitchen preparing a meal for us, needing to be active. I realised how frail she was.

Mark told us about where they lived. He said they were very happy and brought out photographs for us to look at. Michael was quite big for his age and in answer to my question, 'Can he swim?'

'Like a fish' Mark replied. 'We have a pool in the garden at the back of the house. One that is above the ground and I have built a platform around it leading off the veranda.'

'It sounds beautiful,' I said wistfully.

'Why don't you come and visit us and see for yourself. It would do you good to get away from here for a while and you'll have to leave the house, so before you make any decisions about where you are going to live and work why not come and see your nephew and how grown up he is.'

'That sounds a good idea to me' said Grandma Powell, 'go and see that sister of yours and Michael,'

'I'll see,' I replied.

The next morning I had a call from Mark 'Grandma's gone' he cried, his voice choking.

'I'm coming straight over,' I told him.

'I took her a cup of tea,' Mark's voice was full of anguish, 'I thought she was asleep, so left it by her bed, when I went back later I opened the curtains, she still didn't wake up. Even before I touched her, I knew she had gone. She was a mother to us,' he wept, 'I shouldn't have left her.'

I put my arms around him; he had lost his grandmother who had replaced his mother for most of his and his brother's lives. He really needed Jenny to be comforting him but I would have to do. I knew how he was feeling.

We managed somehow with the help of good friends to arrange for the funerals together. We both felt that Martin and his grandmother would like it that way, to be together.

We had only had a small wedding at the church – but for Martin and his grandmother's funeral, people gathered outside, as there was no room inside the church.

Martin had been born in the town and was known for miles around, playing in the football team in winter and the cricket team in the summer. As a local bobby he was respected by the young and old alike. Grandmother had lived there all her life too.

I sat in the pew looking at the coffins. There was a rustle of noise all about me from the many people in the church, but it was as though it had nothing to do with me, it was on the perimeter of my mind. A sort of muffled hush came about, I knew that the service had begun and I heard a voice as the Vicar spoke his words, words of praise and remembrance, but I was not there. I was a bride again and where the coffin lay, I saw Martin – my Martin turning to look at me as I walked down the aisle on my Uncles arm. Mary was not sitting next to me but standing, waiting to take my bouquet, a bridesmaid once more. The words being spoken were not of the past but for our future. 'To have and to hold from this day forward, to love and to cherish' Oh! How we had done that, loved and cherished, how can I bear not to feel your arms about me again? Someone moved, taking my arm. I was guided down the aisle and, as we passed the font, I felt another wave of tears well up inside me as I recalled Martin and I, only a few short weeks ago taking responsibility for being Godparents to Mary and Ian's twin boys.

A hand took hold of me, maybe my pause at the font made them think I had stumbled, I don't know, but I was lead out of the church onto the steps where we had taken photographs, laughing and taking turns at holding the babies. Two years since our wedding and my sadness at such a happy time for my parents not being there to share it with us. The thought of my parents gave me a warm feeling. I knew they were with me, supporting me. It was a feeling, just like I knew my mother was listening to every word about my wedding dress when I was in the cemetery. I knew that ~~Michael~~ Martin was with them and at some time in the future we would all meet again. I felt an all-consuming awareness of time taking care of everything. A deep, deep peace entered my being and spread through every cell in my body, I knew, I just knew.

Mark had to stay longer than he originally intended; there were things to sort out with the solicitor. Mrs Powell had left everything she had to Mark and Martin. Because Martin died before her then Mark inherited. He asked me if there was anything I would like.

'Thank you for the thought, there really is nothing I need. Is there anything Jenny would like? Perhaps something from when you boys were small that Michael could have when he is old enough to understand.'

'I'll look,' replied Mark.

'I told him that I would see to as much as possible so that he could get back to Jenny and Michael.

'You have enough to sort out yourself Maggie.'

'A bit more won't do me any harm,' I replied.

'I can't thank you enough,' Mark said as he gave me a hug. 'I don't know what I would have done without you. Do come and see us, I really mean it.'

'Yes,' I answered.

It was three weeks later that I received the letter from my mother's friend in New Zealand, Wilf Franklin, or Wilf as he signed himself. We had written occasionally since his coming to our wedding and I had sent him Jenny's address. My first letter to him had been to thank him for our lovely wedding present. The parcel had arrived in the post after we returned from our honeymoon. Such a large box; by large I mean long. I took our layers and layers of packing, obviously done professionally. I realised why there needed to be so much when I came to the beautiful, delicately carved boat. In the enclosed letter, Wilf explained that it was a 'Waka,' a Maori canoe, the type the Maoris had travelled in for thousands of miles to find New Zealand hundreds of years earlier. The figures sitting inside rowing the many delicate oars were individually carved. The sides and front of the boat were decorated with shells in blue green and pink, Paua shell as Wilf explained. Wilf had answered my letter of thanks, telling me a little of life on his farm, of the sheep, cows and horses. He rode a horse to move the stock around the fields, found it a good way to keep fit and healthy although the regular way was to use a motorbike.

I wrote to him about the news of Martins job and little incidents that happened I thought were amusing. I told him how Martin had bumped my car and broken the front bumper as he turned into the market place in town,

'What were you doing' I'd asked.

He gave his slow smile and admitted that he had been looking at a girl in a mini dress.

'It was so 'mini' that it was almost not there' he had said.

Apparently the name for such is a "pelmet," like the short frills at the top of windows.

I had laughed too and said 'I would let him off as long as he repaired the car.'

We wondered how Mark was coping with Jenny in a mini skirt the way he was so jealous of men looking at her.

Martin said 'Mark would be used to it by now, with the climate they had, it would be bikinis rather than minis that were the problem.'

Wilf's letter expressed deep sorrow and concern for me. He asked what I was going to do. He knew it was early days but understood I would have to leave the Police house that came with Martins job. My Aunt Phyllis had written to Wilf, she had found a great rapport with him at the wedding, recalling the days when he had lived in the area. She had met him before briefly when he worked in the bank for a few weeks at the end of the war. Aunt Phyllis was my father's step sister and older than my father by quite a few years. Perhaps she was being just plain 'nosey' about Wilf but whatever, she had written to him of Martins death, telling him the circumstances.

Wilf urged me to go to New Zealand. "Just come for a few months, our summer will do you good. Give you time to think of where you want to be, where you want to work and live." The words were almost a repeat of Mark and Grandma Powell's words and also Jenny's letter. She too begged me to go to Australia, "I need to see you," she had written, "and I feel so hopeless."

As I read the word I thought that she had meant to write "helpless."

"Michael would love to see you too," she wrote "he knows you from your photograph and says Maggie when I show it to him. You could easily get a job out here, they are needing good teachers. I know you haven't had any work experience yet but you would be accepted to live here I am sure and we would vouch for you. Oh! Please, please Maggie, I need you." It was those last words that set my heart beating faster. Did she really mean hopeless and not helpless. Reading between the lines I started to be aware of a feeling of dread, perhaps all is not as it should be. We, Martin and I, had always joked about Marks jealousy. It had always been an underlying factor, not quite wanting to really know the truth of the matter.

35

Wilf had said in his letter that he wanted to pay my fare to go to see him; it would give him so much pleasure. He couldn't see himself ever getting this way again and there was so much of New Zealand he still wanted to see, he would take great pleasure in showing it to me; would I accept my fare?. He had enclosed a blank cheque, already signed. All I had to do was fill in the name of the travel agent and the amount. He knew that I could afford my own fare as I had told him about my parents leaving everything to Jenny and myself, also I would get a Police pension as Martin's widow. But he begged me to give him the pleasure of this holiday; it would be his gain in having my company.

I spent many hours with my friend Mary. I don't know what I would have done without her and Ian to help me. She had a strong sense of dependability I had not noticed before, but it must have been lying dormant from our youth waiting to be developed by such occasions. She had always seemed so much younger than me, looking to me for direction when all the time she was this reliable deeply understanding woman. That's what it was, she was a woman in every sense of the word. I saw her for the first time as Ian saw her, not as just a school friend, I guess we had just grown up. I remember thinking I had done that, years ago.

Mary had read the letters from Wilf and Jenny and I had voiced my fears for Jenny. She told me that she had told Ian of our antics years ago, our watching Jenny's eyes. Mary had wanted

Ian to explain what "Come to bed eyes" meant to him.

He had laughed, grabbed her round the waist, put his nose to her's, looked her straight in the eyes and said, 'come to bed.'

Mary had pushed him gently away saying, 'Please be serious, I want to know.'

He explained that with some girls there was a look about them that oozed sexuality, not just niceness or cleverness, but just pure "come and get me, I'm interested in you". Whether intentional or not, they gave over vibes and most women enjoyed the ego boost of knowing they were attracting men, a kind of power. It could become a habit in the way they moved, walked, spoke or looked at the male species, even when not consciously intending to send out vibes to attract.

'This was how Jenny was,' Ian said.

'Mark was attracted and knew others were also. Men know every girlfriend can attract other men but in a close relationship form a trust and confidence about each other.

'I know what you mean,' said Mary, 'you take us for granted.' She laughed and put her arms about his neck, tilting her head, pursing her lips for a kiss. 'I love you Ian Greenwood.'

'I love you too Mary Greenwood.'

Mary and I discussed the letter from Wilf and his wanting to pay my fare. It was decided I should pay my own fare but it would be easier for me if, when with him, he paid for what expenses we incurred. In that way I knew that I would only need my own personal spending money and didn't have to concern myself with the cost of wherever we stayed on our journey. I realised that as we talked like this, I had already made up my mind to go, in the fact that I was planning what might happen when I got there.

'Seems to me,' said Mary, 'it's not if you go but how long you go for. I know you can stay for six months so why not take advantage of it and get away for the whole winter.'

Mary and Ian lived in a large Victorian house, lots of rooms and space to absorb my furniture and possessions. It was their suggestion to store my things for me.

'Make the house look more lived in,' Mary said, 'and the attic is almost empty, except for a few of Ian's old things.'

Ian had pulled a face at Mary when she said that, 'One day those "old things" will be antiques; then you will want them to be on show, not up in the attic.'

They had a wonderful rapport with each other and Ian was fantastic with the twins too, dealing with one each when feeding, then changing around the next day so they would all grow up to enjoy sharing each other. Such wonderful wisdom.

Ian and a friend of his came in a van to take my furniture. It didn't take them long; I had spent hours packing the china and glass, wrapping each piece in newspaper. It didn't seem that long since I had been unwrapping many of the pieces, gifts for our wedding. Other items were from my parent's home, things I had grown up with and didn't want to let go of when my mother and father died. The tears rolled down my cheeks, silent tears, I felt bewildered by what was happening in my life. I wiped my cheeks with my hands then saw that my hands were black with newsprint from wrapping the last few items. I went to the bathroom to wash the ink off my face and, as I stood before the mirror looking at the sad face before me, I heard a large howl, it was coming from me. I wept and wept. Now that the house was empty I felt empty too. It was as though it was saying it was time to move on. On to where?

The day of my departure came quickly once I had put everything in the hands of the travel agent. When Jenny and Mark had gone to Australia it had taken them five weeks in a ship and here I was flying there in a few days. Ian and Mary took me to the airport, hugged me and told me to have a wonderful time. I know Mary was concerned about me although she smiled brightly. As I turned to give them a last wave before I went through departures I saw Mary bury her head in Ian's sweater, tears rolling down her cheeks, as though she would never see me again. I had intended to fly straight to Australia then go back to New Zealand, but Wilf suggested I make a break on route, firstly in Singapore, then three or four days in Auckland. The farm was over three hundred miles south but he wanted to show me around Auckland, then when I returned from

Australia, we would go straight to the farm. So this was the plan and as I said, the travel agent soon had it all arranged.

Chapter 5 Wilf

As we approached New Zealand, and the pilot told us we were starting our descent into Auckland, the woman sitting next to me started to cry. She was "coming home", she said. I looked out of the window beside me down to the green countryside and ribbon of the coast line meeting the sea. What is in store for me here, I thought. My answer was a wave of feeling I had never had before but I knew what the woman who sat beside me meant when she had said "she was coming home." It was a strange but comfortable feeling I was to remember many times.

Wilf met me at the airport. I was quite apprehensive about being here in a strange country, meeting and going to stay with a man who was a virtual stranger, but as he waved to me when I passed through the door from the custom's hall, all my fears swept away. Here was a genuine man, a man my mother had as a friend, and everything would be alright. Once more I saw his face, bright and smiling as he recognised me.

He put his arm across my shoulders, hugged me and kissed my forehead. 'It's so good to have you here.'

It was 7.30 in the morning, everything was so bright, the sky clear and blue. I needed my sun glasses as soon as we left the airport building. I felt quite exhilarated as I thought that, in a few days I would be doing this again in Australia and Jenny and Mark would be meeting me. How lovely to see Michael too, but first I am going to see this lovely city.

Wilf took me to a hotel on the water front. My room looked over the harbour and down to the busy street below. He suggested that, from his experience of jet-lag, the best way was to sleep as soon as possible, not try to keep awake. Not to worry about him, he had business in the city, so would come and collect me later for dinner and show me the city at night.

'Order anything you need from the hotel reception,' he said.

I stood by my window absorbing every detail of the view. I wanted to be able to tell Jenny everything. A ferry boat was leaving the harbour to cross to the other side of the bay. I could see the land across the water but found it difficult to see where the bay would become the sea. I realised that my eyes were stinging through lack of real sleep and became aware of an overall drag of weariness taking me over. I undressed and got between the clean white covers, glad Wilf had put the 'do not disturb' sign on my door. I slept.

I awoke leisurely stretching my limbs, feeling good and rested. I lay a while deciding what clothes to wear and what in the unpacked case would not be creased. The blue, light wool dress would be suitable I thought, with my navy jacket. I hung up my clothes in the wardrobe then had a long hot shower. I felt calm and relaxed, more so than I had felt for a very long time, a time that seemed to be never ending tension. I was aware of the extremes and the relaxation seemed to put everything into a slower gear. I revelled in this awareness. There was no hurry now, just time to enjoy soaking up the atmosphere of my new surroundings.

There was a knock on the door.

It was Wilf saying, 'I'll be having a drink in the bar, don't hurry there's plenty of time. Come down when you are ready.'

I liked his attitude and wondered if it was typical of all New Zealanders. I was almost ready when he had knocked at the door, so it wasn't long before I joined him in the bar. He was sat on a stool talking to the barman. The barman looked up as I entered, his movement indicating to Wilf that I had arrived. He turned on his stool and his face brightened; I liked the way this happened when he saw me. He came towards me smiling and admired my dress.

'What would you like to drink,' he asked.

'I would like a long orange juice, please,' I replied. I had a pot of tea and a sandwich in my room earlier but felt quite thirsty.

Wilf told me that flying was dehydrating so I must drink plenty of fluids. He asked if I would like to eat at the hotel or go somewhere else.

I said, 'somewhere else please, somewhere typical of New Zealand.' This hotel was very nice but modern. Then in the next breath I said, 'Where-does the ferry go to?'

43

'Now that's a good idea, just give me a minute.' He disappeared out of the room. In no time at all he was back. 'Come,' he took my arm and led me across the road in a hurry.

'I think we can make it,' indicating the ferry. 'That was a good idea of yours, now you can eat in an old New Zealand hotel and look at the lights of the city too. We must see as much as possible in your short stay here but not too much to tire you out; there will be time later when you return.'

There was a young man playing a guitar on the ferry boat and for a second or two a wave of sadness came over me, jogged by the memory of where I had heard the tune before. It was Wilf touching my arm to attract my attention that brought me back to the present. He was pointing out places on the landscape.

'The town we are going to is a part of Auckland called Devonport. It is a Naval Base and in the war, when ships came into the dock, people used to go down to the dockside and invite the sailors back to their homes; some for a meal, others for as long as they could stay.'

How lovely, I thought. These people especially parents, must have hoped that their sons' were being looked after in a similar way, across the world from home. In some cases, Wilf told me, there were lasting unions made when a young man met the daughter of the house and after the war came back and they married. He knew two couples who had met and married in that way and were very happy.

It must have made him remember his time in the war because he suddenly took my hand and said, 'I want to tell you about when I was in England in the war years. I would like to talk to you about your mother, would you mind?'

'I would love to hear all you wish to tell me.'

Just then we realised we were coming into dock. We let the other people go before us as there wasn't any need to hurry. We had the whole evening ahead.

We walked along the front, the sea on our right, and across the road was a park area with a band stand.

'Just like home' I said.

'Yes, you have to remember that most of the people here had ancestors who came from Britain and brought the way of life with them. The treaty with the Maoris was only in 1842, the early years of Queen Victoria's reign.'

We came to a large wooden building. By large I mean two storeys as most of the buildings around were on one level.

'This was the first hotel at this side of the bay, they have a wonderful reputation for good food I hope you like it. I telephoned from the hotel before we got on the ferry to let them know we were coming.'

The table we were given was by the window to be able to see the view. Wilf had said he was bringing a visitor from England. I felt quite important.

'Do you like sea food?' Wilf asked, as we were handed the menus.

'Oh, I love it,' I exclaimed.

It took ages reading the menu the choice of fish and sea food immense, or to me it was, scallops, crabs and oysters. I made my decision thinking there would be other days to try other dishes. As we ate the sun went down and the lights went on.

'You were going to tell me about my mother,' I said to Wilf.

'It's a long story; let's leave it until tomorrow if you don't mind. I'll take you to the top of One Tree Hill; we will look out over the whole city from there.'

Wilf could see that jet-lag was hitting me again. We walked back to the ferry, a very satisfied feeling inside of me, well fed and content.

'I agree with the reputation of the hotel. That was a beautiful meal, delicious.'

'I'm glad you enjoyed it.'

Watching the city as we approached across the water was a wonderment, a myriad of lights of all colours, thousands and thousands of lights and we were heading into the centre of them. As we got closer I could define certain buildings such as the hotel we were staying at. I knew I would need no rocking tonight, as my mother used to say.

I said goodnight to Wilf' and it wasn't long before I was climbing back into bed; it seemed such a short time ago, in one way, but so long in others. What a wealth of lovely memories I had of

New Zealand already. So much to tell Jenny, I must keep a diary, were my last thought as I drifted off to sleep.

When I awoke I drew back the curtains to clear blue skies. It was so bright; I had only seen such brightness before when I was on holiday in Spain. Was it only a few months ago? I thought of my friends back home, Mary and Ian, in their house with my furniture around them. They would be going to bed soon and I was getting up, how strange it seemed. I was brought out of my reverie by the alarm clock starting to buzz. I turned it off quickly, not wanting to disturb people who may still be sleeping in the next room. It was 7.30, an hour before I was to meet Wilf for breakfast.

'Have a good sleep,' he had said last night, 'it's going to be a busy day and believe it or not it can be hard work being a tourist.' I had laughed at that.

I dressed quickly, having decided the night before what I would wear; navy trousers with matching jacket and a pink sweater. Ready for anything, I walked into the dining room.

Wilf was already there at the table, reading a newspaper. 'I'm a very lucky man,' he said as he stood up and held out his hand.

I took it and gave him a peck on his cheek. 'What do you mean? I asked.

'Well, look around you.'

I did just that as I sat down at the table. Most of the other people in the dining room were men.

'Business men,' said Wilf, 'all wishing they were in my shoes at this moment having breakfast with a very attractive young lady.'

I laughed. I liked the way it was easy to laugh with Wilf. I knew he was teasing me. No wonder my mother had liked him.

We set off in Wilf's car and drove for miles and miles along the sea front from one little bay to another, each with its individual style of houses, shops and sea front. I loved the architecture, so many variations of style. We had lunch in a little cafe on the water's edge then walked along the beach. I took off my shoes and paddled in the sea. There were so many shells on the beach, I picked some up and put them in my pocket to take home.

'Don't take too many, you'll be overweight on the plane,' Wilf teased.

'I thought I would take some for Michael. 'When Jenny and I were small we used to bring them from the sea side and paint them, then Daddy would make holes in them and we would thread cord through to form a necklace. I just thought I could show Michael how to do it.'

We made our way back to the car.

'Now I will take you up One Tree Hill.'

As we drove back towards the city Wilf pointed out the hill and there really is only one tree on the top of it. We wound our way up the hill side; the view from the top was magnificent. The harbour in the distance, the bridge to the North shore where we ate last evening, a panorama of buildings and shining sea dotted with boats and yachts of all sizes.

'Look at those roof tops!'

'What do you mean?' he asked.

'The colours, there are so many different colours.'

'Oh, yes, we paint our roofs.'

'What colour is the roof at the farm?' I asked intrigued by this.

'Red, but you will see for yourself soon.'

'I must take some more photographs, will you stand by that wall please.'

I took some photographs then joined Wilf by the wall. We both sat down.

'Would you like to hear about your mother now?'

'Yes please,' I replied making myself comfortable.

'As I told you,' Wilf began, 'when I was in England I was interested in my ancestors; my father had a book, which is mine now of course. It is about most of the sailing ships and steam ships that brought people to New Zealand with the Captains names, cargoes, number of passengers and all sorts of other information in it. This book fascinated me as a child and I think it was the instigation of my interest in the other side of the world.

'My research had lead me to your town and I had a few days leave so decided to investigate and took the train from London where I was based. When I arrived I went to the church yard looking at the names on the grave stones. A man stood by a grave; I could tell it was a recent grave. The man asked if he could help and if I was looking for a particular name. I was wearing my uniform so the man knew I was from New Zealand. I told him my name and my interest. He introduced himself as Adam Mathews and his wife had recently died. The man was of course your grandfather.'

Wilf continued, 'Adam showed me the inside of the church, telling me some of the local history. As we walked down the path together we chatted and he told me he was a bank manager and most days' walks up to the church for a breath of fresh air in his lunch break. He asked me where I was staying and I told him I had managed to get bed and breakfast in the area. He invited me to come and eat with him and his family that evening at 6 for 6.30 pm. I accepted and he gave me the address and directions then left to go back to work.

'On the dot of six I was at the door. It was opened by a little girl. Big brown eyes looked at me and she asked my name. I told her and asked if she could tell me hers to which she answered, "Jenny." Then the door opened wider and the prettiest woman I have ever seen stood there, her hair so fair and golden, blue eyes twinkling at me and at the same time telling the child to invite Mr Franklin in; which she did very sedately.

'I went through the doorway into a hall where the woman held out her hand and introduced herself as Sarah and told me her father would be along in a minute. I shook her hand and repeated her name, then followed her into a sitting room. It looked and felt very comfortable as I sat in a big armchair, a fire crackled in the grate sending shadows on the walls of the room. Sarah turned on a lamp in the corner and another on a small table remarking how dark it was now getting. A food smell was coming from the kitchen, I could see through a door a table set for a meal.

'Sarah asked if she could get me a sherry and I stammered, "Yes please." I felt as though all sensible conversation had gone from my head. Jenny saved the day by bringing me a book to look at. I asked her if she could read and she proceeded to show me how clever she was, turning the pages and reading the large words at the bottom of each picture. Suddenly she jumped up from where she had been perched on the corner of the armchair to greet her grandfather; telling him to come and say hello to Mr Franklin who lives at the other side of the world. "Mummy showed me," she called as she ran out of the room. Adam shook my hand and apologised for not being there when I arrived. Jenny rushed back into the room holding her world; a spinning globe, her finger pointing to show Great Britain then turning to the other side to show New Zealand. Her grandfather sat down and lifted her onto his knees. Sarah came from the direction of the dining room holding a glass of sherry which she handed to her father, "Dinner is almost ready," she informed us.

'We had a lovely leisurely meal, talking about so many subjects. Then Sarah noticed Jenny was falling asleep. "Bedtime for you my lovely," she said to Jenny, picking her up and heading for the stairs.

'"Say goodnight to Mr Franklin."

'A whispered good night came from a tired little girl whose eyes were drooping.'

'Adam stood up and took Jenny from Sarah saying he would take her up then winked at me and whispered, "Don't like washing up, well that's my excuse anyway."

'I heard a sleepy voice asking, "Story Grandpa?" Sarah and I talked as I helped with the washing up; drying as she washed and piling the dishes on the table for her to put away later.

'"That was a lovely meal and I have really enjoyed being here."

As Wilf was telling me this, I couldn't help my memory turning back to the previous night and being told how people invited sailors into their homes and how I hoped it happened in Europe. Here I had proof it had. This was a lovely side of my mother and grandfather that I never knew. How little we know about our parents and mine died so young.

It was Wilf moving his position on the wall that brought me back. Maybe he felt he had lost me.

'How do you feel,' he asked, 'are you alright, not tired?'

I answered that I was fine and begged him to carry on with his story.

Wilf continued, 'Sarah told me she had only come to live with her father two months previously, when her mother died. She had been living on her own with Jenny and it seemed silly her father being on his own too. Her husband Ted had been lost at sea two years before. As she loved this house she had been born in, it seemed the right thing to do.

'Sarah made coffee and we sat quietly by the fire. After a while she excused herself and left the room. When she came back she beckoned me to go with her, her finger to her lips to denote silence. I followed her up the stairs to a door with a plaque and the name Jenny painted on it. Jenny was fast asleep, also in the chair by the bed, book still in hand, Adam slept peacefully with Jenny's little hand stretched out resting on her Grandpa's knee.

'I signalled to Sarah not to disturb him and we crept back down the stairs. I thanked her for spending a wonderful evening with me.

'"My father will be very upset with himself for falling asleep. What are your plans for tomorrow?" she asked me as we walked to the door.

'"Do you have any suggestions what I should do or where I could go?"

'"Come for coffee about 10 o'clock and I'll think about it in the meantime."

'"That sounds good to me," I told her, and thanked her again.

'The next morning when I came down to breakfast there was a note on my plate. Apologies from Adam for his rudeness and would I please eat with them again before I left to at least prove he had some good manners. After breakfast I managed to buy some flowers for Sarah. When I arrived at 10 o'clock Sarah was delighted with them, she led me into the dining room asking my forgiveness for the mess on the table. The table was covered with material and paper patterns. She picked up a vase and took it into the kitchen to fill with water, then arranged the flowers in the vase and put them on a table in the sitting room. I asked her what she was making and she went on to explain that she was making dresses for the "sunbeam" in the pantomime. I asked if she was in it too but no, not this year as she had enough to do making the dresses and getting material these days was a problem. Sarah told me that in the past she had much more involvement and fun with her late husband, Ted, who enjoyed being Widow Twanky or an Ugly Sister, depending on which pantomime it was. She was quite wistful as she said Ted had a lovely strong voice and she had made the rank of principal girl at one time, then other times in the chorus.

"'Have you given any thought to what we can do today?" I said 'we' in the hope she would not turn down my presumption that we would be doing whatever together. Pointing to the table she said she would be tied up with sewing until lunch time as it was needed for that night's rehearsal but could join me for the afternoon. She suggested between now and then I visited the museum which is very interesting. I told her I could find plenty to do and had better let her get on. Draining my coffee to leave I heard her say to come back at 1 o'clock for a sandwich. I suggested a better idea, lunch at The Golden Lion which she accepted. I left the house and walked down the path with an extra spring in my step, it felt good to be alive.

'How are you feeling Margaret?' Wilf asked.

'I am feeling fine,' I smiled. 'I realise how important those times were to you, for you to remember in such detail.'

'I have relived those times over and over again in my memory,' Wilf told me.

'Please go on, tell me more.'

'Right, where were we?'

'Oh yes, lunch at The Golden Lion,' he continued. 'I must admit I can't tell you what we ate. No, my mind was not on the food; I just felt wonderful being with Sarah. I remember we sat by a big open fire and a black Cocker Spaniel kept nuzzling her hand, wanting to continue being patted and having its head stroked. I envied that dog.

I remember in that wonderful haze hearing Sarah's voice telling me it was getting late and we would be falling asleep in front of the fire after the wonderful lunch. We walked for miles and miles, Sarah pointing out landmarks, telling me the history. She asked what had interested me in the museum. We talked and talked having so many interests in common.

'"You must come and eat with us again this evening. My father insisted I ask you and I agree with him, will you come?"

'I remember that invitation vividly. I told her of her father's note on my breakfast plate and would come if I could help in some way. There must be something I could do, peel potatoes perhaps. We agreed it was a deal and she held out her hand to shake on it. Her hand felt so good in mine it fitted perfectly. I didn't want to let it go. I brought myself back from reverie as I heard Sarah talking about me taking the morning train and asking if I would be back again. I wanted to say, yes next week but knew it wouldn't be that easy. I dared to venture if she would like me to come back because I would love to come back I told her. In a quiet voice I heard her say that I had been like a breath of spring in their lives and hoped I would come back. I asked if I could write to her and felt so elated when she said she was hoping I would suggest it.

'Sarah looked at her watch, it was time to go. A friend was meeting Jenny at school and she said she would be back before it got dark. We walked back quite briskly, following each other where the path narrowed. We called at her friend's house to collect Jenny. Sarah asked her daughter if she had a good day at school.

Jenny proceeded to tell us she had and reached into her pocket to bring out a piece of grey looking paper. She unfolded it and showed it to her mother. "This is your portrait," she proudly pronounced; Sarah took it and said it was a work of art.

'"What do you think Mr Franklin?" she passed it to me.

'I took the portrait paper and perused it seriously, aware of Jenny's face full of anticipation. I held it from me at arm's length as I had seen artists do. "The making of a great artist here I think but needs plenty of practice."

'"I will draw you if you would like me to," offered Jenny, seriously.

I bowed and told her, "I would be honoured."

'"You can keep Mummy's portrait too if it's alright with Mummy," she said.

'"That's a very nice thought dear," Sarah told her as she handed me the paper.

'You know, Margaret, I still have that drawing and the one that Jenny did of me later. I'll show you when you come to the farm, don't let me forget will you?'

'No, I won't forget. You must have loved my mother very much.'

'Yes I did,' he answered softly and continued. 'I had a wonderful evening with Sarah, Jenny and Adam. We listened to the news and talked about the situation.

'"The war must soon be over," Adam remarked.

'I agreed with him, but for the first time I realised how happy I was to be in England at war and not at home in New Zealand. I didn't want the evening to end. Leaving that house was like leaving a part of me behind; it was my heart. Going back to London on the morning train, my mind was racing with ideas. It would soon be Christmas, what could I get for a little girl and a big girl for that matter. Suddenly, I had other people to think about and my mind was full of happy thoughts, not just for tomorrow but for the future.

Wilf stood up, rubbing his back, commenting he was stiff with sitting so long. As I stood up I knew what Wilf meant, I ached too. I had been so interested in Wilf's story I had not noticed.

'Time we had a drink and something to eat. I'm hungry, how about you? It's gone quite chilly,' Wilf said, putting his arm around my shoulders and giving me a hug. 'Come on, race you to the car.'

We ran across the car park laughing, a mere fifty yards and we were panting at the sudden effort. It was nice to get back into the warmth. We hadn't noticed how the wind had risen. We must have been in a sheltered spot.

'Where shall we eat tonight?' Wilf asked me.

'Depending on that, do I need to go back to the hotel to change?' I questioned.

'If you are hungry now then no problem, we can easily find somewhere where we are perfectly dressed as we are now.'

'I know something I would like and I haven't had for a long time,' I said.

'What's that,' Wilf asked me.

'Fish and chips, they must be good here.'

'There is a wonderful fish and chip restaurant on the waterfront where you can eat inside or take them out but I think eating in for us, don't you?'

'Sounds marvellous,' I agreed.

It was warm and cosy in the restaurant and the smell made me hungrier than ever. When the fish and chips came, accompanied by tea, bread and butter, I couldn't believe my eyes at the size of the portion of fish. I thought I'd never eat all that but it was so delicious and the batter so thin and crispy, it just melted in my mouth. I devoured the lot.

We had been so intent upon our food that we hardly spoke other than to comment on how good it tasted but as we sat with our last cup of tea Wilf asked me, 'Do you remember your grandfather?'

'Yes, but not very well. I wasn't very old when he died and I don't know if my memories are really mine or more what Jenny told me she remembered of him. Jenny loved him very much. She was very upset when he died. I used to hear her crying in bed when she thought I was asleep. She kept a photograph of him and herself by her bed.'

'He was a wonderful man,' Wilf said wistfully. 'Your mother wrote and told me when he died. It was such a shock for everyone. It was so sudden. He wouldn't have liked to be ill for a long time. He was an active man, always making or doing something and, of course you must remember, he filled the part of Jenny's father for many years in the war.

'I wish I had known him better,' I said.

'What about your own father Margaret?'

'Oh, he was good fun, well a lot of the time, but sometimes he used to get quite down and depressed. Jenny and I had a term for it. We used to say he was having a "grey day" but mostly I have good memories. He was caring about all of us. Maybe, being away in the war made him appreciate what he had. It must have been difficult adapting to one arm. I once heard him say to someone who asked him how it happened. He said that he was lucky. Some chaps don't have any. He liked his job; I think that goes a long way towards someone's attitude to life. He liked being with and meeting people, everyone seemed to like him. I suppose he was a bit of a ladies' man when he was younger. He was very good looking you know. Did you ever see his photograph?'

'Yes I did. Your mother showed it to me. The main thing is that you were happy. Childhood is such an important time. It must have had a great effect on some children, their fathers being away for years, but Jenny seems to have come through that alright, wouldn't you say?'

'Yes Jenny seems happy to me. I can't wait to see her and Michael and Mark of course. I can't imagine that in two days' time I will be with them.'

'Less than two days now,' Wilf corrected.

'How time flies when one is having fun,' I laughed, looking forward to the 10th October.

We drove back to the hotel along the waterfront. There had been a shower while we were eating and the lights reflected on the wet road.

'How about a nightcap?' Wilf suggested.

'That would be lovely, the end to a perfect day, one that I don't want to end.' We sat in the hotel bar in deep comfortable chairs. I felt so relaxed, I wanted to savour every moment of this feeling. I couldn't believe I could feel so good. I looked across the table at this lovely man, trying to see him as my mother had seen him. He was obviously in love with her; I wondered how she had felt about him. My father had been presumed dead for two years by that time. Mother must have been feeling lonely. Had the war not ended, perhaps Wilf and mother would have been together but what about my father then; so much was going on in my mind.

'A penny for your thoughts,' Wilf was saying.

I told him how my mind was wandering. If my father had not returned from the war, perhaps mother and you would have been married and lived in New Zealand. That also means that you would have been my father.

'Would you have minded that?' Wilf asked.

'You mean, you being my father?

Oh no, I think you would have made a wonderful father. It's a pity you didn't have any children or maybe you have,' I teased, smiling at him with my head on one side questioningly.

'Oh my dear Margaret, if you only knew,' he said with anguish in his voice.

Suddenly, everything seemed to become serious. I was aware of something special. It was as though we were in a large room but in a cocoon at the same time. This moment in time was planned a long time ago.

'Tell me,' I said.

'You are my daughter Margaret,' Wilf said.

'How I have wanted to say those words, ever since we met in the cemetery at your mother's grave. I hope it isn't too much of a shock for you my dear.' I heard his words and realised why I had been reflecting along those same lines only a minute ago. I was being prepared or was it telepathy I was picking up from Wilf,

'I don't understand,' I realised I had spoken aloud.

'I will explain,' Wilf was saying. 'I don't want you to get the wrong idea about your mother and me but there is a lot to tell and it's late now. Perhaps you would prefer to leave it until the morning. I do hope I haven't spoilt your day?'

'Oh Wilf, you haven't spoilt my day, I have never felt happier, confused but happy. It explains so much that I couldn't understand. I always felt that Jenny was so special to my father; I knew I was special to my mother but father was always reserved. Yes, that is the word I would use now on reflection. I think he liked me, even loved me but I think he was conscious of it, sort of made an effort to try to treat me like Jenny. He always seemed to do things spontaneously with Jenny, then me as an afterthought, as though he should remember me but now you are telling me that my father is still alive. Do you realise what you are saying; you are alive!'

'I hadn't thought about it in quite that way,' Wilf said.

'What a relief. I may have never known you,' if you hadn't have come to the cemetery,' I said, 'Would you have ever told me?'

'I don't honestly know. For twenty years I have done what your mother asked of me. I could not see me doing any differently. She did not ask in the letter she left with a friend for me to contact you but I had such a strong feeling to go to England when I knew there was no point really as she was dead. So, who knows Margaret, perhaps your mother did bring us together. I know I was so happy to meet you and, when you said you would come here, I could not believe how lucky I was to have the chance to spend time with you; to get to know you and you to know me. I could not believe it possible after all those years of just letters and photographs. I wanted so much to make up for those years my dear, so, to hear you say, "your father is alive." I think I am going to cry, excuse me.' Wilf disappeared in the direction of the men's room, taking out his handkerchief as he went, blowing his nose.

I sat back in my chair, not realising how I had been leaning forward towards Wilf as he spoke. I felt a warm glow come over me, a pleasurable feeling of contentment. I was not alone, I felt safe. Wilf came back across the room and I stood up and went to meet him, taking his arm.

'I think you are right about bed time. I could go on talking and asking you questions all night but tomorrow is another day and it is going to be a full one. I am giving you a chance to get some sleep before I bombard you with questions tomorrow. I don't think I will sleep very much but I feel wonderful. I understand my mother much more and feel that, if it is possible, at this very moment she is happy too.'

'That makes three of us then,' Wilf said smiling.

'I am looking forward to tomorrow.'

'Me too,' I said, 'Goodnight.'

I stood by the window looking down on the waterfront, the lights reflecting in the rain. I thought of how short a time since I first looked at that view and of how much had happened in that time. Wilf, my father, after the way he had talked about my mother and how I was aware of his deep feelings; then it was no surprise and, as I had already told him, it covered many spaces in my father, Ted's, attitude, that I couldn't understand. I climbed into bed feeling like a little girl again, how strange life is. I had never believed I could say I felt really happy again after losing Martin but now I could doubt that, as I was aware of a different sort of happiness coming over me. I snuggled down the bed feeling safe again. I was not alone.

We arrived in the dining room for breakfast at the same time. As we sat down, Wilf said he must make a quick phone call. 'Order my toast and coffee please. I'll not be long.'

The waitress came along in a couple of minutes and I gave the order. Wilf returned and sat down just as the waitress brought our breakfast, putting poached eggs before me and saying,

'Toast for your father,' as she placed the toast rack on the table with the coffee.

'I am the happiest man alive,' Wilf said, his face glowing with pleasure.

'What happened?' I replied.

'Do you realise what you said to the waitress, "toast and coffee for my father."'

'Yes, it sounds good to me too, my father; my father. I am proud to say my father.'

'I too am proud to say, "my daughter."'

'We sound like a mutual admiration society,' I said and Wilf laughed.

'Will you bring your swimming costume with you today?'

'It's too cold to swim isn't it?'

'Not where I am taking you,' he replied.

We ate our toast in companionable silence or as silent as one can while crunching toast. We enjoyed each other's company as one does when

65

with someone you know likes you and you like them. To an onlooker we were together. It had rained through the night but now the sun was shining. We set off out of the city on the road north, over the harbour bridge. The water was living up to its name, 'Shining Waters,' the translation of the Maori name for the harbour which was dotted with boats of all types and sizes. What a beautiful city, a lovely way of life I thought. Wilf said we would not go the direct route but take a road in and out of many bays. My head turned like I was watching a tennis match, not wanting to miss anything. I don't know how Wilf kept the car on the road as I kept attracting his attention with 'look at this, and look at that, oh the view.' Had he taken any notice of my demands we would have had an accident but Wilf just kept smiling, getting great pleasure at my excitement.

We had lunch at a lovely old hotel, sitting on the veranda overlooking the sea. We watched a kitten in the garden trying its prowess at climbing a tree. We thought it had gone too high at one point and would need help to get down, but it seemed to just close its eyes and fall, landing on its feet and scampered away. For lunch we had a crunchy ploughman's, various cheeses, bread rolls, crisp lettuce salad and pickled onions. After this we walked along the beach allowing our food to digest. Wilf had brought me to the 'Hot Pools' which were lovely warm outdoor baths, hot water coming out of the ground from a natural spring called a geyser, controlled of course.

'These are not swimming baths as you know them,' Wilf told me, 'there are different pools of various heats, so some are for swimming but others for just sitting in, very therapeutic, that's why there is a ledge around the edge of the pool under the water.'

The steam rose around us, it was quite eerie but, as I grew accustomed to it, I felt myself relaxing and enjoying the sensation.

Later I asked Wilf if he would continue from yesterday's story.

'Oh yes, where was I?'

'It was soon to be Christmas and you sat on the train wondering what to get for Christmas presents, remember?'

'That's right,' he confirmed. 'My first priority when I had a few minutes, was to write to Adam and Sarah to thank them for their hospitality, for being such wonderful, friendly people and welcoming me, a virtual stranger, into their home. I posted the letter already anticipating a reply, working out how many days it would take to get there and how many for a reply to return, if answered straight away, which I did not dare hope for, so I added another few days onto my calculation so that I would not be too disappointed if it took longer. I would be delighted if a reply came sooner.

'Over the months I had struck up a friendly association with a woman in the NAFFI, Jessie, a big, jolly woman who claimed to be a genuine

Cockney having been born within the sound of Bow Bells and very proud of it. She served the meals and always had a happy word. I do not know how, not when she lived down the Tube station where whole families were camping on the platforms and coming up each morning, not knowing if their homes were a pile of rubble. People living in London during the war all deserved a medal,' Wilf said, going off his story.

'Anyway, back to Jessie, a marvellous woman. I asked her one day what she could suggest I get for Jenny and Sarah for Christmas. She asked if I knew Sarah's size and when I sort of held my arms out

She laughed saying, "that's no good but can she sew?"

'I told her that Sarah was very good at sewing.

'Jessie with hands on her ample hips said proudly, "My idea is that you get them some dress material. I have a friend who has some lovely stuff. What do you think?"

'"What a good idea I told her, you are a marvel. Will you arrange it for me?"

'"Leave it to me Luv," Jessie said.

'Not smoking myself, but claiming my allowance, enabled me to do a bit of swapping, so I acquired a few other goodies as well. The material duly arrived, one large piece and two smaller ones. I liked the patterns and colours; they would suit Sarah and Jenny. I felt like the cat that had the cream as I parcelled up my gifts, including a big box of chocolates with Adam's name on it, knowing it would be shared and also a book for Jenny.

'My calculations of getting an answer to my letter had been correct; the letter from Sarah was lovely and quite funny. She described the rehearsal of the pantomime and said how she wished I could have seen it myself. She asked what I was doing for Christmas and invited me to stay with them as they had plenty of room. How I wished I could spend Christmas with them, just a day would be wonderful but I knew it could not be. Maybe in the New Year I could go up again. Jenny enclosed her drawing of me as promised. I had bright red hair. I wrote back saying that I was sending a parcel, not to be opened until Christmas. Although I would love to be bringing it in person, I would be thinking of them all on Christmas day opening their presents. I hoped they liked them. I sent off the parcel with a letter and card enclosed, not knowing how long the parcel would take to get there.

'Christmas came and went as did New Year. I felt quite miserable. I thought how I would not have felt like that had I not wanted to be in the North, I would have accepted being in London. I watched the post every day. I received a letter from home, how everybody was, how the farm was doing. My mother concerned about my father's health. "He does too much," she wrote. There were no answers, not until this war was over.

'It was Easter before I could go north again, three whole days before I was due back. It took hours and hours on the train. We seemed to stop at every station, changing at Doncaster and waiting for a connection. Sarah and Jenny met me. It was a chilly day but Jenny could not wait to open her coat and show me her skirt and blouse.

'I said "You look lovely. Your Mummy is very clever."

'We walked back home from the station. There were daffodils along the roadside and in the gardens of most of the houses, so bright after a long winter. We entered the house and Sarah went straight to the fire, did marvellous things with the poker and it burst into crackling flames. Jenny and I sat watching the fire and the dancing shadows it made on the walls while Sarah brought in a tray filled with tea and cake. We sat there, eating and drinking in the firelight, warm, cosy and content.

'The front door opened and Adam came in. Jenny ran to him for a kiss. "Have you had a busy day Grandpa?" she asked, obviously having heard a grown up say the same.

'"Yes my dear, I have; and what sort of day have you had?"

'"We have been very busy," Jenny said, "We have been in the kitchen all morning, baking lovely things to eat."

'"That sounds good to me," Adam replied.

'"I have tried the cake and can recommend it," I said

'"It smells good," Adam said as he reached for a piece. Sarah handed him a cup of tea and he sat down with us by the fire.

'"Did anything exciting happen today Grandpa?"

'"Well, a little bird told me that there is a fair over on the common this weekend."

'"Can we go Grandpa, can we?" said Jenny jumping up and throwing herself onto his knees.

'"What do you think Mummy?" he said turning to Sarah.

'"I think we can manage that."

"Would you like to come too, Mr Franklin?" Jenny said.

'"Try to stop me," I replied, grinning at her.

'The days flew by too quickly. We went to the fair and had fish and chips for tea.

'After Jenny was in bed, Adam suggested I take Sarah for a drink at the hotel. "I will be here for Jenny, you go and enjoy yourselves."

'We walked down to the pub; it was a beautiful evening. We sat in a corner and in the public bar a darts match was in progress. Sarah asked me why I was stationed in London and I explained how I had been injured and given a desk job. I went to the bar to get another drink and when I came back a man was talking to Sarah.

'"Oh Wilf," she said, "I would like you to meet my cousin, Jack." We shook hands.

'"Jack has a garage; we passed it as we walked here. I was telling him that you farm in

New Zealand and round up the sheep on a motor bike."

'Jack and I got into a discussion about motor cycles and I told him my father collected old motor bikes and also had a 1929 Sunbeam car.

'"I'd love to see them," Jack said.

'"You will have to come over to New Zealand when the war is over. You will be welcome at the farm," I replied.

'"Come and see the garage before you go back. Have a ride on my bike." He left us to return to the darts match in the next room.

'"Nice chap," I said to Sarah. "I'll take him up on that offer."

'I did just that the next morning. Sarah was busy and I walked along to the garage. Jack was delighted to see me. We went through into the back of the building, into his treasure trove. Partly built bikes and bits and pieces everywhere, some hanging from the walls, others from the beams of the ceiling.

'"My father started the garage," he proudly told me. "He had the first motor bike in this area." We sat with great pint size mugs of tea and talked and talked.

He showed me the bike he was using himself. "Take it out for a run around the town if you like."

'So, off I went. It was good to feel the wind on my face. It was so long since I had ridden a motor bike, years in fact. I remembered the days of racing on the farm tracks in my teens until my father objected strongly. By the time I got back to the garage I felt quite exhilarated. I thanked Jack and told him how much I had enjoyed it.

'"Take it for a proper run the next time you come."

'"I'll keep you to that," I told him.

'It was lunch time when I returned to the house. I told Sarah what a good morning I had had and how the next time I come, "that's if you'll invite me again," I added quickly, "then we could go for a run on the motor bike. What do you think of that?"

'"I'll look forward to it," Sarah replied smiling at my enthusiasm.

'Sarah, Jenny and I went for a long walk in the afternoon. We walked along the path on the river bank, climbing over styles which divided the fields. Jenny was full of energy on the way out, clambering over the styles and running ahead of us, but she soon started to flag on the way back. I carried her on my shoulders.

'"It's lovely up here, I can see for miles and miles," she cried.

'We stopped on the river bank for a rest. Sarah produced some biscuits from her pocket and we all munched away happily.

'"You have not worn your new dress Mummy. Will you put it on when we get back?"

'"What made you think of that?" Sarah asked.

'"I was remembering Christmas," Jenny replied.

73

'When we got back home Adam surprised us by having prepared tea. "Thought I would give Sarah a break, now all just sit down, it will soon be ready."

'Sarah kissed him on the cheek and thanked him for the lovely idea. Jenny showed me her latest pictures and how she could write her name "properly," as she put it. Jenny looked up, I turned around, and Sarah stood in the doorway wearing her new dress made of the material I had sent her for Christmas.

'She looked lovely, the colour suiting her hair. She did a little twirl, the skirt billowing out. "Do you like it?" she asked.

'"It's absolutely lovely, you are so clever," I replied.

'"Dinner is ready," Adam announced, "All changed for dinner I see," he said when he saw Sarah. "You look lovely my dear."

'I did not want the evening to end. After we washed up and Jenny was in bed, once more Adam suggested we go for a drink.

'Sarah and I went back to the pub but only for one drink. We came out and went for a walk. It was a very bright evening, almost a full moon. We sat on a seat and looked at the man in the moon, wondering what it was really like up there.

'I asked Sarah about Ted. "Were you very happy?"

'"We were most of the time," she said, "but I regret that last year."

'"What happened?" I asked.

'"Oh, it was my jealousy I suppose, but Ted was very attractive, the girls all liked him, he was very popular. We belonged to the Amateur Dramatic Society as I told you and this one girl was always around Ted. I was pregnant at the time so that probably made me overreact, making me more suspicious than I needed to be. I just felt that they were too friendly. When I tackled Ted about it he said it was my imagination. I was the only girl for him. I never, ever, felt quite happy about it though. We parted for him to go to war with this between us and I was sorry."

'It was a bit chilly and she shivered. I put my arm around her to keep her warm; she turned her head towards me and smiled. I put my lips gently on hers. Her lips were so soft, and I wanted to stay like that forever, my heart beating as though it would burst. I dare not believe what was happening. Sarah wanted to kiss me, to return my kisses, we held each other closely. The wind grew stronger and it became cold, so we walked home hand in hand. I did not want to go back to London in the morning, or ever for that matter.

'When we got back to the house Adam had already gone to his room. Sarah stirred the fire with the poker and the coals leapt into life. She made some hot chocolate and we sat by the fire until it burnt away, putting off the moment of parting. How soon could I return I thought; soon I hoped.

'When I returned to London I enquired about leave in the near future. '"Nobody is going anywhere," I was told. There was a very busy time ahead of us.

'Sarah and I corresponded frequently, but I could not visit her. The end of the war in Europe was getting near; we all knew that and the day in May finally arrived. The lights went on in London and all over Britain, people danced in the streets and the men started to come home.

'It was a long hard time getting them repatriated. They came into Britain first; then the married men were given priority to be sent home to New Zealand. As I said earlier, single men like me were given the chance to do something worthwhile for their careers; while they waited to go home and so I contacted Adam to see if I could join his bank for a few weeks instead of staying in London. The army would be paying, if you could call it pay, it was so little. Adam replied that it was a wonderful idea.

'I returned to the north a happy man. It was like going home. Everything went so smoothly. I settled into the bank easily, thinking what a good idea to be doing this before returning to New Zealand. Most of the customers were the same as back home, farming people. The north of England is so like New Zealand, country wise, sheep, sheep and more sheep with some cattle thrown in.

'The routine, both at the house and work went like clockwork and I looked forward to going home each evening to Sarah. One weekend we took up Jack's offer to take his motor bike for a proper run.

'Adam said he would look after Jenny and suggested we go over the moors to Whitby. "Climb the steps to the Abbey and watch the sun go down from there. It's wonderful."

'We went to Whitby on the motor bike, crossing the moors, the heather was a sea of purple; we stopped to pick some to put on the front of the bike for luck.

'We walked around the many narrow streets, gazing in the shop windows, watching the fishing boats in the harbour, listening to the noise of the gulls waiting for fish. The path up the hillside was steep. As we passed the hotels we looked in the windows then climbed down to the beach. Walking along the sand, we joked about Dracula written by Bram Stoker who lived in Whitby.

'Across the harbour, on the other side of the town standing proudly on the hilltop, was the Abbey; a beautiful old ruin. After we had eaten we climbed the ninety or more steps leading up to the Abbey, stopping every so often to get our breath and look back at the view of the sea and harbour.

'The light was the soft light of early twilight, a golden hush around everything. Walking around the Abbey time seemed to stand still, a silence enveloped us and we sat on the hillside looking out at the sea. We marvelled at Captain Cook, also from Whitby and his discovery of New Zealand and how small the world really is.

'I told Sarah about New Zealand and how bright the stars are there and the Southern Cross so easy to see in the night sky. I told her about the water going down the plug hole in the opposite direction to here in the Northern Hemisphere. She laughed and said I was joking.

'Suddenly she flung herself against me, as a bat dipped and zoomed in the air about us. I put my arms around her, putting my mouth against her neck pretending to be Dracula and going to bite her. She laughed and giggled. Then things changed, her skin felt so soft beneath my lips, I did not want to bite, I wanted to kiss.

'I kissed her neck beneath her ear, the faint smell of her perfume rose to make me dizzy. I kissed her throat then the other side of her neck. I opened my eyes to see her eyes were closed, her chin tilted upwards and her lips waiting for mine. Then I kissed her eyes one by one, then her lips again, this time more deeply. I felt her hands move up my back, gently, each vertebrae coming alive to her touch like a spark of electricity. We lay down in the long grass as the sun went down over the hill; everything was in slow motion as though we were in a time warp.

'We made love. It was the most wonderful experience of my life, the deepest gentlest feelings I have ever known, yet I felt afire with a passion there were no words for. I was in love.

'The lights had come on all over the town. Lights that a few weeks ago were not allowed. All would have been darkness with blinds at every window. Now everyone wanted their lights to show. Down had come the blinds and people left their curtains open, part of the feeling of freedom after fear and restriction over the past five years.

'I felt the future as a bright star and asked Sarah if she would marry me and come to New Zealand and Adam too if he would.

'I told her I wanted her to see the Southern Cross and how the stars are brighter. She laughed and hugged me and said she wanted to see the water go down the plug hole in the other direction, so she would have to come with me.

'"What an excuse to get married," I said and we hugged each other and did a little dance around and around, one way then the other way, pretending to be the water going down the plug hole.

'It was very late when we arrived home, everyone was in bed. Quietly we entered the house and sat in the kitchen having a cup of hot chocolate speaking in whispers. It was our last weekend together alone. One more working week then I would go back and explain the circumstances. Tell them that I wanted to defer my return to New Zealand as I wished to get married first. We stole upstairs into my room at the back of the house where we held each other closely and made love once more.

'The next morning I awoke feeling on top of the world. I, for once, knowing the meaning of those words. I went down into the kitchen and there she was, sitting at the table, tears rolling down her cheeks, a letter in her hands. She looked up at me and motioned for me to take the letter. It was from the War Office, Her husband was alive, he was to be in hospital for tests and, if all was well, he would soon be home. I did not know if the tears were for joy or despair.

'Sarah decided she could not leave Ted and take Jenny away from him. Those last few days together were agony. I desperately wanted her to say she would come to New Zealand. I knew I was going back soon and would never see her again. I prayed that she could come over to me, and it was a mistake about Ted. We didn't know she was pregnant at that time of course; it would have made all the difference.

'"Put yourself in his place," Sarah had said "All those years away and then to come home to find your wife and child gone." I tried to understand how Ted must be feeling too, I thought about my homecoming and how it could be me. I understood.

'When Sarah had realised that she was pregnant her feelings were of joy and sorrow. Happy to be having my child but sorry we could not be together. Sarah had told Ted about me and he had been very understanding. She could not leave Ted now she wrote. She told Ted the child was mine but he said he would bring it up as his, no one would ever know.

'Sarah wrote to me later explaining that when Ted's ship had blown up he had been thrown into the water, the explosion made him deaf, he had lost an arm and his sight in one eye. He had been found on the beach and saved by the local people. These people had moved away inland for their own safety from the Japanese, taking him with them. He had eventually regained his memory and partial hearing but knew he would have been reported dead. No one should have survived that explosion and distance from the mainland.'

Wilf was almost in tears as he relived the memory of those early years. I sympathised with his highs and lows of emotional turmoil. One day picking heather for luck on the Yorkshire moors and a future of happiness, only to find the next day every hope dashed in one short letter.

He told me that he came back to New Zealand and threw himself into work. He did not go into a city bank but stayed local to home so that he could help his father on the farm. In the long term this would have affected his future career in banking but as it happened it was for the best as he left banking to take over the farm. Building up the business filled his every waking moment and, looking into the future to see which direction to develop. That led him into the haulage and crop dusting businesses; also, buying more land as it became available. He filled his life with being successful in a man's world of achievement.

'Sarah wrote and sent photographs regularly,' he said. 'I must admit that there were times when I was very angry at the way things were and wanted to shout out what had happened and the injustice of life. Then, I would read

Sarah's letters and you both seemed happy in England and I would calm down and carry on as usual.'

'Sarah probably intended to tell you about me when you were older, or maybe never. We will never know, but she would not have expected to die so young. It's so easy to keep putting intentions off until another day, another time more suitable, that time never seemed to come.'

I was to remember those words often in my future as I did a similar thing as my mother had done. We drove back to the hotel in silence, each lost in our own thoughts. I had told Wilf how I understood about him and Sarah, my mother, and once more repeated my happiness at finding him, my father, alive.

For our last evening in Auckland, we dined at the harbour watching the boats coming and going. Wilf seemed quite weary after dredging up all that old emotion but, after a couple of drinks and some good food, he brightened up considerably and we talked about when I returned to New Zealand and the many places he wanted to show me.

'I'll not waste any more years,' he promised me and himself. 'There is a lot of catching up to do.'

Wilf took me to the airport. There was sadness and happiness, not too much sadness because I would be returning and was happy about seeing Jenny, Mark and Michael in a few hours.

Chapter 6 Australia 1966

I thanked Wilf for all he had done for me and especially telling me he is my father. I could not wait to tell Jenny. We hugged and kissed each other, not wanting to part after so short a time together in our new awareness but knowing that we would be together again and how much I would have to tell him about my experiences in Australia. I waved as I went through departures and he waved back.

The plane took off into a clear, blue morning sky. I loved the feeling of being up there, floating along in a cocoon of time and space, looking forward to arriving in another country and meeting my family.

I could not understand what had happened to Jenny. I expected them to be there to meet me, when I came through customs, as we had arranged. I stood about thinking they may have had trouble with the car or traffic. Eventually I went to the information desk to see if there was a message for me but there wasn't. Wilf had given me some small change in case I needed anything at the airport.

'But Jenny will be there,' I had said.

'You never know,' he'd replied.

How true I thought as I mentally thanked him. Now I could try the telephone. The number rang and rang; a funny continuous noise but then again, I thought, it could be a different sound here.

No answer, so they must be on their way. I went to the coffee bar, ordered a cup of coffee and sat down where I could see people passing to and from the entrance.

A man left a newspaper on a nearby seat, obviously finished with, so I reached over and picked it up. I became quite absorbed in the paper and suddenly realised that over an hour had passed. Something is definitely wrong I thought. I returned quickly to the information desk again, no message. I telephoned, still the same noise, no reply. Perhaps Jenny had got the wrong day or flight. I checked the date on my ticket, 10th October.

As I returned to the coffee bar the girl recognised me; I asked her to change a bill for me as I needed to get a taxi. She was sorry but she didn't have enough change and pointed to the bank just along on the left. I had my large notes changed into smaller ones at the bank, also cashed another travellers cheque. I might as well do it now as later, I thought. I went out of the airport entrance pushing my trolley to the taxi rank, still looking and hoping to catch sight of Jenny before I set off.

The taxi turned into the road, or at least tried to, there were police cars everywhere. An ambulance stood by the gates of a house. I looked at the number of the nearest house and automatically counted off the numbers. Jenny's house!

My heart dropped, I felt a prickle of fear rise from the base of my spine to spread up my back to tingle at my neck, my breathing felt as though it had stopped. I felt leaden in my feet as I tried to walk forward from the taxi.

A woman was standing nearby, holding a small child. I recognised him from the pictures that Jenny had sent, it was Michael. I moved forward with a new spurt of energy and relief. I told the woman that I was Jenny's sister.

She burst into tears and held the child out to me. As I took Michael in my arms I heard the woman say,

'They are dead.' Just like that.

I spoke to Michael and told him who I was. 'Aunty Maggie, do you remember me? You have seen pictures of me, haven't you?'

He raised his little head from my shoulder to take a better look at me as we moved away, the woman leading towards her house.

'Maggie,' Michael was saying, 'Maggie, Maggie.'

As we entered the woman recovered enough to introduce herself.

'I am Louise, your sister's neighbour. Perhaps you had better leave Michael with me before you go on.'

I turned to look back at the scene behind me. What was happening was like when I found John Hunter at my door when Martin died. I knew they were dead, that was enough to cope with, the details were not necessary at that moment.

A man was coming out of Jenny's house. He was wearing a blue short-sleeved shirt and grey shorts and my sharp impression was how grey he looked and how can that be possible with such a gorgeous tan. He was almost six feet tall with powerful shoulders and a strong neck, his legs and arms were muscular and a golden brown, his hair was a shock of blonde probably bleached by the sun. That was my first sight of Alan.

'I'm hungry,' the little voice said I gave a sob of despair as I remembered my mother saying, "There can't be much wrong with you if you can eat."

We gave Michael some cereal and as he ate he started to fall asleep, his eyelids kept drooping. What had those eyes seen I wondered? Lifting him gently from the chair I took him upstairs to the bedroom and placed him into the turned down bed. He turned on to his side and I tucked the covers around him and he was asleep. I was invited to sleep there too and, not knowing what to do otherwise, I gratefully accepted.

What kind people. They told me that they were also from England, from Devon. They had not lived in this house for long but had already realised that, when loud music was played next door, it was to hide the sound of raised voices and things being broken. The next day Jenny would not be seen. It was this not seeing her that made them suspicious of the reason for the loud music plus when she did appear she would be wearing long sleeves and skirt, even on the hottest days. It was never her face that showed any signs of being beaten.

I knew I had to inform the police who I was, so, I went across the garden to Jenny's house.'

The police were just putting the covered stretchers into the ambulance when I went into the house. There was broken glass everywhere, furniture turned over, and there was blood on the walls.'

'Sorry lady, you should not be in here,' a young policeman said.

'I am her sister,' I said and then felt myself floating away as the floor seemed to come up and hit me. That was my first meeting with Alan; he had seen me enter the house and realised I was coming to see Jenny and Mark. He caught me as I fainted. When I came round I was back in the house next door again with Alan sitting at my side on the sofa. He told me who he was and of course I knew of him from Jenny's letters.

'What happened? - Please tell me everything, I must know.'

Alan told me of his concern for her safety after various incidents that had happed but first he would tell me about that day.

'I had returned from a two-day flight duty, 'he began, 'I don't know if Jenny said I was a pilot, in her letters, but I had just got home and taken off my uniform and had a shower. I turned on my answer phone while I looked through my mail. There were a couple of messages then a faint voice said, "Help me," then silence. It was Jenny's voice, very weak, I felt a surge of panic hit me. I checked what time the call was made and dialled

Jenny's number from memory. The line didn't connect. I ran to the door to get my car at the same moment my mind told me to call the police. I dialled emergency and sent an ambulance to 8 Orchard Road. "Someone is very ill," I told the operator.

'My mind went into automatic gear as I backed the car out onto the street. I cursed the fact of living at the other end of town; I thanked God that all the traffic lights were with me. As I turned off the main road I heard the sirens of a police car. I entered the road at the same time as the police car coming from the other direction. We drove side by side to the end of the road and jumped out of our cars simultaneously. Running down the path we heard a loud bang, a gunshot. We stopped in our tracks.

After our initial caution we rushed the door together. It gave easily and swung back against the wall. Glass and broken ornaments were everywhere, the furniture was turned over and soil from plants spread across the carpet. Mark was sprawled across the bottom of the stairs.'

Alan stopped talking and looked at me in concern.

'Go on,' I said, 'I need to know everything, I have to face it sometime, better now.'

Alan continued, 'The force of the bullet had knocked Mark's head back, giving a startled look to his lifeless face, blood splattering the white painted walls. I rushed up the stairs, the police officer going into the downstairs rooms, everywhere was carnage. Jenny's body was sprawled on the bed, her face covered with thick red lipstick. On the wall above her head was scrawled the word "S L U T" in the same red. I touched her face and her head lolled off the pillow twisting to a strange angle as her broken neck gave no support. I took her hand, I wept.'

'"Don't touch anything." It was the police officer at the bedroom door. I looked up at him, he looked back at me, and we both looked up towards the ceiling in a silent question, WHY?

'A tiny whimper brought me down to earth, I had forgotten Michael. I rushed into the next bedroom; the bed was turned over against the wall, the lamp on the floor. I gently eased the mattress away and there was Michael, rubbing his eyes as though he was just waking up. "Alan," he said. I picked him up and held him close to me. When we came down the stairs, I held Michael's head into my shoulder, covering his face with my hand so he would not see his father. I carried him outside and Louise, here, took him from me that must have been around the time you arrived.'

Louise placed cups of coffee in our hands and I thanked her automatically. I asked Alan what were the incidents that had aroused his concerns and he continued relaying the happenings.

'I had evidence of Mark's jealousy before, not of me, there seemed to be some special trust he had for me. Mark knew I had lost my fiancé in a road accident, so apart from the occasional match making, he never bothered me about my private life. He seemed to know that time would heal and take care of things and when the time was right the girl for me would be there. He had a deep understanding, an awareness of time being precious in some way.

'In this, at times, he seemed to be in a rush to do things and I would have to say, "Hey slow down, you'll burn yourself out; there's always tomorrow."

'He would give a grunt and say, "yes, you're right." It was Mark's reaction to other men that was the problem.

'One time, we were in a bar with a group of friends, sat having a quiet drink, when suddenly Mark jumped up, rushed across the room and grabbed a man by his shirt front and punched him in the face. At first I thought he was in a rush to get to the men's room so was amazed to see the man with blood all over his face and his nose obviously broken. Mark said the man had been staring at Jenny, which may have been true, but so had half the men in the room. She was beautiful.

'The next unsettling thing was when I went over to the house after being away for a few days and came onto the porch to see Mark watching Michael playing on a blanket on the lawn. Michael seemed to hurt himself on a toy. Mark sprang from the porch, took the toy and smashed it against the wall. Michael sat watching his daddy. I looked from father to child, not quite sure of what I had witnessed.

I spoke to Michael as I came down the steps, both heads turning at the sound of my voice. "I hope this one won't break that easily as I handed Michael the little wooden car I had brought for him."

'"Damn thing was dangerous," Mark mumbled, but he knew I had meant that it was no way for a child to see his father behave. I must admit that over the past few months I had noticed a change, a sort of intensity that I had not seen before.'

Alan told me how he had become friends with Mark. He knew him as a generous kind of man, a man with a terrific sense of humour, a dry humour but could take a joke at himself. They had worked together when Jenny and Mark first came to Australia but Alan now worked for a commercial airline company and, as such spent more time away from home, training men in other areas as well as flying his own duties.

They enjoyed the time they spent at sea on Alan's yacht, The Princess, and never had a wrong word, being able to give and take as they parried words at each other, knowing neither meant harm in what they said, feeling completely at ease with one another.

What happened about a week earlier had given Alan great concern for Jenny. Mark had been doing some work on The Princess and Jenny had gone to the yacht to take a picnic lunch to share with Mark. Michael was being looked after by their neighbour so Jenny had taken advantage of the time to relax at the beach. They had a lovely lunch together on the yacht, which was out of the water to have work done on the hull and laughed about being "Up in the World" as they sat on the deck, high off the ground in dry dock. After clearing away the picnic things, Jenny left Mark happy at work, took her towel and went down to the beach. Not the public beach but small area of sand just below the dry docks, not too far away and very private.

The sun was hot but there was a slight breeze, enough to keep the temperature comfortable. Jenny enjoyed her few precious moments of peace from everyday living with a baby and husband to look after. She had oiled herself with lotion so as not to get her skin burnt and adjusted her bikini so as to get as much of a suntan as possible.

Suddenly a man's voice brought her out of her reverie, what had he said? She lifted her hat from her face to see a young man looking down at her. She wasn't quite sure what he had said, she may have been mistaken, but felt it was something she did not want to hear. It was a dirty suggestion. She started to cover herself, to adjust her bikini. He seemed to think her movements were consent. He straddled her body, still standing in a very domineering stance, one hand on his crotch; he leaned forwards staring into her eyes as he reached out to grasp her bikini top with his other hand. Jenny tried to sit up. Suddenly, he lurched backwards and rose up off the ground into the air and landed with a thud on the sand. Mark was on top of him, beating him from one side then the other, the rain of blows knocking the young man senseless.

As if the last breathe had gone out of him, Mark turned from the beaten man to face Jenny. Jenny was crying, huddled in a heap. He went towards her and she put up her hand for help, he took it but, instead of giving her a pull to get to her feet, he wrenched her arm around and dragged her bodily up the beach. She tried to get away but couldn't.

"Dirty slut," he was cursing. "I'll show you what you'd get from that animal."

He pulled her across the gravel to the dry dock underneath the Princess. There he tore off her bikini top and savagely bit her breasts, one hand held her hands behind her back whilst the other tore off her bikini bottom. He threw her face down across the bottom girder and raped her. The sun heated metal searing into her stomach with each furious thrust of his body.

'I found her in the galley. I don't know how she had managed to climb up the ladder; she was huddled in a corner, an old sweater I wear for painting pulled over her.' Alan said, 'She told me what happened but would not go to the doctors or report him to the police.

"It's my fault," she kept whimpering, "I hate myself, I hate men looking at me but they do. Mark says I'm a witch, it's my fault not his; I make him angry."

'I took her, home making her promise she would call me if she needed anything. I confronted Mark and said I would go to the police if I saw or heard anything again.

'He was sorry by that time and said, he did not know what came over him and he hated himself for what he had done. It was as though someone else took him over. A rage built up inside of him and seemed to take control. I told him that was no excuse and he should see someone about it. He said he had been to someone to get help to control himself and was trying very hard, but sometimes the over control made him worse, as though it turned in on him, bringing out some demons, he saw red mists.'

While the police sorted out Jenny and Marks house, no one was allowed in. I slept that first night at the neighbours with Michael. A woman arrived the next morning from the Social Services, saying that she would have to take the baby into care.

'Oh no,' I cried, 'I am his mother's sister, I can look after him.'

'I am very sorry,' she said, 'but I gather from the information that I have been given you are not resident here. Is that correct?'

I had to admit that it was true.

'Please tell me what is going to happen,' I begged.

'We will take care of Michael, until he can be fostered,' she said.

'Could I foster him?' I asked. 'He was born in England, they have only been here for three years, and I am his only relative. Perhaps I can take him back to England, or maybe I can apply to stay here.'

My mind was racing fifty to the dozen. I explained how my husband had died a few months earlier and I had come to visit my sister and her family with the intention of looking into staying in Australia with them.

'There will be a lot of red tape,' she said. 'Do you have anyone to help you?'

I told her of Alan's offer and my father in New Zealand.

'You have a father in New Zealand?'

'Why yes, he was born there. He met my mother in England during the war.'

'He's your best bet,' she told me. 'New Zealand and Australia have reciprocal agreements; may I ask how old you are?'

'Twenty, I'll be twenty one in February.'

'That's good,' she said smiling, 'can you get your father over here?'

'Yes,' I said, hoping it was possible.

'The sooner we take Michael away from here the better,' she was saying.

Just then Alan arrived. I told him what had been said and he replied, there was no problem;

'You can stay at my place. I am going away tomorrow for two days, it will give you a bit of peace to get yourself together. How does that sound?'

I thanked him for his kindness then turned to the woman,

'Can I take Michael?'

'I am so sorry,' she said, 'he will have to come with me, but you can visit him and stay with him all day if you wish, but it must be at the Children's Home.'

'Can I come with you and Michael now?'

'Yes, of course, the more time with you the better,' she replied.

'What about Michael's things?' I asked.

'We have all we need at the Home, don't worry, better to leave those memories behind him. We have clothes and toys to suit him, you'll see, he will be fine.'

I thanked the neighbours and said I would be in touch; what a terrible experience for them, I thought. We all left, Alan following behind in his car.

We settled Michael into the Children's Home then Alan suggested he take me to his apartment and show me how everything worked. I looked back at Michael sitting on the floor playing with another little boy surrounded by toys. As I had kissed him and explained I was going shopping but would be back soon.

'Soon Maggie,' he said, and turned back to his toys. He will be fine, I told myself, I will see to that.

When I got to Alan's apartment, I telephoned Wilf. He was not in the house but would be contacted and would phone me back I was told.

Alan showed me around the apartment, it had a balcony and this was the first time I had really looked around me, apart from in the taxi.

I took a deep breath and shuddered, one second aware of the tragedy that had taken place and the next, of what I had taken on. I prayed at that moment that I could have that responsibility; please let Michael be mine.

Alan brought me back to reality. He was handing me a cup of coffee. 'Do you take sugar?' he was saying.

'No thank you. You have a lovely view.'

'Yes, when I come home from work I only have to step out here and I feel relaxed. Here, have a seat, rest and enjoy your coffee. A few moments won't hurt. You are not going anywhere until you hear from Wilf. You said he is your father; can I ask, are you and Jenny half-sisters?'

I sat on the chair Alan offered me. I told him how Wilf had met my mother, how I had only known of this two days before, whilst in New Zealand with him. I had so much to tell Jenny. I burst into tears. Standing up my coffee spilt over into the saucer. Alan took the cup away from me, put it down and reached over to me. I was aware of big arms drawing me to him, I wept and wept.

'I'm so sorry,' I said to him trying to compose myself.

'Just what you needed, have to get it out you know.' His voice was thick with emotion. 'Time for another coffee,' he said.

The telephone rang, it was Wilf. I took a deep breath to calm myself, and then started to relate the happenings of yesterday.

'Oh my dear, you should have called me sooner, I'll be over straight away.' I did not have to ask him to come; tears rolled down my cheeks. I passed the telephone to Alan to give directions to Wilf as I could not speak.

'Give him my love,' I managed to snuffle to Alan.

Alan explained that it would be evening by the time Wilf arrived so I went back to the Children's Home to spend time with Michael. On the way back Alan pointed out the route for me to come while he was away.

'Drive your car?' I said in dismay.

'Of course, it's a long walk otherwise,' laughed Alan.

How kind people are, I thought, how kind.

'Thank you for everything Alan,' I said.

'No problem. Just remember though, I am not a mind reader, so if there is anything you want or I can do then please do say so.'

Alan took me to the airport to meet Wilf. He came through the barrier and once more I felt myself swept into comforting arms, my nose buried into his soft wool sweater. The two men introduced themselves as I sniffed again into my handkerchief. We had not eaten; I was not hungry but Alan insisted that we must eat something so we went into a Bistro. I played at eating some spaghetti, the fork going round and round in my dish.

Alan told Wilf what he knew of the position with Michael. Wilf reached out and took my hand. 'Don't worry about Michael, it can all be sorted out, no strangers will get him if that's what you are thinking.' I smiled at him as much as I could smile.

I then excused myself to go to the ladies room before I made a spectacle of myself at the table. I wept with relief; looking in the mirror I saw a red eyed, sorry looking female. What a mess I thought. Bending to splash cold water onto my face I resolved not to let Michael see me like this. I put on fresh eye makeup. Amazing what can be done with a bit of powder and lipstick I thought as I look at the result in the mirror.

Wilf had booked into a hotel not far from Alan's apartment, so we dropped him off there. We were all ready for bed. Alan had an early flight so was gone when I got up. There was a piece of paper propped up against the toaster. It was a round circle, supposed to be the sun, the mouth an upturned curve – keep smiling was printed underneath.

I telephoned Wilf to say I had surfaced and he said he would walk round to me. He would drive the car I thought, relieved. I didn't feel like facing that task at the moment. Wilf took me to the Children's Home where he came and said hello to Michael first then disappeared into the office.

All day I helped doing one thing and another. I wanted to make myself useful, not to be in the way. That evening Wilf told me I had to be twenty one to be able to have Michael, there would be no problem then and, with him as sponsor, there was no reason we could not go and live in New Zealand with him. I told him I did not think there would only be Michael and me. I was pregnant. His face lit up.

'You mean I am going to be a real grandfather,' he said.

'I hadn't thought that far but, yes you are.' I got another hug for that, a gentle one as though I was made of glass. 'I won't break.'

'Are you alright, have you seen a doctor?' Wilf asked anxiously.

'No, I haven't, I only started to realise when I was with you. I seemed to put on so much weight around the middle; I had a problem fastening up my waistbands. That's when I started to think. I've had no morning-sickness, which is the first give away usually. I thought I was suffering stress from Martin's death and that had upset my monthly cycle. I'm over three months pregnant, Wilf. Can you cope with all of us?'

'You try me,' he replied. We discussed many things. I told him I thought it better that no one knew that Michael was not mine. He agreed and had not told anyone at the farm, only that he was having a visitor some time next February. A visitor, not three.

'I never was any good at maths, everyone knows I can't count,' said Wilf smiling. He took my hands and put them together in his.

'You have no idea how happy you are making me. I am only sorry that you are having so much sorrow in doing it.'

'I don't know what I would have done without you Wilf. If there was ever a better time to find a father then I don't know one. Thank you for finding me.'

'I'm hungry and I know you are going to say you aren't, but mothers need nourishment and may I remind you that you are now eating for two.'

'You are so right,' as I patted my tummy.

Michael seemed fine at the Home. If he asked for his Mummy then no one told me. When I went in he always held out his arms to be hugged. 'Maggie,' he would say. He showed me his books and I bought him new toys, letting him choose some things himself.

Wilf arranged for me to have an apartment near the Home which was at the other side of the city from where Jenny and Mark had lived, almost in the country, a small suburb by the sea.

'I have been to see a doctor and my baby will be born in February, maybe on my birthday,' I told Wilf.

Wilf had to go back to the farm. He said he would be back over within days if I needed him. I assured him it would be fine and not to worry about me.

'But I like it,' he said. 'I have never enjoyed worry like this before. If this is what you call worry then I can take as much as you can throw at me.'

'I love you. I can understand my mother falling in love with you. I thank her for giving me you as my father,' I said.

'We're back to the mutual admiration society again,' Wilf teased.

I don't want to remember too much about the funeral, so I am not going to. It was very quiet.

Alan was wonderful. He helped me to settle into the apartment; it was furnished but I wanted one or two things of my own. I bought a new bed cover and some bright cushions for the settee and chairs, a lamp and a bright mat for the sitting room floor to match the cushions. It looked more homely. Michael liked it. He was allowed to come and spend time with me at the apartment and sometimes we brought another child too.

I was to stay in Australia until my baby was born. By then I would be twenty-one years old and Wilf and I would be able to take Michael to New Zealand. When I arrived there, it would be thought that I had brought both children from England. I had married very young so it was possible.

One day I sat helping the children with their painting when the Matron came and asked if I had trained in teaching. I told her I had but never actually started teaching. She asked if I would like to work there on a part time basis. That would be wonderful I said smiling from ear to ear. I had a flash in my mind of Alan's drawing of the smiling sun. That's me I thought.

'We will sort out the details,' she told me.

I telephoned Alan to tell him and he was delighted and suggested dinner to celebrate. Of course I agreed. I would keep the surprise for Wilf when he came over.

That night as I lay in bed, I couldn't believe that I could feel such happiness again. I thought of Michael, he is fine, I thought of Wilf, he is fine. I thought of me and my baby, we too are fine. Out of all the tragedy has come some happiness, please don't let it be spoilt, I prayed.

The months passed quickly, as my stomach grew. I told Michael that I was going to have a baby indicating my large bump. He would pat my tummy and say baby, and would look at a baby in a pram and then would look at my tummy and back at the baby in the pram.

Wilf insisted on coming over for Christmas. 'I'm not missing Christmas with you,' he said, 'I missed one with your mother in 1944 and I've learnt my lesson.'

When Wilf arrived he had a massive suitcase.

'You look as though you are here for six months,' I teased him. 'What have you brought?'

'Ha ha, you will have to wait and see.'

I found out the contents on Christmas morning when the suitcase had been opened before I woke up. I counted six presents for Michael and the rest for me, funny shaped parcels, at least six long thin ones and then a longer box that rattled when I shook it, a big fat parcel and many more.

I couldn't wait any longer. 'Let's go and get Michael. I can't stand the suspense.'

We collected Michael from the Home. He was carrying a cuddly toy, a tiger I think it was supposed to be. All the children were occupied with their or someone else's gifts. We took Michael back to my place and when he saw the pile of brightly wrapped parcels he pointed and looked up at us questioningly.

'Now, let's see what we have here. This one is for Michael,' Wilf handed it over.

Already an expert from the earlier session at the Home, he started to break into the wrapping paper. We had great fun, I had bought things for Wilf; a pair of blue swimming trunks in case he didn't pack any, a box of mixed sweets to enjoy sharing, the latest paperback book on the market and I can't remember what else.

For Michael I had bought the usual crayons, paper, books, and other toys, all to leave here at the apartment. Also his own bed cover as he was to be allowed to stay with me at the weekends to help him adjust when we left for New Zealand. This was the first night he was to stay. My parcels were a mystery with lots of long pieces of wood and many screws to eventually assemble into an artist's easel, just what I needed. There were tubes of paint in every colour I could imagine, all any artist needs. I was thrilled and showed it with big hugs. Michael helped Wilf assemble the easel while I went to make coffee. Had anyone told me six months ago that I would be so happy come

Christmas, I would have called them crazy. How strange life is!

It seemed strange having Christmas in the middle of summertime, with school summer holidays and the beach packed with children. Michael loved the beach as Mark had told me. We ran in and out of the water time and time again, giggling and splashing each other. We made sandcastles then jumped on them, then made another one to let the sea run into. Each day was paradise; I had never known such continuous sunshine before. I used bottles of sun screen lotion on Michael and myself but we both still acquired beautiful golden tans. What a time to be pregnant in that heat. I thought I would melt.

New Year's Eve was spent quietly and I reflected on what my friends were doing. I remembered Mary's intention to have a real drink and we all wondered what we would be doing a year later. I realised that it is for the best that we don't know. I could not have coped with all that knowledge. I looked back as though looking at a balance sheet, on the left hand side I had lost my husband, his mother, my sister and brother-in-law. On the right hand side I had gained a father, a nephew, whom I intended to call my own son and a baby on the way. A baby my husband, Martin, would never see, and all this in a year.

The doctor told me I was fit and healthy. I certainly looked it. I was sad when I thought of Martin and how proud he would have been. Sometimes I would feel he was near me, silly maybe, but that's how I felt. Wilf told me that all the paperwork was ready and just waiting for me to put aged, twenty-one. He asked what I would like for my birthday but I couldn't think of a single thing I needed. It is a special year he reminded me. I asked him what he got for his twenty-first birthday. He pondered for a while.

'It was a long time ago, the war had just started. I remember I got a watch from my parents. I still have it somewhere at home. There were some gold cuff-links from an Aunt and Uncle and yes, my father gave me his father's signet ring. I still have that too of course.'

My work at the Home really interested me. I developed the painting side with the children, the smaller ones not attending school in the mornings and the ones attending school as an after school hobby. Nobody was forced to join in but I gathered quite a group. I must admit that, with Wilf's generosity with the paints, it was easier to show them more scope than they ever learnt at school. I busied myself, helping as much as I could to keep the children occupied, through those long hot weeks of summer holidays.

Michael spent more and more time with me at the apartment. I noticed how he sometimes said Mummy instead of Maggie, more noticeable because it was not a word used at the Home. I listened to it wondering if it related to a problem, maybe missing his Mummy. He must wonder where his Mummy and Daddy are, I thought. I asked for advice and was told that maybe he did wonder but, being with so many other people and children, he was not lonely so did not miss them as such. If he was calling me Mummy, instead of Maggie, then it showed he was accepting me into that role. I wondered how he would react when the baby came and we went to New Zealand. Wilf had told me that there were quite a lot of people about the place. I asked him to tell me about them, then they would not feel like strangers when I met them.

He told me about his Girl Friday in the office, Liza, said he would be lost without her. 'Her husband, Bill, is my stock manager. Then there is Jonesy, she's a treasure and is my housekeeper and a very good cook. Her husband, Bert, works with Bill on the farm and her son Peter works with me.

'We are contractors, Peter and I. This is the crop fertilizer side of the business. We fly over acres and acres, feeding the grass. You have to remember that this is sheep rearing country we are talking about.

'You didn't say you had a plane. Is it dangerous?' I asked.

'No, not unless we are stupid, it's our necks we're risking so we don't take risks. It's a busy life, farming. I told you that when I left the bank to work with my father. We had to develop or go bust. I negotiated a large loan and we bought a plane. There were government grants after the war. Another side of the business is haulage; you may see our trucks on the road and recognise the name.

I'll show you when we get back to New Zealand. I guess it always gives me a thrill to see the name on the trucks, I feel I have achieved something for all the years of hard work.'

'You sound as if you have achieved a great deal, your father would be very proud of you.'

'I am letting Peter do more of the flying, these days, he's very good and I am going to want to be home more in the near future. I'll get someone else to work with him. I want to spend time with you and my grandchildren. I cannot believe this is happening to me, I have to keep pinching myself to make sure I am not dreaming. Have you thought of any names for the baby yet?'

'One thing for sure,' I said, 'it won't begin with an M.'

Wilf laughed at that.

'Do you have a second name?' I asked Wilf.

'Yes I do; it's Alexander, my father's name, although he was known as Alex.'

'I love it,' I cried. 'If my baby is a boy, it will be called Alexander.'

'What if it's a girl?' asked Wilf.

'Why, then it will be Alexandra.' I felt very happy. I asked about Liza.

'Well let me see. I was just going away to work in the city when she was born, so that makes her about thirty years old.'

'When you say city, where do you mean?'

'I mean Wellington, the capital of New Zealand; we always refer to it as 'The City.'

'Liza is part Maori, her mother was Maori but her father was European. She is a very good horse woman, like her mother, Ruth, she grew up on the farm and my mother adored her. I had a sister who died when she was only three years old, so Liza filled an empty space in my mother's heart and Ruth was only sixteen when Liza was born.

We planned to send Liza away to college; when she was old enough, she didn't want to go; to leave the farm.

'She caught me one day in the stables. "Please Wilf," she begged "don't let them send me away to college. I'll run away."

'So defiant, I thought, like mother, when she was sixteen. I said to Liza, "Come on, ride with me."

We saddled two horses and headed out to the beach. I talked to her about the future and how I visualised the business expanding. I asked Liza what work she wanted to do.

'"I want to stay at the farm and work with the stock; I'm good, I can do anything."

'I pointed out that we did have to employ men for these jobs and, although she was strong, not strong enough for some work. I said that I would make her a promise; if she went to college and did well, especially in the business course, I would give her a job. I would employ her to help me run the business, to be my Administrative Assistant. I had already explained how I saw the business expanding and if she took her work seriously and did well in college, then yes, I would honour my promise.

'"Would you really do that for me?" she asked. "Do you think I am clever enough?"

'I told her she was very clever and to stay on the farm as she wanted would be a waste, in my opinion.

'"I suppose you are right," she said eventually, "I will go to college and make you very proud of me."

'Did she do well?' I asked Wilf.

'Oh yes, once she got her teeth into the course, she blossomed and became a very sophisticated young lady. She met Bill while he was doing an agricultural degree; they married and chose to work at the farm together. It all fell into place.'

'Do they have any children?' I asked Wilf.

'No, I think that is upsetting Liza, but she's only young yet.'

Chapter 7 Ruth

I found the story of Wilf's farm in New Zealand fascinating. 'You mentioned Liza's mother, Ruth,' I said. 'What happened to her?'

Wilf told me that Ruth had appeared on the farm when she was no more than a girl herself. She was heavily pregnant and starving. His mother took her in and looked after her. Wilf was at home at the time, having finished school and waiting to go to work in the city.

Ruth gave birth to Liza two weeks later. Wilf's mother told Ruth that she could stay and help her if she wished. She gave her the small house where she and Wilf's father had lived before they built the big house. It had been used as shearers' quarters, until some new ones had been built and now stood empty. There was a lot to be done with it but everyone gave a hand. The veranda was repaired along with the guttering and steps, paint was applied inside and out making such a difference, then furniture appeared from somewhere. It looked quite lovely by the time they had all finished. Ruth couldn't believe that she had a home of her own. We were all besotted with the baby girl and my mother was so happy to have female company. It was quite lonely for her, being miles from neighbours and town.

As the years passed, Ruth found she could trust him. They liked to ride the boundaries together, looking for broken fences, when he wasn't working. He came home as often as he could, to get away from the city, to the peace of the farm. Ruth was an excellent horse woman. She would ride into the bush and stay away for days, that was all the, so called, holiday she ever took and she never left the farm boundary.

'There is a lot of bush land and quite deep gorges that are dangerous, if you don't know what you are doing, but Ruth was brought up in such terrain. One day, we were out checking the stock we stopped to mend a fence, then sat in the shade for a rest.

'My father had died a while before and we were talking about life, death, the past and the future and "what's it all about!" I asked her what had happened to her when she was young and where she came from. It was not my habit to pry into other people's lives and I started to apologise for my question.

'But she said, "No Wilf, I've never been able to talk about it in the past but feel I would like to explain now." It took a lot of doing on her part but slowly she told me her story.

'This is what she said. "I lived on a farm with my father, I was happy until my mother died. I was expected to take on all the work my mother had done and I became resentful. I saw other girls doing things that I wanted to do, going off into the city to work and coming back to the village, showing off their clothes and with money to spend. I decided I would go to the city and make a lot of money, maybe one day be famous, so that when I returned my father would be proud of me.

"'One day father and I had a big row. I couldn't stand it anymore; whatever I did was not right, I could not do things the same way my mother had done, and he would get very angry. I made my decision; I would go to the city. The opportunity arose when father went to town to meet his friends for a drink. I knew it would be a long session and he would not miss me as he would have to sleep it off. I packed my things and set off down the road to catch the local bus.

"'I left the bus at the main highway hoping to hitch a lift to the city and I was lucky. A truck pulled up, I had not been waiting long and thought how lucky I was. There were two men in the truck, we chatted away and they seemed quite nice. The miles passed and I became weary. I closed my eyes for a few minutes but awoke to find one of the men holding my arm. He had placed handcuffs from one wrist to the door handle. I felt very scared. I asked them to let me go, to drop me off on the roadside, but they laughed at me.

"'Don't be frightened, we'll look after you,' one of them said and they both laughed again, a nasty laugh. I begged them to let me go but I knew it was no use. I felt angry at myself for being so stupid as to take a lift with two men. We travelled for miles and miles, away from the main road and eventually came to a lonely farm house in the hills. One of the men pulled me out of the truck and pushed me towards the house. The other one opened the door and shouted, 'hey, look what we've brought you,' as I was shoved through the doorway.

"'Must be Christmas,' said one of the two men inside.

Another man sitting at a table asked them, 'where did you get that?'

'Ruth couldn't talk to me for a while, the memory was too painful, and so I just sat and waited until she was ready to go on,' said Wilf. 'After a while she continued,'

"'Let's see what we have then. The man at the table stood up. 'Come on then, strip off.'

"'He was addressing me. I ignored him.

"'Come on, need some help.'

"'He came towards me and put his hand at the top of my jacket and wrenched it open, the buttons falling on the floor and rolling under the table. He did the same thing again with my blouse, hitting me across the face as I tried to protect myself.

"'I said strip off,' he leered at me.

"As my blouse fell open I could hear the suck of breath as they saw my skin. Another of the men joined in and pulled down my trousers. I soon stood naked in front of them, their eyes feeding on my un-clothed body.

"'Let's see what she's made of.'

"The first man grabbed me around the waist and with his other hand grasped my face and kissed me, his stubble scratching my skin. I reeled back at his touch but he pulled me back to him by my hair, his hands groping all over my body. He struggled to open his trousers with one hand, holding onto my hair with the other, then half carried, half dragged me through into another room and threw me on to a bed. I felt a searing pain as he entered me and I let out a scream.

"'No one to hear you here,' he said, as he took his pleasure of me. Then suddenly it stopped, he had rolled off me and he laid breathing heavily at my side. Each in turn they raped me. One man fastened me with a chain to the bed.

"'We ain't going to let you go far, are we,' he sneered as he turned to the others for agreement.

"Dead sure," another laughed.

"I felt as though my whole insides were on fire, I was bleeding and raw. I told them that I needed to go to the toilet and one of them took me to the privy at the end of the house. I could hardly walk and as I passed water the pain was so bad that I fainted. The man must have heard me fall and pushed open the door as the next thing I knew was waking up in a bed. It must have frightened them as they left me alone the next day.

"The two men who brought me to the house left the next day. I was chained by my ankle to a ring in the floor, it was a long chain as I was expected to clean and cook. The two men who stayed in the house used me in their beds each night but, when the other two returned, a fight broke out. They had been drinking a lot of whiskey and playing cards until one of them decided to go

117

to bed. He undid the chain to take me with him, when another one said he wanted me, they started arguing which led to fists being raised.

"'Let's toss for her,' a voice said.

"'Yeh good idea,' someone agreed.

"The first man didn't win and objected furiously.

"'I won't be long with her,' the winner said, 'then she's yours.'

"After they had been satisfied, I lay there awake, I realised that they had not fastened me up again. The man next to me was snoring; his mouth open; how I'd like to pour acid down that throat, I thought as I quietly rolled off the bed. I grabbed my clothes and crept into the living room, the floor seemed to be creaking loudly. I lifted the latch on the door praying it would open quietly. Suddenly, the door came open and there stood one of the men, he had been to the privy.

"'Caught you' he said as he grabbed me and flung me back into the room where I hit my back hard against the table. 'Trying to run away were you, can't have that now can we.'

"He took me across his knee and thrashed me with a shoe.

"Another man appeared in the doorway. 'What's all the noise?'

"'She was trying to get away,' he answered.

"'Oh hell, do you know what time it is? Fasten her up will you and we'll see to her tomorrow.'

"The next morning two of them left again so the night before was forgotten. I had to get away somehow. I asked to go to the toilet but was told to use a bucket. It was raining outside and the men were slouched in chairs almost asleep. I begged to be able to go to the toilet. One of them undid the chain and told me not to be long and he'd be angry, if he had to come after me. I left the room as he dropped back into the chair. I didn't go near the privy but took off across the fields. I had to get away.

"I thought I was doing well until I heard a noise behind me. I hit the ground with a thump, as his body landed on mine, in a rugby tackle. The wind was taken out of me, I could hardly get my breath and felt a pain in my chest. He dragged me to my feet and frog marched me back to the house; the chain was put around my ankle again.

"'Get that bloody floor washed,' he shouted as he pushed me to the ground.

"I stood up, poured hot water off the stove into a bucket and got back down on my knees, as far from the men as I could. I started to wash the floor, knowing they were watching my every move.

"'Nice bit of tail there,' he said to the other man. 'I fancy a taste of that.'

"He raped me on my knees, my stomach wretched and I was sick on the floor in front of me. He barked and yelped, like the dog he was pretending to be, as he used me and I knew I would get my revenge one day, even if it killed me.

"I only tried to escape one other time and my punishment was to be stood under the dart board as they threw the darts above my head. I looked straight at them as the plonk of each dart hit the board; I felt the shudder of the board on top of my head. I pictured each of them chained to the wall in front of me and I was playing darts with them as my target, starting with the forehead, one in each eye, the mouth and working down their bodies. I was so deep into my mental pictures that I did not realise they had stopped using me for their fun. It became the way to survive, to use pictures in my head to get away from the reality and I enjoyed planning what I would do to each one of the men, it became my game.

"I realised that I had to gain their confidence, make them believe that I wanted to be there. The house was filthy and the bedding stank so I started to make things clean and boiled water to wash the sheets. I had to be let off the chain to hang out the washing but one of the men was always sprawled in an old chair on the back porch watching me.

"There were signs that there had been a garden. Someone who had lived there before had made a vegetable plot and roses grew along a fence. I picked some to put in a jug on the table, then went back outside to check the washing and started to pull up some of the weeds, enjoying being outside. I did more and more around the house, making it much more homely, if they ever knew what homely meant. I could not imagine them ever living in a decent home or having a family.

"The two men who stayed in the house, I believed had escaped from prison. They never left the property. One was a bit slow and tried to copy whatever the other one did.

"Each night became a ritual after supper when I had washed the pots and pans, I had to take a pan of hot water, pour it into a bowl and wash myself all over. It was their entertainment as they sat with their homemade grog. The one whose night it was with me getting more excited and the others jeering him on. It was better this way as it was all over and done with quickly and he would roll over and sleep. There were occasions when this happened and one of the others would try their luck but then I would hang on to my partner and threaten to wake him up or tell him the next morning.

"There was a sort of 'honour among thieves,' once they had made a bargain with each other as they had done about me. They knew they could not go on treating me as they were and, if I was ill and became infected, then no one would have me and I could die.

"I knew this washing in front of them each evening had to stop. I was pregnant and they would see. I didn't know or dare to think what they would do to me if they found I was of no use to them anymore. Perhaps kill me. I had to get away so I formed a plan. The next time the two of them went away I would do it.

"When I had been out in the garden I had noticed a herb growing; I did not know what it was called but my grandmother had used it to help people sleep, there were also some toadstools under a tree I did not know if they were poisonous or not but I would try everything. I did know that the rhubarb growing in the corner of the garden was my best bet as the leaves are deadly. So, my plot thickened and I just had to be patient and wait for the right time.

"The weeks went by and I brought more grog onto the table, encouraging them to drink more and more with their meal, hoping they would drop off to sleep. One day the two came back and said they would be away for four days, that's long enough, I thought. They had brought lots of provisions, food for me to prepare.

"Two days after they left I set to, making a big pan of mutton stew. I put in the herbs and the toadstools, chopped the rhubarb leaves into small pieces and added them to the stew. I made pastry for a rhubarb pie. As it all cooked it smelt delicious. A small pan was kept for me without the special ingredients. I placed the plates of stew on the table with the grog and waited. I ate my portion and refilled their plates. It was good stew and they had more. I waited. Eventually one of them went to the privy and I heard him groan as he came back and drank more grog. The other one went to the privy. He came back holding his stomach and drank more grog. I waited.

"I sat quietly watching. One went to bed groaning and the other one had another drink and took it with him to bed. They had forgotten about fastening the chain. Should I leave now? Has it worked? Gathering my things together quietly, taking all the bread and other food I could carry in a sack. I heard them both groaning, they were not going to bother me tonight for anything, I was off.

"Keeping off the road, I knew the direction because when the wind blew in a certain way I could hear the whistle of a train. Half walking, half running, all night, through the bushes and streams, stopping only to drink the water, I found the railway tracks.

"Which way to go? I did not want to end up in the town, where the men were working. I decided to go down the track. It must be going south as the sun came up on my left hand side. The dawn was beautiful and I felt free. I walked and walked then saw buildings ahead of me; I needed to read the timetable to know where I was and when a train would come. Creeping along the platform to the office to look at the information, I saw the next train was at 10am, plenty of time. I walked back up the track and into the bushes and slept.

"The noise of the train woke me. I rushed down to the station to pay the man the money I had taken from the house. How far would it take me? He looked at me strangely, shrugged his shoulders and gave me a ticket. The train went south through the mountains. The ticket collector came around for the ticket and said the name of the place I was going to. He asked if I was visiting relatives. I replied that I was. He asked me if I had been there before, said it was a nice place and moved on.

"Eventually, he called the name of the next station, it was mine. 'Have a good visit,' he called as I alighted. I looked about me, then followed the other people out of the station and into the town. As I walked from one end to the other I noticed an empty shop. I turned into the alley that went up the back of the building. There was a door, with a broken pane of glass, I pushed against it and it creaked open. The place was filthy, littered with broken bottles, old lino, and wooden crates, but it would do for tonight or a few nights, I thought.

"I wondered if I could find any work that I could do? 'With my coat hung open no-one could tell I was pregnant,' I told myself. After resting, I went out into the town and passed a bakery. It smelt good and made me so hungry. I ate a little of my precious bread, but felt so weary I went back to the empty shop. Curling up in the corner, I went to sleep.

"It was dark when a noise woke me, a scuffling noise. I felt something on my leg; it was a rat and another one on my bag. They could smell my food. I grabbed my bag and ran out of the shop. It was late and the streets were empty. Turning south I started walking.

I slept in barns, under hedges, hollows, anywhere. I stole food, vegetables, out of gardens, picked berries off the bushes; stole the dog's food at a farm and eventually came here. You know the rest," Ruth finished.

'She was exhausted at the end of telling me her tale,' Wilf told me, 'reliving the memory of that dreadful time had drained every ounce of energy from her. She looked very weary and I told her to close her eyes and have a rest and to think of the good things that happened after she came here.

'I walked away and sat by the river to give her a few minutes to herself. A while later I rejoined Ruth. She opened her eyes as she heard me approach.'

'"It did me good, telling you about my past. You are the only person I have ever told and now I feel lighter in some way."

'"You are sharing the load with me now," I told her, "and I'm pleased you felt you could talk to me." We climbed on our horses and rode home, our bond of friendship strengthened.'

I asked if Ruth ever married

Wilf said that she hadn't. 'She died not long after I returned from England. My mother died first, next was Sarah and then Ruth.' His voice was sad. We sat in silence for a while then Wilf started to speak.

'There was a lot of work to catch up on when I returned from England and I was fully occupied so I always regretted not having time to talk with Ruth. I don't know if anything was bothering her, I don't think so but I do not know for certain. I will never know now.'

He went on to tell me how some steers had broken loose from the herd and wandered off into the bush. 'We had found a break in the fence and repaired it. There was no problem really because we knew where they had gone. Ruth said she was going to fetch them in. "A lovely day for a ride," she had said as she climbed onto her horse.

'"Expect me back when you see me," she called.

'From past experience that could mean a couple of days as she loved to be out in the bush country. No one thought anything of it when she didn't return that evening, or the next day, but her horse was found in the top paddock the following morning. A search party was sent out, the stray steers were found in a gully but we couldn't find Ruth. We had to get the dogs out and give them her scent and they found her body. It will always be a mystery as she was an excellent horsewoman, as I have said many times.

'All we could think was that her horse had been frightened by something; she was unexpectantly caught off balance and fell down a deep gully. She must have struck her head on a rock but we will never know.'

When Wilf had finished his story about Ruth I felt very sad, and we both sat quietly, reflecting upon our past.

Eventually, Wilf stood up and said, 'It is time to go, are you going to run me to the airport?'

'Silly question,' I replied. 'Although I would rather you were staying longer.'

'I would second that one,' he said.

When we arrived at the airport he said, 'don't come in, no point in you sitting about here, anyway you are having dinner with Alan aren't you? So go and get dressed up for the occasion.'

'I can't do much dressing up at this size, just change to another tent.'

'Soon be over.' Wilf smiled as he gently put his hand on my large tummy. 'I wonder what is in there.'

'I'll tell you as soon as I know,' I replied as I reached over and kissed his cheek.

Chapter 8 Alex

I drove home and had a long hot bath. As I relaxed, and looked at my enormous tummy, I remembered Wilf's words; "I wonder what's in there." It must be a footballer I thought, the way I feel sometimes when it's kicking me.

I chose a green tent dress, white necklace and earrings at least my tan looked good in contrast to the white. Alan arrived and told me how good I looked as he handed me a bunch of flowers.

'Pour yourself a drink,' I said as I indicated the drinks cupboard while I went into the kitchen to arrange the flowers.

'I'll have orange juice.'

We sat a while talking.

Alan looked at his watch, 'Time to go, I reserved a table for 8 o'clock.'

He reached to help me out of the chair, when I felt a sharp pain. That was silly I thought as I took Alan's hand.

We drove to the restaurant; it was a beautiful evening. We had a balcony table, the view was magnificent. I told Alan what the doctor had said about Michael calling me Mummy instead of Maggie and that I was going to bring him up as my own. When I got to New Zealand no one would know that he wasn't my child.

'What do you think?' I asked.

'It sounds a good idea to me. I'm quite sure that Jenny would agree.'

The mention of Jenny in that way confirmed my intention. It had to be the best way I thought.

'What about the people in England?' he asked.

'There are no relatives over there,' I said, 'I have written to my close friend Mary and told her I am going to live in New Zealand. She's upset at not seeing me again but I said I would visit her in the future or maybe she would come and see me. Mary says that she won't say anything to anyone.'

I felt I had made a decision I was totally happy with. We had a lovely meal.

It wasn't until I tried to get up from the table that I felt another twinge. This was not indigestion. I felt goose bumps all over my skin.

'I think you are going to be an uncle soon.' I whispered calmly.

'Great, I fancy being an uncle,' he laughed. Then he realised what I really meant. 'Oh are you alright, stupid question,' he admonished himself. 'What do we do next?'

'Take me to the apartment first to pick up my case, then we can go to the hospital.'

'Shouldn't we go straight to the hospital,' he asked. I think he had a vision of having to deliver my baby in the car.

'No, plenty of time,' I informed him, keeping my voice matter of fact. We went carefully down the stairs to the car.

'Keep your eyes on the road,' I reprimanded. Alan kept looking over at me, 'otherwise we may both end up in hospital.'

'Oh yes,' he said like the very worried man he was. As we stopped outside the apartment, another spasm caught me and Alan heard me gasp.

'I think you should pant or something' and he started to pant in demonstration. I too started to pant while the contraction finished then my anxiety turned to laughter as I watched Alan's antics. Once he realised that my pain had gone and I was laughing, not crying, he stopped too.

'I wish I had a camera,' I said and we both laughed with relief.

'Tell me where the case is,' he asked taking the keys. 'We had better get you into safe hands as soon as possible; I can't take any more of this excitement.'

We were soon at the hospital and I was tucked up in a clean white bed counting the minutes between the contractions. It was the next evening before Alexander was born; Valentine's Day and a little earlier than expected.

Alan had called Wilf to say I had gone into labour but not to return so soon after going home. Wilf was delighted to hear he had a grandson and wanted to come back straight away but I thought a week was better to give me time to get over the birth. He understood and did as I asked. I had a hard time over the next few days, not having Martin with me. The doctor said I was suffering from exhaustion. I didn't want to go into a depression so concentrated on how lucky I was to have a beautiful, healthy baby boy that Martin would have been so proud of. There was Michael to think about too.

When Wilf arrived I couldn't see who it was behind the enormous bouquet of flowers advancing towards me. He was coming to take me out of hospital and back to the apartment. We were ready, Alex and I, with everything packed. Wilf left the flowers and a large box of chocolates with the nurses saying, 'There are plenty more at home.'

We took the coast road back to the apartment. The sea sparkled in the sunshine, children played on the beach, sails dotted the water and I felt wonderful. Weak but strong at the same time. Wilf pulled the car up so that we were facing the wonderful view. 'I have something for you,' he said and handed me a parcel wrapped in lovely shining paper with a bow on the top.

'Happy Birthday and I'm sorry I missed it.'

I undid the paper and opened the box. Inside was a beautiful watch.

'Do you like it,' Wilf asked anxiously.

'I love it; it is beautiful, thank you so much.' I leaned over and kissed him.

'Here let me help you put it on. I hope it fits.'

He fastened it around my wrist and I held out my arm to appreciate it.

'You gave me the idea of a watch when you asked me what I had had for my twenty first birthday. Here is something else,' he offered me another package. A smaller one this time.

'You are spoiling me.'

He laughed, 'Yes, isn't it lovely.'

I opened the small box and it contained a ring. It had three diamonds on a twist in a very beautiful setting.

'Oh, it is so very delicate.'

I put it onto my finger and held it out to show him. He took my hand and said it was his mother's engagement ring.

'I know she would love you to have it and I am just sorry that she is not here to enjoy this moment to be bringing home her great grandson. I am sorry I never told her about Sarah. Oh, she knew about my friend in England but she never knew she had a grand-daughter. I feel I let her down in that way, I had not realised until recently how much she must have wanted me to marry and have children. She must have hoped but never voiced those hopes to me.'

I told Wilf how I had felt in the hospital when Alex was born and how I had missed Martin. How I had felt that he was near me, that, when I was depressed and low, it was Martin who had lifted my hopes for the future.

'It was as though he had been standing there,' I said, 'saying that if I let myself be ill and depressed then I would be spoiling all the happy memories of the past that we had together. They would be wasted.'

'I am sure your mother is aware of what is happening.'

I took Wilf's hand. 'There is so much that we are not meant to know but sometimes it is as though we are allowed some flash of knowledge, it's a knowing, deep down inside.'

'I hope you're right. It's comforting to think that way,' he agreed.

'I'll always treasure this ring, and watch of course, but the ring is special and I thank you for allowing me to wear it.'

Wilf had arranged everything; he had to go back to New Zealand but a nurse was going to be at the apartment, just until I felt I could cope on my own. 'She can help you pack your things as well as look after Alex and Michael.'

I was twenty one two days after Alex was born. Michael could now be with me too but the Home had been reticent about that, knowing I had a new born baby to see-to. So that's why Wilf had hired a nurse to help me. He asked if he had done the wrong thing and I assured him it was a wonderful idea and it would be good for Michael to be in at the beginning with Alex.

When Wilf said in the hospital there were plenty of flowers at home he had not been exaggerating. The apartment seemed full of them; it looked beautiful. Alan was there and the nurse whose name was Kathleen.

'What did you give Maggie for dinner the other night,' Wilf joked with Alan. 'Whatever it was it certainly got things moving.'

I looked at these two men who I had known such a short time who were now playing such a big part in my life.

The first time I saw Alan and Kathleen together I knew he was attracted to her. What man wouldn't be? She had lovely red hair and a soft Irish accent. Kathleen had trained as a nurse in Ireland but wanted to emigrate and was waiting to start a new job at the hospital in a months' time. She had enrolled with a nursing agency until then. As the days went by, and I saw Alan and Kathleen together, I guessed I would be hearing a lot about her when I got to New Zealand and I was right.

Not only was Kathleen lovely to look at but had a lovely way with her too. I liked her very much and will always thank her for all she taught me in such a short time. We became very good friends.

Chapter 9 THIRD LETTER

New Zealand 1993
It is two days since the second letter and four days since the first one. Once more, in a plain white envelope, one sheet of white paper, the words cut out of a magazine.

I KNOW YOUR SECRET. 10TH OCTOBER 1966

WHO WILL PAY YOU OR THE
NEWSPAPERS?

Enclosed was a newspaper cutting with a photograph of Michael and Janet's wedding. The words "mother" and "son" were underlined in thick pen and a big question mark. Underneath this were added:

BE ALONE – BY THE PHONE.
TOMORROW AT 6.30 pm FOR
INSTRUCTIONS.

I have had time in the past few days to try and think who can be doing this to me, in fact I have thought of nothing else; I go to bed thinking about it, I get up thinking about it and still I am no wiser.

The cutting from the newspaper gave me a clue as to the reason for all this. It must be someone who has discovered that Michael does not know of his past but knows that a scandal could harm his career.

Not the sort of career for having secrets, as the newspapers had proved in the past. If one secret comes out of the closet there may be others, I can hear people saying. Some people are easily swayed by journalist's interpretation of the truth. I can see some reasoning in this and, where as I thought it was to do with me, I can now see it is someone getting at Michael through me. Some sick person who is jealous of his career probably. Oh, why had I not told Michael about his past? I know full well why.

The psychiatrist at the children's home, back in 1966, had specifically said that if Michael did not show any abnormal signs, no nightmares, then leave well alone. Only if there were questions from Michael about his past, was I to open any doors in Michael's mind as a way to clear hidden things that might be upsetting him.

There had been no nightmares, no questions from him relating to that time, he was a normal happy child. I think having Alex as a baby brother must have filled a gap somewhere, and he continued calling me Mummy instead of Maggie, especially as Alex started to talk and say Mummy too.

The time was never right or necessary for me to change anything, even as the children grew older, I put off churning up unhappy memories for all of us. Our names were the same, Powell, and

Michael believed that his father was Martin, the same as Alex. Martin and Mark were brothers. They had the same initials as mine and Jenny's; she being Jennifer Mary and mine, Margaret Jean. Everything was so similar. We had joked about this in our letters, Jenny and I. It's a good job we live twelve thousand miles away or we would be always getting the wrong mail Jenny had written.

I will tell Michael one day, I consoled myself with that thought. How naive I chose to be. No use making mountains out of molehills I could hear my father's voice. So, time went on and Michael grew into a fine young man.

I turned over in my mind all the people who knew about Michael. Thinking back to England, I had written to Mary but asked her to say nothing. Telling her what the doctor said about Michael and it would be better for his future if no one knew. Being Michael's only relative and caring for him as my own, I told her I was pregnant and would bring the children up together. How can you manage, I could hear her say, so I told her about Wilf being my father and that he would arrange everything at this end and if possible we would all stay in New Zealand.

I remembered being in Australia and the people I had met. No one there can be doing this to us. If this isn't sorted out soon I would be ill. I couldn't live under this tension, reliving all those months in 1966. That time had already taken its toll on my health and I couldn't afford that stress upon me again.

139

Who should I speak to? Should I tell Michael? He is away until next week and under enough stress at the moment. I must tell Wilf, he will be back home tomorrow. Yes, I will tell Wilf. How silly not to have told him sooner, I could have called him but never mind. I feel better now I have made a decision and can wait until he gets home.

I sat thinking about Wilf, of him waving goodbye to me in New Zealand the day he saw me off to visit Jenny in Australia, 10th October 1966. What would I have done without him so many times since?

Chapter 10 Honeymead 1966

The day arrived when we were to leave Australia and start our new life in New Zealand. My time in Australia had been so extreme. I had arrived on my own and now in less than six months, was moving on with two children and a father. Wilf flew over to take us back.

We said our goodbyes to everyone at the Home and Alan and Kathleen came to see us off at the airport. There were mixed feelings, as over the last few weeks there was a sort of security amongst these lovely people, now I was leaving them behind to start life in another country.

I was glad I had spent those few days in New Zealand; at least it wasn't completely new and we would be landing at Auckland again. Wilf had left his car at the airport, only being away for two days, so we were soon on our way.

We broke our journey about half way and stayed at a hotel on the side of Lake Taupo; a very big lake in the centre of the North Island. We were all very weary, from the journey, so we relaxed, enjoying the view and had a stroll around the small town. It was an early night for all of us and a leisurely start the next morning.

Wilf pointed out sights to me along the way. 'There is so much I want to show you but all in good time.'

I had a feeling of anxious anticipation as we got closer to the farm. Wilf had described it in a fashion, each time forgetting to bring photographs with him to Australia.

We turned off the main road into a long wide avenue of poplar trees; under the trees were clumps of blue and white flowers, such a brilliant blue, almost three feet high with big pompom heads. As we drove around a bend the house came into view; it stood on a softly sloping hillside, the land around being terraced and landscaped with flower beds and shrubs.

A long veranda went the full length of the house and there was a wing at each end of it forming rooms that were almost circular with turrets on the top. The sloping roof was high, giving the impression of more than one storey. A lovely red trailing plant ran along the veranda, which was furnished with canvas chairs in a blue colour and white wrought iron tables.

Wilf drove the car to the side of the house and pulled up at a door where there was a comfortable looking woman standing beneath the porch. When the car stopped she came rushing down the steps towards us

'Let me help you,' she said, as she opened the door at my side.

My heart lurched, she sounded just like my mother, the same lilt in her voice. I could have burst into tears, I felt so overcome I couldn't speak. I would have to explain later, I thought, as I handed Alex to her. She took him in her arms and cooed in delight.

'Maggie, this is Mrs Jones,' Wilf introduced us.

'It's lovely to meet you,' I said.

Michael scampered out of the car, chatting. He was asking Wilf all sorts of questions. Wilf was being ever so patient as he unloaded the boot of the car, trying to occupy Michael by giving him parcels to carry into the house.

We followed Mrs Jones down the hall into the kitchen. There was a wonderful smell of baking. It was a large kitchen with a cooking range at one end and a large table at the other. A massive window looked out over the fields and the sun poured in onto the table. This was already set with cups, saucers and plates in a bright yellow and blue pattern. Everything looked so clean and fresh. The atmosphere was of a very friendly place.

I remembered Wilf telling me about Ruth and how his mother had welcomed her to this house and then she had the baby girl, Liza. I could imagine Ruth's utter relief at finding such a sanctuary as this. I too will never want to leave, I thought.

'Cup of tea?' Mrs. Jones was saying.

'That would be lovely,' I replied, having recovered my voice. She handed Alex back to me.

'Just a minute,' she said as she disappeared through the door; in a few seconds she was back carrying a lovely wooden crib which she put by the table. She took Alex from me and laid him in it. He cooed happily.

'How lovely, Mrs. Jones.'

'Oh please, call me "Jonesy," everyone does.' She pulled down the blind a little, to shade the table from the sun.

The tea tasted special and I was tempted by the freshly baked scones.

'I have to lose weight,' I told her. 'I put on so much with the pregnancy.'

'That will soon go my dear, you will have lots to do here and there are some lovely walks you can take, yes you will soon be fit again.'

'Not if I keep eating your wonderful baking,' I laughed.

Wilf came into the kitchen.

'There you are,' he said, 'Jonesy mothering you is she?'

Michael was at his heels.

'Drink please,' he asked, then added, 'cake,' as an afterthought.

Wilf picked him up and placed him on the bench close to the table. I poured him a glass of milk and cut him a piece of cake. He took a good drink, leaving milk around his lips, he picked up his cake and took a large bite.

'There's nothing wrong with a wee lad with an appetite like that,' Jonesy said.

Once more I could have burst into tears at the words my mother used to us. This time I replied,

'Yes my mother used to say that,' and, having said it, I felt so much better.

After we had all had enough to eat, Wilf and Michael took me on a tour of the house. As I knew they would be, the rooms with the almost circular bay window were beautiful and so was the view over the fields and hillside. One room was a sitting room, a baby Grand piano stood in the window space with a beautiful arrangement of flowers on the top of it. There was a formal dining room.

'Hasn't been used much,' Wilf was saying, 'must get it out of moth balls now though, we will do some entertaining to introduce you to the neighbours.'

'Not too soon,' I said, 'I like eating in the kitchen.'

When we got to the other end of the house we went into a large room with my cases in it.

'This is your bedroom,' Wilf said as I went to the window to look out. 'There is a smaller room here', he opened another door into a room just right for Michael. We moved on to another round bayed room.

'This is your sitting-room; I thought you would like this end of the house. I'll leave you to unpack and settle in. Ask Jonesy for anything you need. I am going to the office but will see you later. Are you sure you can manage?'

'I'm quite overcome, it's lovely,' I said, putting my arms around him, 'I don't know what to say.'

'Actions speak louder than words,' and he returned my hug. 'See you later, bye Michael.'

Michael waved bye bye. I realised that he was getting too tired to speak so I took off his shoes and held up the top cover on the bed for him, he crept into it. I placed the light cover over him and he was asleep in no time.

Looking around the bedroom, there was a large clothes closet, dressing table, chest of drawers, large arm chair and a small desk and chair. In the bathroom there was everything I needed for the baby; towels, powders and lotions and a baby bath.

On the top of a high chest of drawers in my bedroom was a tray with two cups, two saucers, an electric jug, tea, coffee, sugar, powdered milk and a tin of biscuits. How very thoughtful.

Going back to the kitchen to feed Alex, I found he was awake and Jonesy was talking to him; I lifted him out of the crib,

'I must change his nappy,' I said.

'Do it here on the table, or I'll do it for you if you like, while you make his bottle.'

I had told her that I could not make enough milk to feed him myself and I could see that she couldn't wait to get her hands on him; I thought of my mother and her few precious weeks with Michael, before Jenny and Mark took him to Australia.

'That's very kind of you.'

'My pleasure,' she answered and meant it. 'By the way, the tray of tea things in your bedroom; I don't want you to think you are not welcome in the kitchen but I just thought that it is a long way from that end of the house, especially when you are keeping an eye on the baby and

Michael, this is your home and you must enjoy every room in it.'

'You are so kind,' I said my heart feeling full for such thoughtfulness. I told her how I had felt when she first spoke to me, how she reminded me of my mother.

'That's a lovely compliment,' and she kissed me on the cheek.

By now Alex was changed and sucking happily on his bottle, a little bit of back rubbing brought up his wind. I laid him back in his crib and carried him back to my bedroom. I too lay on the bed, pulling the folded cover up from across the bottom of the bed, I fell asleep.

When I woke it was 9 o'clock, the room was dark, and it was Alex stirring that woke me. I switched on the bedside lamp, the curtains were closed; someone had been in and closed them. Going through to the next bedroom Michael was still asleep. After changing Alex, I took him through to the kitchen to prepare his bottle. A lamp was on in the sitting room, I went in Wilf was sitting reading in a big comfortable looking chair. He stood up, put his book down and came towards me and kissed my cheek.

'It's so good to have you here, you can't imagine how good.'

'I feel so good too; I am so emotional I keep wanting to cry.' Alex stirred, 'I am going to prepare his bottle; do you mind holding him?'

'Dare I,' said Wilf as he gingerly took hold of him in his arms. When I came back with the bottle, I stood a moment by the door looking at them. One with a Grandson he never expected and the other with a grandfather he may never have known. I realised that we could not keep secret the fact that Wilf was my father, the children needed to know who he was and, maybe selfishly on my part, I needed Wilf to fill in the roll of the father they did not have.

Wilf turned his head and I handed him the bottle, 'me?' he said.

'Why not,' I replied. Carefully Wilf put the teat to Alex's mouth. He took it and sucked lustily. A smile spread over Wilf's face, a smile of amazement.

'I was thinking, Wilf,' I began, 'I would like everyone here to know that you are my father. What do you think?'

'I think those are the best words I could possibly hear, but I'll leave it to you when you choose to speak about it.'

We sat in comfortable silence while Alex had his feed.

'I must check on Michael, he may be hungry by now.' Michael was just stirring as I went into the bedroom, I must be getting a mother's intuition, I thought, that's good.

'Hello Michael, did you have a good sleep?'

'Yes Mummy,' he replied.

'Would you like a drink and something to eat?'

'Yes please.'

We went into the bathroom first then joined Wilf in the far sitting room.

'Look who I have here.'

'Hello Michael, I bet you are thirsty, I was just going to make some hot chocolate. Would you like some?'

'Yes please,' he replied.

'Is that three?' Wilf asked looking at me. I nodded my head and took Alex from him.

'Can you climb up on the settee Michael?' I reached to take his hand.

I gently stroked Alex on his back and he gave a hefty burp. I settled him in the corner of the settee propped up by cushions and I sat in the middle of the two children. Michael snuggled up to me; my two children I thought, feeling very satisfied. Wilf came in with a tray of hot chocolate and the biscuit tin. He handed Michael his in his special cup.

'Not too hot,' he said as Michael carefully took the cup.

We sat peacefully, and I remembered many such occasions from when I was a child and hoped Michael's memories would be happy ones.

'All gone?' Wilf said as Michael emptied his mug. Michael was almost asleep again.

Wilf picked him up and carried him back to his bedroom, stopping in the bathroom on the way. I followed and I placed Alex in his crib.

'There's a good boy,' I told Michael, 'now you will sleep all night.' I undressed him properly and put him into his bed. We both kissed him goodnight.

Wilf kissed my cheek, 'Goodnight my dear daughter.'

I slept so soundly it was Michael climbing into my bed that woke me.

'Wake up Maggie,' he was saying.

I pulled the sheets over my head as he came close, then quickly turned it back,

'Boo,' he laughed and we repeated the action a couple more times.

I could hear Alex gurgling away in his crib, then he let out a howl, he wanted to be noticed and join in too. I asked Michael to talk to Alex while I went to fetch his bottle.

Bathed and dressed, we all went along to the kitchen.

Jonesy was there just pouring boiling water into the tea pot. 'Just in time, did you sleep well?'

'We all slept very well,' I replied

'Good morning Michael,' said Jonesy.

'Good morning,' he replied.

'Can you say good morning Jonesy, my name is Jonesy.' Michael tried the new name.

He really is a clever child, I thought.

The door opened and a dark haired woman came in.

'Come for your coffee Liza?' Jonesy asked.

'Yes,' she replied as she came straight over to me extending her hand.

'I am so pleased to meet you, I hope you will be happy here; my name is Liza.'

'Hello Liza and thank you,' I took her hand. 'This is Michael,' and she held out her hand again and Michael took it and shook it up and down as he had seen Wilf do. 'And this is Alex.'

'May I?' she held out her arms to take Alex from me. I passed him over.

'You are beautiful,' she whispered, as she held him in the crook of her arm and swayed to and fro.

I remembered Wilf saying that he thought Liza wanted children; she would be a natural mother, was the thought that came into my mind.

'I'll help you with the children whenever you need it,' she was saying.

'I'm sure there will be an abundance of those times,' I told her.

It nearly slipped my tongue to say that I was a beginner then I realised that I am supposed to be Michael's mother, I must be careful.

'Have you unpacked yet?' she asked.

'Well no, I haven't started yet, we were so tired yesterday, and it was a long journey.

'What if I take Michael for a look around while you do it and we can meet up again for lunch?'

'Sounds great to me,' I said.

The morning flew by as I arranged the closet; quite amazing how much I had accumulated in such a short time. I made a cup of coffee in my room and sat a few minutes, planning what to put in what drawers. Michael could reach some of the low small ones so some of his things could go in those.

In no time, it seemed, Michael ran into his bedroom and stated that lunch was ready. The kitchen seemed full of people. Wilf introduced them. Liza I had already met, Bill, her husband and Bert, Jonesy's husband. The table was loaded. Two large quiches and a big bowl of salad, chunks of homemade bread, a round pot of butter and an enormous bowl of fresh fruit. Michael, with a little help, climbed onto his adopted spot on the bench.

'Tuck in,' said Jonesy as she passed Michael a glass of milk. Michael seems to have organised himself very well, got his priorities right, I thought; why did I worry how he would adapt.

I noticed Liza watching me; she would look at Wilf then back at me, obviously having difficulty weighing up the situation. Wilf had told her about me and my husband's death and how he had known my mother in the war years. This is a good time as any to tell her about Wilf and me, I thought.

I sort of coughed, it attracted everyone's attention, and all eyes turned to me. Looking at Wilf I said, 'Wilf has something to tell you.'

'Yes,' said Wilf realising what I meant.

'I told you that I knew Margaret's mother in the war in England, well, we were more than just good friends. I am proud to tell you that Margaret is my daughter.'

'Oh, how lovely,' Jonesy clapped her hands together.

'I did not know this myself until six months ago,' I told them, 'and I am so happy that Wilf is my father, he is wonderful.' Liza, Bert and Bill all said how marvellous and started asking questions.

I noticed that Liza seemed quite relieved; her face had dropped when I had said we had something to tell them. Perhaps she thought we were going to say we were getting married. Whatever it was she now seemed quite happy with the situation, enrapt with Wilf's answers to the questions being put to him. I felt better now that was out of the way, I don't like secrets, they lead to lies, but I must adapt myself to that in Michael's case; it will be worth it I know.

The weeks and months passed so quickly; Michael started attending a morning pre-school group in the village, so met other children in the area. He thrived on it and seemed to get on with everyone. By the time Christmas came round again, Alex was crawling, getting into everything; I had never realised how inquisitive children can be. He had to investigate everywhere.

'Full of adventure that one,' Jonesy said, 'not a book worm for sure, he will experience things not read about them.'

I was to remember those words so often. Alex had to be able to do what Michael did. He grew into a sturdy boy, solidly built. "Good rugby stuff," I heard Bert say one day as he watched Alex playing.

Michael became tall and slim, more refined in his actions, he loved cricket at school, and he played rugby as all the boys did but was not so keen on the game. No, cricket, tennis, swimming, and boating, of course, were his preferences. Whereas Alex seemed to like tougher games, he always made a struggle of competing. I think he tried too hard, set his aims too high then became disappointed in himself so had to try harder still.

Whilst all this growing up took place, I too developed my skills. I found that the painting I had done with the children had given me great satisfaction and I wanted to continue this, I didn't want to leave home each day to go to a school to teach, I preferred to do something from home. I love the place, the whole atmosphere, and did not want to waste a minute of it.

Perhaps in the future I would venture further, but not yet. I had been quite some distance accompanying Wilf on his business ventures and seen many lovely places, I had even flown in the plane but was happy to let Peter carry on with that. I always said I was not much of a city girl but I went there occasionally when it was necessary to buy clothes for the children.

It was through a friend of Wilf's that I started my new career. He was a publisher and wanted someone to illustrate children's books. It was just up my street, as the saying goes; I had a few anxious moments of doubt, could I do it well enough for instance.

Wilf came through for me once more. 'Sort of thing you did for the children at the Home, I would have thought,' he said, 'you did that beautifully and what about the pictures you do for Alex and Michael.'

Chapter 11 Stephen

It was these pictures that had started it really. Stephen Brand, a friend of Wilf, had come for dinner; he saw the pictures and drawings I had done for the children in the kitchen and sitting room, where they had left them. It was soon all settled, I had a job. It was good to feel I was really earning a living, I had my police pension but it was so satisfying to be achieving personally. I was able to work from home, with occasional visits to the city of course, and with Jonesy and Liza to help keep an eye on Alex and Michael, I could relax and concentrate on my work. How very lucky I am, I turned my eyes up to the sky and said, 'Thank you.'

Liza taught me how to ride. She was very patient with me. 'We will go at your pace,' she said.

I had never been on a horse before. Once I did get up there, after a few attempts and feeling utterly stupid, it did seem a long way down. As the horse started to move I felt the equivalent of seasick but Liza's voice instructing me took my mind off the feeling. Now you're up you may as well get on with it, I thought. After a while of gently walking I started to feel the movement and go with it.

Dougal was quite an old horse and not inclined to want to regain his youth, happy to plod around the field. He was wise and knew full well that he had a novice on his back. As I improved we would take the road to the beach and I learnt how to trot and canter. I started to feel the exhilaration of achievement, a power I had not known before.

It was a year after we arrived that Liza told me she was pregnant. I was delighted; we had gone for a ride to the beach and enjoyed a good gallop along the hard wet sand.

'Should you be riding,' I asked her.

'I think that will be my last good gallop for some time, but there's nothing wrong with a gentle ride I am told.'

As we trotted back along the path, I did a bit of mental psychology; there were two ways that my arrival here with two children could have affected Liza. One, she could have felt more need for her own children, or two, which seemed to be the case; she welcomed and enjoyed my children and stopped worrying about having her own. Alex and Michael filled the space and so she became pregnant. This often happens when parents adopt a child, I thought, and I was pleased with the course it had taken.

My work absorbed me, I felt totally fulfilled or so I thought. Until, one evening Wilf asked me what I thought of Stephen Brand.

'What do you mean?' I asked, 'You know I like him, he's a very nice person to work for.'

'I mean personally, not someone to work for.'

'Why do you ask?'

'Well, I think he's interested in you more than as an employer. He asks me some very personal questions about you.'

'Oh,' knowing my face was going red, 'I think he is very attractive but I hardly know him.

The next day I had a telephone call from Stephen asking me to go down to the office as he had a new book layout he wanted to show me. I said that I would go in two days' time, which will be Thursday, if that would be alright. He said that it would be fine and looked forward to seeing me. Going to the city always meant staying overnight, being too far to go and return in the same day and I usually took the time to shop for birthday or Christmas presents; thinking well in advance was appropriate, living miles from a decent size town.

As I dressed for my visit to the city, I was aware of a difference in my choice of what to wear. My conversation with Wilf came back to me and I blushed at his references to Stephen's attraction to me.

I looked in the mirror and recognised a feminine woman, my suit was soft blue wool, the skirt swirled gently as I turned and the jacket hugged my waist. I looked back at the bed to the straight severe business suit I had rejected. Should I wear that one? I thought. No Maggie, I told myself, brighten up a bit, anyway, you can take it with you, and you can always change if you want to. The fact of having a choice made my decision and I did just that; put the business suit into my case and closed the lid.

I couldn't believe how I felt as I approached the office. This is a business meeting, I kept telling myself, stop feeling like a school girl on a date. As I went into the outer office, a door opened at the other end of the room and Stephen came straight towards me, his eyes were shining as he looked into mine. He took my hands and said how happy he was to see me. I blushed, I know I did, I felt as though my face was on fire. The receptionist must have noticed as I felt tongue-tied. Stephen led me into his office turning to ask for coffee for us.

'Now tell me how you are,' he asked, sitting me in a comfortable chair.

'I'm fine, really well, thank you.'

'Yes, I can see that, something is making you bloom, you look lovely, really lovely.'

I felt myself blush deeper. I changed the subject. 'What do you have for me to see?'

The door opened and coffee was brought in.

'We will just have this then I'll show you. First can I ask you; is there any chance we can have dinner together this evening?'

'That would be lovely.'

'Do you have any preference of where to go?' he asked me.

'Oh no, you know better than I do, it is up to you.'

'Good, there is a new place opened up on the hill, I have been told that it is very good and the view will be magnificent over the harbour. 7.30pm alright with you?'

'Perfect,' I replied.

After coffee we went to look at the new layout. It was for a series of children's books.

'Are you interested?' Stephen asked me.

'It will be quite a challenge, but yes, I would like the chance.'

I felt quite excited at the prospect of such an absorbing project. I left the office and did a quick look around the shops before going to my hotel to have a shower and change for dinner. My quick look around had acquired a beautiful evening sweater. I was glad I had brought my business suit along as the straight skirt together with my new sweater would be perfect for dinner and I could wear the jacket over my shoulders if it became chilly. I could not remember the last time I had considered my appearance to this extent.

Dinner was wonderful, the restaurant was all it was made out to be; a perfect place for a romantic dinner with a special man.

'You know how I feel about you,' Stephen said.

'No, I don't,' I replied, 'my eyes have been closed in that way for a long, long time.' Then I told him what Wilf had said.

'I never dreamed that you could care about me Maggie, I ask Wilf questions so that I can feel in contact with you; I had not realised I was being so obvious, although Wilf is a very clever man.'

'I always thought you were married,' I said.

'I wish I could say no to that one, Maggie, but yes, I am. My wife has been in a home for six years, she will never come out. We had a son,

Barry, who drowned in a boating accident when he was sixteen years old, and Mary, my wife, turned in on herself and has never spoken since.

'The waiting for news went on for days. She became more and more hysterical until his body was found and she screamed and screamed until suddenly she stopped. She has never uttered another word since. She doesn't seem to recognise me or anyone. I go to see her only once a week now, there seems no point anymore. She has her own little world where she seems secure. The doctors say she couldn't cope with the outside world anymore now.

I was not interested in the physical side of life, after Barry died and Mary became ill, that is, not until I saw you. When I first came to the farm and met you, I felt alive again but knew it was hopeless in my situation and so all these years I have just dreamed about you.

However, when you came into my office today, I felt there was something different about you, I felt that you were noticing me, not as in the past as working colleagues, but more in a man, woman capacity. You blushed when I held your hand, you never did that before you just shook my hand in friendship, today was different. Dare I ask? Am I right?'

I told him how I was aware of wanting to look attractive, when I chose my clothes, and that this had happened after Wilf told me his thoughts. Something must have stirred somewhere as I felt like a woman again.

I told him how sorry I was about his son and his wife. It must have been happening at the time Alex was born and I was feeling so unexpectedly happy after the horrors of Martin's death. I told him how Martin had drowned too, and I understood the waiting time until the body was found. The build-up of the pressure, until the final knowledge that there was no mistake and reality set in; the forever and ever time.

Stephen said he was going away for the weekend. He had a "batch" a few miles around the coast, just a small place in a quiet bay. He enjoyed fishing and walking. Would I like to go with him and get to know him better? He did not want me to answer him there and then, as he feared I might say no if I answered too quickly.

'Think about it,' he said, 'and tell me tomorrow. I know I won't sleep all night praying you will say yes.'

We walked up to my room and at the door he kissed me gently on the lips. As he held me in his arms I felt so warm and safe, a coming home emotion that I remembered as I flew into Auckland on my first visit, but with more, much more, intensity. Feelings, only in my memory since Martin left me, being stirred into physical awareness. I kissed him back as I have not kissed anyone for six years.

'I don't want you to miss your beauty sleep,' I teased him; 'I'll come with you this weekend.'

'You really mean it, are you sure? No forget I said that.'

'Yes, I mean it. Yes, I am sure.'

'You don't know how happy you have made me. You remember Gene Kelly in "Singing in the Rain," well, if it was raining, that's what I would do.'

'I don't want to bail you out of jail for disturbing the peace, please drive home carefully; I'll see you at the office in the morning.'

'I can't wait,' he said, giving me a last hug and kiss.

I did not sleep well; my mind was full of the implications of my acceptance to go with Stephen for the weekend. I must call home and see if they will look after Alex and Michael. The boys were not used to me being away for more than a couple of days at a time.

Eventually, I drifted off to sleep and awoke feeling remarkably good. I felt as though I had taken an important step forward in my life, one that I was ready to take. So, happy with my decision, I had breakfast and set off for the office. Will Stephen be the same, I thought, as I entered the building. I had always been aware that he was a very attractive man but now, when I remembered his kiss last night, I felt a tingle up my spine and lightness in my heart; I understood what he meant about Gene Kelly, dancing in the rain, I felt like dancing too.

Yes, he's lovely as ever, I thought when I entered the office and saw him. Why did I ever doubt it; I can't believe what is happening to me, I suppose. He was obviously delighted to see me and quickly took me through into his office, put his arms around me and kissed me.

'I've been waiting to do that since last night,' he said grinning from ear to ear. 'I have been in and out of this office into reception a hundred times watching the door, the minutes crawling by.'

As we stood there his arms around my waist and my arms around his neck I felt so comfortable; the most natural place to be. I gently pulled his head down as I raised my lips to his for another kiss. We could have stayed like that all day, but there was work to be done and a knock on the door brought us back to earth.

I made my telephone calls to the farm.

'No problem, stay and enjoy your weekend,' I was told. 'The weather forecast is good, have a great time and don't worry about the boys.'

What would I do without these wonderful people around me? I raised my eyes upwards and said, 'thank you.'

It was a busy morning but Stephen said we could get away by 3 o'clock. As my clothes felt unsuitable for a country weekend, I nipped out for an hour to go to the shops. I realised looking around for clothes in a large department store, my eyes seeking, for the first time in ages, really looking, not just getting something to wear, but choosing clothes and colours with an expectance of being noticed.

It felt good as I chose a pair of beige slacks with a thick wool sweater, in a mixture of turquoise and peach, a plain peach scarf to match, some flat shoes and socks. Next to the cosmetic counter for a lipstick the same colour as my sweater and scarf, nail polish too. It is a country weekend; I reminded myself as I went to the ladies room and applied my new nail polish.

Sitting waiting for it to dry I watched other women coming and going, do I look different I wondered? I certainly felt different, surely it must show. Looking in the mirror, I thought, yes, I look happy and the new peach lipstick suited my fair complexion; lifting my hand to my face to admire the perfect match of lipstick and nail polish.

It was over an hours' drive around the coastline to the cottage, or 'batch' as the New Zealanders say. It was well off the main road, through miles and miles of forestry, but we eventually came out of the trees to a view over the sea. We stopped and looked down over a small hamlet.

'Mainly holiday homes,' Stephen pointed to the left, 'there is a shop, hotel and garage over there to the right.' In the middle of the bay was a jetty, we watched as a motor boat was being manoeuvred into place at the ramp and onto its trailer. 'Quite a community here at the weekends,' Stephen was saying, 'I'm going to enjoy introducing you.'

'Which is your place?' I asked.

Stephen put his arm along the back of the seat as he leaned over to point out of the window towards a log cabin amongst the holiday homes. 'You smell so good Maggie,' he nuzzled into my neck. 'I could eat you. Talking about eating, we could go to the hotel tonight, make everyone envious, then we can shop for food tomorrow. How does that sound to you?'

'Sounds great to me,' I laughed.

We drove down to the bay and parked the car beside the batch. There were three lonely shrubs at the front of the place and a small square of grass.

'I'll soon get the fire going, and then I'll make some tea or coffee.'

I can make tea if you show me where the things are.' I volunteered.

'Everything you need is in the cupboard by the sink.'

'Right, I have found it,' I called back to him from the kitchen, 'tea coming up soon.'

I heard a crackling sound and went into the living room; the wood burning stove was well away, the flames showing through the glass door. Bringing in the tray with mugs of hot tea we sat before the stove, enjoying the warmth.

'The place soon gets warmed through, I'll leave the doors open when we go out and every room soon gets aired,' said Stephen.

After our tea I took the mugs back into the kitchen and rinsed them under the tap, then went into the bedroom to change into my trousers and sweater. There was an enormous wooden bed; it must have been made for the first settlers, I thought. Stephen must have read my thoughts.

'It belonged to my grandparents. I could not bear to throw it away, so I kept the head and base boards and fitted a new modern mattress; look how comfortable it is,' as he flung himself onto the bed and bounced up and down. 'Come and see,' he pulled my hand and I fell onto the bed. We laughed together like children.

'Now it won't be strange later, will it?' he questioned.

He kissed me gently but with no urgency, as he knew not to rush me.

'Come on or we will be too late for dinner.'

He took both of my hands, and pulled me to my feet giving me a hug. It was getting dark outside as we walked to the hotel. The bar was brightly lit and seemed full of people chatting to each other in a friendly manner, everyone knew everyone. I couldn't remember all the names, there were so many but the atmosphere was warm and Stephen took the light banter in good part, obviously proud to have me with him.

Eventually, we moved into the dining room, most of the tables were occupied. People who had not been in the bar said hello and Stephen introduced me. We had a beautiful meal. I had fish, freshly caught in the bay and Stephen had a steak, it almost filled his plate. The vegetables were cooked just right and the side salad was crisp and fresh. We lingered over coffee and Stephen asked if I wanted to go back into the bar or leave by the side door. I chose the latter.

We sauntered back to the batch along the beach, our arms around each other, gazing at the bright stars. When we got inside we did not turn on the light, the glow from the stove gently filled the room and the warmth enveloped us. We sat on the big settee and held each other, knowing that this night was a special time and there was no hurry to make it pass quickly. We wanted to savour every second of it.

Voices woke us, people jogging along the beach. I stretched my arms above my head, I had never felt like this before, not even with Martin; so at peace with myself. I snuggled back under the covers and put my head onto Stephen's chest, he kissed the top of my head; it all seemed so wonderfully natural, as though we had known each other forever.

When we eventually got out of bed, Stephen wrapped me in a large dressing gown and I went into the kitchen to make tea whilst he tried to salvage a glimmer out of the stove, which had not been dampened down the night before. We had had other things on our minds. By the time I carried the tea into the sitting room I could hear crackling as flames leapt into life. We snuggled together on the settee watching the wood burn and enjoying the warmth coming from the stove.

After a leisurely breakfast we decided to go for a walk. We walked miles and miles, firstly along the beach then turning inland through the bush; the idea being that we make a circle and end up where we began. Stephen asked me if I was any good at navigation and I told him I had a good sense of direction but not in the middle of the bush and would prefer the help of a map. I was sure he had, or we wouldn't be going along this path.

'I bet you were a boy scout,' I laughed.

We came to a farm house, a long, low, rambling place, similar to home. As we walked up the drive, a couple came out onto the porch and two dogs came running down the path towards us, their tails wagging in friendly greeting. One was a golden Labrador and the other a black Cocker Spaniel. I bent to pat the dogs as they came to sniff at me. Stephen introduced me to his friends Ann and George Trent.

'Hope you can stay to lunch,' George said.

'We have plenty,' Ann added. 'Don't run off, we don't see much of you these days.'

'You will in the future, if Maggie can arrange it,' Stephen said, turning to me.

They were wonderful people; we enjoyed our lunch on the patio. It was a very sheltered spot. The garden was beautiful; so many plants. Shrubs and trees of all kinds, including my favourite Punga, which is a tree fern and the Phoenix Palm that looks like a pineapple at the base.

'This garden looks like a full time job to me,' I said admiringly. They both enjoyed gardening and had more time to give to it since they had retired.

'Time to smell the roses,' George said as he stretched out his arms above his head in a relaxed fashion.

'The children are all away living their own lives, so we can take it easy,' Ann added.

We left them, promising we would call again, when we next came down.

'Come and join us for a meal at the hotel,' Stephen invited.

We walked and walked, every so often stopping to listen to the wild life; Stephen knew so much about the trees, plants and birds. I am quite ignorant about such things, and wished I had paid more attention to nature study classes at school, but it was much more interesting learning from Stephen. He made it fun with little rhymes to remember things with. Suddenly, we came through a clearing and, like magic, there was the back of the batch. I recognised the car. I was so surprised and congratulated Stephen on his navigational skills with a big kiss on his cheek.

'How about a cup of tea?' he asked.

'Just what the doctor ordered,' I replied.

It was so cosy in the batch, the log fire in the stove still burning away merrily. I sat by the fire on the settee and Stephen appeared in no time with mugs of steaming hot tea and a packet of biscuits.

'We didn't do any shopping,' he said. 'Usually I bring food down with me, but it's only fair to patronise the shop as well, so after we have finished our tea we can go to the shop, or you can stay by the fire if you are tired. I'll go and it won't take me long.'

'I'm not really tired, just weary after all that fresh air, but this tea will revive me, I'm sure, and I would like to see the village shop. Is it as interesting as the hotel?'

'They pride themselves on having most things so I go in for one thing and come out with a dozen.'

Stephen was right about the shop. It had everything. I would have hated to "stock take" the place, it must take them days and days. We chose some lamb chops and vegetables, a tub of ice cream and a big bar of chocolate for later. When we got back to the batch, there was a note pinned on the door inviting us for drinks. It was from Bill and Betty, who I had met the previous night in the bar; I had a faint recollection but there had been so many people.

We went into the warmth, put the food into the fridge then collapsed onto the settee; preparing dinner could wait.

The next day we went out on a fishing spree. We had been invited the night before by friends who were at Bill and Betty's house. It had been a lively little party, nice background music and intelligent conversation; most of them worked in the city. It was an early start, no lying in bed this morning, and it was mid-afternoon by the time we returned. We had lunch on board; I was amazed how much room there was in the galley. I was happy being at sea but not too happy about catching the fish. I had to have a go but could not bear to take the hook out of the fish's mouth. I thought how much I would be hurting in such a situation and felt I wouldn't eat fish again.

We had let the fire go out at the batch as we knew we would be leaving as soon as we returned from fishing. It was quite cold so we wasted no time packing up and getting on our way, but it soon got warm in the car and we travelled comfortably back towards Wellington. I was staying at Stephen's apartment; he had sold the house two years before when he realised that his wife would never live there again and bought an apartment which is much easier to look after.

As we drove along I pondered on how my life had changed in just a few short hours; all the things I had done and all the people I had met. I remembered how I had stood outside my empty house in England knowing I had to move on – move on to where? This was another step along life's journey, only this time it was different, this time I was enjoying it.

By the time we arrived back at Stephen's apartment it was almost dark. The apartment was on a hillside overlooking the bay and as the last rays of sunlight disappeared over the horizon, the lights came on all around the edge of the bay and dotted on the hillside. It looked like fairyland.

This really is a beautiful country, I thought. Here we are in early spring, going into summer, whilst in England they are in autumn with the lovely golden red colours of the trees and soon into winter. How my life has changed, from my hopes and dreams at Jenny's wedding, when I first met Martin, the only romance in my life. Now I am embarking on a new pathway, with a new romance. I wonder where it will lead me.

'Do you like Chinese food?' Stephen was asking, as he broke my reverie.

'Yes, I do, why?'

'I thought I would get some takeaways, unless you prefer to go out to eat?'

'No, I think that is a good idea, is it far to go?'

'No, just around the corner, you make yourself comfortable, I'll be back before you have a chance to miss me; on second thoughts, I would like you to miss me a little bit.' He bent to kiss me and I kissed him back.

It had been such a perfect weekend, and I walked around the room looking at his books and photographs; there was a photograph of the three of them when Barry would have been about six years old. They looked a very happy trio.

I put some plates to warm then went back to look at his music cassettes. I selected one and put it on the machine. The music filled the room and I put my arms around myself and swayed to the music; I felt so happy. When Stephen returned we sat on the floor to eat our Chinese meal, our backs to the settee.

'Have you tried using chopsticks?' asked Stephen as he handed me some.

'Only once, many years ago, but I'll try again.'

We laughed at our efforts, and then tried again; the meal lasted a long time.

'How do you feel now?' Stephen asked, as he put his arm around my shoulders.

'Wonderful,' I replied and laid my head back onto his shoulder; he kissed me and I melted into the moment.

The next day I went back to the farm. I did not go back into the office with Stephen but he said he would call me that night. Travelling home I wondered what the boys would think, and how to explain my sleeping in Stephen's bed or him in mine. I would ask Wilf's advice; he always came through for me.

Chapter 12 New Zealand 1972

Michael would be going away to boarding school in a few months, he was going to Wilf's old school and Wilf was very proud of that. We had been to see the school years before and Michael and Alex had been accepted when they were the right age. What should we do this summer? Michael will want to play tennis all of the time and Alex loves swimming. It seems funny the way we acquired a swimming pool and a tennis court.

It was back when Michael was coming up to six. Wilf asked him if there was anything special he would like for a birthday present.

'A tennis court,' he told Wilf.

'What a good idea. You will have to help me organise it though. What do you know about tennis courts, other than how to play on them,' Wilf asked.

Michael went to the bookcase and came back with a thick heavy book.

'It's all in here, Grandpa; how long, how wide and all the lines to put on it.'

'Well fancy that, we will have to get on with it straight away if it is to be ready for your birthday. Bring the surveyors tape off my desk and we will go and find the right spot. 'They trooped out of the house absorbed in their task.

So of course when Alex's birthday came around eight months later, Wilf asked him what he would like for his birthday.

177

Obviously schooled by Michael Alex replied 'A swimming pool, Grandpa.'

'What a good idea,' said Wilf, to his eager grandson, his own eyes twinkling. 'But you will have to help me design it. Can you do that?'

'It's a big hole Grandpa,' Alex smiled at his cleverness.

'Ah, but where do we put the big hole?' asked Wilf.

'I'll show you Grandpa,' and he took Wilf's hand to lead him out of the door; Michael followed quietly behind.

Never would a tennis court or swimming pool be used so much. Everyone took advantage of them and Wilf wondered why he had not put them in sooner. Michael played tennis from morning till night as long as he had someone to play with and even on his own he would serve all the balls to one end, then collect them and serve them back again; over and over. We all belonged to the local tennis club and Michael became an extremely good player.

Stephen called, he said he was missing me, his whole life had changed and we had to talk. When could we meet again, could he come up next weekend? I told him how I did not know how to cope with the boys seeing us in the same bed. I wanted them to get to know him better. I knew they already knew him but it had only been for short times before dinner, their bedtimes and as someone I worked with in the city. If he came for the weekend then I could not accept him into my bed at this stage and did he understand my sensitivity.

Yes, he understood and if it was alright with Wilf then he would come up on Friday evening and go back on Sunday afternoon.

I talked to Wilf and explained my predicament. He was delighted that I was happy and said he had high regard for Stephen. He was not too pleased about Stephen's wife, having thought her dead, but he understood when I said that I did not want to leave the farm, there was no intention of me going to live in the city with Stephen at this stage.

I honestly did not want to leave the farm, perhaps a part-time lover was the best for me. I could keep my independence, concentrate on my work and we could see each other as often as we liked.

Stephen might not like this idea, I thought, but time will work it all out. I had become very wise from my past experiences not to ask for too much vision into the future; it does not do to know too much.

And so Stephen came for the weekend; the boys enjoyed his company and he brought them books they did not have; "new off the press."

Michael and Stephen played tennis. 'He's very good,' Stephen told me, 'could enter tournaments if he chose to and who knows where that might lead.'

He swam with Alex; luckily it was a warm weekend and the pool is sheltered and angled to catch the sun.

Michael talked to him about his new school and how he was looking forward to going there.

Stephen told them about the batch and invited them down to it. 'Come next weekend, it's a holiday so you won't miss any school. What about you Wilf, can you come too?'

He was trying so hard, I felt sorry for him.

'Can we go Mummy,' the boys chorused.

I looked at Wilf. 'Will you come?' He knew I needed his support.

'Why not, I could do with a long walk on the beach and we could have a game of cricket.'

'Oh yes please,' cried Michael. 'I'll take my new bat and ball.'

Everyone was so excited, we talked about sleeping bags and blankets, the food we would need and extra plates, mugs and cutlery; you would think we were planning to go for a month. Let's call this a trial weekend and if you enjoy it then we could plan a week or so in the school holidays.

After the boys were in bed, I went back into the sitting room to join Wilf and Stephen. They are so comfortable with each other, having been friends for quite some time.

'I'll just go and check the gate is closed,' said Wilf, being considerate.

'If you don't mind Wilf, I will take Stephen for a walk around so I'll check the gate; it is a lovely evening now, and you can come too of course.'

'No, I have a good book I want to get back to; see you in the morning.' He kissed me goodnight and shook hands with Stephen.

We walked outside in the moonlight; just the opposite to the city. We hugged each other as we sat for a long time on the veranda, until I said I was tired; it had been a long day and I wanted to be up early.

'Would you like to ride tomorrow?' I asked Stephen.

'It is a long time since I was on a horse but yes, I would like to ride again.'

We parted reluctantly, but knowing it was the best for us at that time.

'Goodnight my love,' he said, and then gave me a last deep lingering kiss.

The next morning we rode along the beach, we were on our own. Michael was visiting a friend in the village to play tennis and Alex was building something with Wilf in the workshop. When Stephen felt secure on his horse, we had a good gallop; the horses enjoying stretching their legs. We turned off the beach into the bush.

I knew where I was going. When we came to the clearing with the little shack and we left the horses to graze. There was always coffee and tea in the cupboard so I filled the billycan from the stream and soon had the primus stove going and the water boiling. Stephen explored the area then came back to sit on the blanket I had spread on the ground.

We enjoyed our coffee then laid back and looked up at the sky; I took a blade of grass and tickled Stephen's nose. He took it from me and traced the outline of my lips with it, then, he kissed my eyes, the tip of my nose and lastly my lips. I revelled in the teasing, savouring the moment when our passions would be released. We loved each other there in the open, very slowly, enjoying every caress. The birds sang, the sun shone; I felt as though I was in heaven. We lay there for what seemed hours, sharing our private time together, not knowing when the next time would be.

We arrived back at the house in time for lunch. Wilf had been busy with Alex's help; the table was laden with sandwiches, man-sized sandwiches, and hot soup was simmering on the hob.

'Looks like we're feeding an army,' I joked.

'Someone's been very busy,' Stephen added.

'I helped make the sandwiches,' said Alex proudly.

'You did a good job there. Can we start as I'm starving,' said Stephen.

Wilf filled up the soup bowls and we all ate ravenously.

'Horse riding has given me an appetite,' said Stephen looking at me with a twinkle in his eye.

We all waved goodbye to Stephen after lunch and I knew he had had a wonderful weekend just as I had. That was two in a row.

'Drive carefully,' I called as he went down the drive with the window down, waving his arm in a goodbye salute.

All week seemed to be taken up with planning for the coming weekend. Michael and Alex were asking dozens of questions and then going into deep discussions together. We left the farm at 4 o'clock on the Friday afternoon. It was a long drive and I was glad that Wilf was doing most of it, although I would give him a break along the way and take over for a while. As we passed over the mountains and through the gorge, Michael and Alex were thrilled with the deep ravines and narrow roads snaking around the mountain sides.

'Don't go too near the edge Grandpa,' said Alex as some cars came from the other direction. Michael asked Wilf how it had been built and what was holding it up.

'Look back as we go round the bends and you will see how it is built out from the side of the mountain and if you look carefully you can see the railway track fixed onto the other side of the gorge.'

'I can see it,' they chorused. 'I'm glad we're not in a heavy train,' called Michael.

It was going to be late when we arrive so Stephen said he would have supper ready for us. When we entered the batch the stove was glowing, giving a welcoming feel to the place and the smell of cooking came from the kitchen; rich and tempting. We were all starving and were soon tucking into the stew and large chunks of crusty bread. There was ice-cream to follow.

I was going to sleep in the bedroom with the boys and Wilf had the bunk by the window in the sitting room with Stephen on the big settee. In no time the boys were asleep.

'Why don't you have a walk to the hotel,' I suggested to Wilf and Stephen. 'Introduce Wilf to everybody. I have enough to do sorting out the food and clothes and could do with an early night. It is going to be an early start if I know my boys.' Stephen and Wilf agreed. 'You may be back before I have finished but if not I will say goodnight now.' I kissed them both thanking Wilf for bringing us down and Stephen for his culinary efforts, which had been greatly appreciated.

After they left I put the food away in the cupboard and made neat piles of the clothes as I took them from the bag, a pile for each of us. I put on the jug to boil and undressed, changing into my nightdress and dressing gown. Taking my mug of tea I curled up on the settee before the fire feeling utter peace, secure in the knowledge that everyone I cared for was safe and happy. I wanted to hold the frame forever and keep time at that very moment.

My eyes soon started to close so I went to bed, snuggling in next to the boys. Faintly I heard Wilf and Stephen return and their quiet movements in the next room as they prepared for bed; the noise made me feel safe and I remembered no more until Alex was leaning over me kissing my face to wake me up.

'Come on Mummy, come and see.' I opened my eyes to see Michael standing at the window.

'Look, the sea,' he was pointing. Alex jumped about on the bed in excitement.

'You would think you had never seen the sea before,' I said as I climbed out of bed.

'I know but this is a different sea.'

The bedroom door opened and Wilf handed me a mug of tea.

'You will need this.' -'I could hear the rumpus.' -

'In the bathroom first boys, then you can run down to the water's edge whilst I make the breakfast.'

Michael and Alex made a dash for the door.

'Here,' I called, 'take your clothes,' as I handed them their shorts, pants and tee shirts. I sat back and enjoyed my tea.

Stephen poked his head around the door. 'Ready for a refill?' he asked.

'Yes please' as I held out my mug to him and he came over and sat on the edge of the bed; he kissed me.

'Good Morning,' he said.

'I have not even combed my hair.' I put my hand up to my hair, trying to run my fingers through it.

'Looks fine to me, I'd like to see it like this every morning.'

'What about the tea?' I said, pushing him off the bed.

'At your service madam,' Stephen joked as he left the room.

I quickly put on my dressing gown, ran a comb through my hair, went through into the kitchen and sat at the bench.

The boys rushed out of the bathroom semi-dressed, Wilf after them trying to pull Alex's tee shirt down from under his armpits.

'I'll take them on the beach for a few minutes while you get breakfast ready,' Stephen opened the door for the boys and followed them down the path. I watched from the window; the boys running down the beach and Stephen strolling behind. Then he must have been called by Michael who then set off into a run towards the sea. I wondered how Stephen felt at the memory of his own son at that age.

I went to get dressed and when I came back into the kitchen Wilf was at the stove making drop pancakes. He already had a pile made in a basket with a cloth over them to keep them warm. The table was laid and a big pot of strawberry jam played centre stage, cereals and a jug of milk were at the end of the table. The door opened and three smiling pink faces looked in.

'Something smells good - quick, wash your hands.' Stephen guided the boys to the bathroom. Wilf was kept going at the stove making more pancakes as the first pile quickly disappeared.

'What are we going to do now?' asked Alex.

'I thought we might go for a drive along the coast and see the dolphins,' Stephen replied. 'Do you like dolphins?' Everybody agreed that they liked dolphins.

'I know a super place for fish and chips, we can eat them in the paper at the picnic table by the beach; how does that sound?'

The day went beautifully and by the time we got back to the batch, the boys were ready for bed. I made a hot drink and in no time at all the boys were fast asleep.

'You and Stephen go out tonight,' Wilf suggested. 'I'm bushed and could do with a peaceful read.

We walked along the beach and called at the hotel for a drink. I was surprised how many people remembered my name. We did not stay long in the bar but walked further along the beach towards the sand dunes and in a sheltered spot we lay down and held each other close; the closeness stirring our passions. We made love beneath the stars.

The next morning was a replay of yesterday as everyone demanded Wilf's pancakes again. After breakfast Stephen suggested fishing from the jetty as the tide was just right and we can eat our catch for lunch. So we all trooped down to the jetty and took up our places. Stephen bought bait at the shop and showed the boys how to fasten it on to their hooks carefully, and then dangle the line over into the water.

Michael was the first to have a catch; he brought up a flounder. Alex waited patiently but was a little long faced as Wilf caught the next, then Stephen after him. I prayed for Alex to catch a fish. He did, calling to Grandpa to help him pull in his line.

We got enough for a helping each for lunch; so with bread and butter, a salad, finishing off with apple pie and cream, lunch and the fishing trip was a great success.

That evening we all went to the hotel for dinner. I felt very proud as I watched the boys in the dining room, with their clean shining faces and combed hair, behaving like little gentlemen as they copied Wilf and Stephen.

Once more when the boys were in bed Wilf suggested he would be fine with his book if Stephen and I wanted to go out, and I must admit that he did look extremely happy as he sat by the fire and very healthy too. So I told him my thoughts.

'All this fresh air, exercise, good food and, of course, the company must have something to do with it,' he laughed.

Stephen and I walked in the same direction towards the dunes, found our old spot and settled down in each other's arms, knowing we would be parting tomorrow and not knowing when we would be together again.

I tingled at Stephen's touch, I wanted him with an urgency I had never known before and felt the same need in him, as he slipped off my blouse. I undid the buttons on his shirt, spreading my palms on his chest, taking the shirt up and over his shoulders to drop down his arms. We lay together discovering each other's bodies and the sensations of lingering touch, until we could wait no longer and made love until our bodies were satisfied and our energies spent.

The next day we made our way home to the farm. I was quite exhausted, not just with the change of air and exercise but emotionally too. This was all new to me and although very enjoyable and I was deliriously happy, I still felt quite weary. I fell asleep in the car on the way home.

Summer came and went, we had a couple of weeks at the batch and also Stephen took Michael, Alex and me to the Great Barrier Reef for a two week holiday. A friend of his had a motor cruiser we could use to cruise the islands.

We flew to Cairns in Australia and sailed out from there. Our sleeping arrangements fell into place; we were shown to our rooms, the boys in one and Stephen and I in another. The boys taking it for granted.

We were all fascinated by the underwater world we could see in the crystal clear waters. We enjoyed snorkelling and the boys fancied themselves as Captains as they were allowed to steer the cruiser through the open sea.

Another time we flew down to Sydney to visit Kathleen and Alan; I wanted Stephen to meet them. I told Kathleen on the phone how it was serious between us but the problem was where to live.

'There always has to be a problem,' she had said, 'but you will sort it out, that's how you learn about each other and become stronger, but I have news for you, I'm going to have a baby.'

'Oh! That's wonderful, can't wait to see you and the wedding photos too.

'Not many of those, it was very quiet as I explained but it sounds as though we will be coming to your wedding soon.'

'We'll see.' I replied as we finished our conversation.

It was a wonderful trip. The boys enjoyed Sydney and all the sights. Alan took them sailing on his yacht; it fascinated them and I was sure they would want to sail in the future. Stephen has a friend who sails so that will be an attraction the boys will push for.

While the men were away sailing Kathleen and I caught up on our chatter although we do speak quite regularly on the phone, there's always something we can find to discuss; especially with a baby on the way.

'Have you thought of any names?'

'If it's a girl we like Diane and for a boy Andrew, don't know about second names it's no use complicating things yet is it, do you like those names?'

'I really do.'

This was a perfect holiday for Michael before he left for school. He was looking forward to going to boarding school and proud to be going to the same school as his Grandpa had gone to. Wilf had been so proud too when we visited the school. He was paying the school fees.

'Who else do I have to spend my money on?' he rebuked me when I questioned the cost of the term fees.

Many of the local children went away to school and returned each weekend but Wilf's old school was too far away for that, so it was necessary for Michael to be a full term boarder.

The terms were not that long and the holidays longer than the day school which made up for being away from home. This is what I told myself in consolation. I was going to miss him; certainly more than he would miss me but Alex is still here, I told myself.

Stephen asked me to go and live with him in the city. I felt he knew I would say no but wanted me to have the option. Telling him that I would not leave the farm while Alex was at the village school and did not think I could do my work in the city. I needed the space and peace of the countryside and although wanting to be with him more, it would not work for me.

I felt selfish and told him so; he said he would rather leave our arrangements as they were than make me unhappy and spoil things between us. His unselfishness made me feel worse and I talked to Wilf about it.

'Some people are meant to have a little quality time together rather than quantity. Don't spoil it, value it more,' he advised me.

How come this wonderful man, my father, always made so much sense? I told Stephen Wilf's words and he said, 'He is a clever man, I wonder why he never married?' I told Stephen about my mother, then of Ruth's death, who I have my suspicions was in love with him. Perhaps, they would have become closer after my mother died, had there been time.

'Finding a daughter and two grandchildren must have filled a big gap,' Stephen added.

I had a phone call; Kathleen had a baby girl, Diane. Alan was over the moon and could we go over for the christening at the end of the year.

'We would certainly do our best' I told her.

Chapter 13 Life on the Farm

The years passed and Michael proved himself to be clever, he also became the captain of the junior tennis team and played in the rugby team in the winter. He liked cricket too but the games conflicted too often so he concentrated on the tennis. Each end of term he came back to the farm, sometimes bringing a friend with him and occasionally visiting his friend's home instead. He grew tall, with thick black hair.

In no time at all, it was Alex's turn to go to school with Michael. Alex could not wait for the adventure; he was so boisterous and enthusiastic in all he did.

I took them both down to the school; Michael was impatient to show Alex the ropes and Alex keen to learn. I was happy for them but devastated myself. I put on a front whilst I waved goodbye then I drove to a country lane and burst into tears. Telephoning Stephen I could hardly speak.

'Come to the apartment,' he said, 'I'll be there.'

I parked the car in the allotted place, almost running into the building. Stephen answered the door bell, I threw myself into his arms and sobbed. He patiently waited for me to stop, rocking me gently, comforting me in his arms.

'They are so grown up. I feel I have lost them,' I cried.

Stephen poured me a drink. 'Here, drink this,' he led me towards the bedroom where we lay on the bed, Stephen holding me tightly.

I knew that eventually the question of living with Stephen would arise again, and I did agree to spend more time with him at his apartment but I had to keep going back to the farm. I could not leave Wilf alone altogether, although we had Emily, with her daughter Susan, living at the house now.

It had become too much for Jonesy on her own so Emily came to help. She lived in the village and came each day to the farm but, when her marriage broke up and her husband left with another woman, Emily decided she would like to live at the farm and we all thought it a good idea.

Liza's little girl, Beth, was a beauty. She followed Alex everywhere and was very upset when he went away to school. She had tried to do everything he could do, just as Alex had tried to copy Michael. So it was good that Susan and Beth were of a similar age and they became firm friends, travelling to and from school together. They were never far apart. They played tennis and swam together and took turns on Dobbin, the small pony; so children's laughter still filled the house. I taught them how to paint and set up a studio for them in the garden house; we were all helping each other.

My work absorbed me, as it was quite challenging, and I wondered how I would have managed had not Emily come along, to take on some of my household duties. Even with the freedom from Alex's needs, now he was away at school, I still filled every minute of my time.

Wilf complained that I worked too hard and too long; my easel was set up in the sitting room window, the almost circular one. I could watch the children swimming and playing tennis from one side and the open countryside, all the way to the mountain, from the other.

I liked to join Wilf in the main sitting room after dinner to watch the news on television or discuss what had happened through the day. We realised we were very lucky people as we watched what was happening in some parts of the world; the fighting and starvation.

Wilf had now given up flying altogether; he had found someone else to work with Peter. His name was Ralph and, on the few occasions I had been at the gathering around the lunch table, I noticed how his eyes seemed to follow Emily around as she organised the food. That would be very nice for them.

How strange that people have to leave our lives, to make room for others to come into it. Emily had been devastated when she found out about her husband's affair and when he told her he was leaving her and Susan. Watching Ralph, I could see that had to happen, however sad at the time, for good times to come in. Perhaps I should make her aware of Ralph, as Wilf had made me aware of Stephen. We need waking up sometimes, I thought.

Letters came on a regular basis from Michael and Alex. Michael told me about Alex and how good he was in the swimming team and cricket team. Letters from Alex told me the same things. I think Michael wanted to show me how he was looking after Alex and showing responsibility.

It was in June, 1979, just after Michael's sixteenth birthday that Stephen said he had to go to America and England and would I like to go with him? I could not answer straight away. I don't know why but I felt a blockage in my mind and needed to think about it. I wanted to go to America; it was the England bit that worried me.

I knew, instinctively, that I should visit my home town and my old friends, Mary and Ian. It was the sad memories I did not want to be reminded of.

Eventually, I did agree to go so wrote to Mary of our plans and asking her to suggest a meeting. Putting the ball in her court, so to speak, hoping she would suggest our meeting in London as I hinted, feeling no desire to go to the north.

I received a letter back saying they would be in Dorset at that time. They were staying in a cottage for two weeks and would we go and see them there? I felt such relief at not going north. Stephen gave the best dates for him and it was confirmed with Mary. Looking forward to the holiday and shopping for clothes, I felt like a school girl at the thought of seeing Mary again. It would be August in England and then on to America.

Stephen had been to Britain before when he was young; he had travelled around for a year, seeing the world, as many young people do. He was amazed that I had not been to Dorset before but I explained that at the time for me to start to get about, I came to New Zealand instead.

We had a marvellous time away from home for a month. It was turning back the years to see Mary and Ian again. I had written to Mary about why Stephen and I had not married and of Stephen's wife being in a home, so they knew the situation between us.

The cottage they had rented was delightful, roses around the door and small paned windows. We stayed for three days exploring the Dorset countryside. Britain is wonderful in the summer, nowhere nicer, but not in the winter, especially in the North.

Ian and Stephen got on famously, which was lucky as Mary and I had so much "women's talk" to catch up on. I told her about Michael and Alex and how they were doing at school and she told me about the twins, they were away at a school camp, which had given Mary and Ian the idea to have a break without them.

Stephen said we would have frayed tongues the amount of talking we were doing. We extended each day as long as we could, rising early and going to bed late. I savoured the twilight which I had forgotten was so beautiful in Britain. I asked them to come and visit us in New Zealand one day.

'It is your turn next,' I said, wistfully, 'I hope it does not take as many years though.'

We left them and returned to London, calling in at villages in the Cotswolds on the way. Blenheim Palace and Oxford were wonderful places to walk around and Stephen wanted me to see as much as possible in our short time. One day I'll bring you back and we will visit Europe, Paris in the spring, Rome and Athens. It would be nice to take a year off. I knew he was thinking of a honeymoon.

'One day,' I hugged him.

Stephen's business in America was in New York. I was amazed how quickly I felt at home there. In the three days we were there I found my way around so easily; looking at the shops and famous landmarks. In the evenings we were entertained by Stephen's business colleagues. One evening we were taken for dinner to a roof top restaurant, overlooking the lights of the city; a fantastic view.

After our time in New York, we flew to Denver to stay with old friends of Stephens; Mary Ann and Des Donaldson. Mary Ann took me around during the day and we became very good friends. It felt as though we had known each other for years.

Stephen enjoyed his time with Des, not having seen him for ten years, so I reminded Stephen about his comment to Mary and me on "frayed tongues." Stephen explained to Mary Ann and Des and they both laughed.

From Denver we continued on to San Francisco. I had to keep a diary, as my mind could not contain all I was seeing. We ate in the famous fish restaurants and I visited the harbour while Stephen worked. Once more being entertained by his business colleagues, in the evening.

Our last port of call was Hawaii; this was our time together, no work, just the two of us. It was heaven, a true paradise. We did not stay in the tourist area but in a beautiful cottage in the grounds of a hotel in a quiet bay. The flowers and plants were breath-taking and the perfume was out of this world. We swam and sunbathed. I commented I was getting fat with all the good food.

'You are perfect, just my size; look,' and Stephen put his arms around me. I must admit that we did fit together like a jigsaw.

Everybody was delighted to see us back home and I had great fun giving out presents that I had enjoyed buying. The only problem had been space to carry them. It was hard to remember to buy small things. I couldn't wait to see the boys, so after calling in at the farm, we continued to the city, to see the boys the next day. It was not usual practise but I had called the headmaster and he agreed they could have an afternoon out.

They looked so grown up as they came towards me, I felt like I was the excited child. Alex was not quite as tall as Michael but much broader in his shoulders, and as fair as Michael was dark. I knew they were both just bursting to run and hug me but decorum prevailed and we left the building in a sedate fashion. As soon as we were in the car park, around the corner of the building, we burst out laughing and hugged each other; almost jumping up and down. Michael picked me up and swung me round, then Alex did the same.

'Gosh, I feel dizzy,' I said, putting my hand to my forehead.

We climbed into the car and headed away from the school, intent on not wasting a moment of the free afternoon. After I had dropped the boys back at school, I returned to Stephen's apartment, quite drunk with happiness. I felt euphoric, still trapped in the young world of Michael and Alex's excitement. Stephen was not home from work so I relaxed and let my memory relive all the events of the last few weeks. No one can take memories away, I thought, and I have such wonderful ones to feed me for the rest of my life.

Stephen looked serious when he came home, there had been a message from the Home where Mary was; she had had a stroke, not the first apparently but only small ones before. There was nothing he could do, but I thought he felt guilty being away enjoying himself. I assured him that she was getting everything done for her that was possible. He was going to see her that evening. I travelled with him, more for support after the event, but didn't go in. I stayed in the car. We went to a small Italian restaurant to eat and I listened while Stephen spoke about his past. It was a clearing he had to go through.

Mary died before Christmas, so Stephen came to the farm for Christmas and New Year. It was the best tonic he could have had. No one could be anything but happy with the boys around. Together with Susan and Beth, they produced a play. I think it was supposed to be serious but turned out so funny we almost rolled on the floor with laughter.

The dining room table looked a picture for Christmas dinner; the girls displayed great artistic skills with the table and decorating the tree with the help of the boys, or hindrance, going by the amount of giggling and laughter that went on.

Christmas for me was great fun, in the presents I decided to buy.

'Buying in bulk?' the salesman asked laughing, looking at the guitars.

'Yes, do I get a discount?' I quipped back.

'I'll ask the manager,' he took me seriously. The manager came over.

'Are these all for learners?' he asked.

'Why yes,' I replied.

'You will need these,' and he handed me an armful of books.

'Thank you' and I passed them to the salesman to wrap with the six guitars.

There was wrapping paper everywhere. I fetched a box to put it in, in fear of presents disappearing in the bin with the paper later. We closed the curtains to keep out the sunlight, lit the candles and sung carols as Wilf played the piano. Stephen strummed the guitar quietly; he learned to play in his younger days. The atmosphere was quite strange. It will be instilled in all our memories forever.

Michael's exam results were excellent, he was going to do his two higher years then go to University, probably in England; he wanted to do a Law Degree.

Alex said that eventually, he wanted to work on the farm, Wilf suggested he may like to get an Agricultural Degree first, but that was some time away yet.

Michael was not with us the whole of the holidays, as he had entered some tennis tournaments and was expected to do very well. He told me that he had thought of playing tennis as a professional, but after discussing it with his housemaster, realised that tennis is a short term career and it would be too late to go into law after that, so he would keep tennis as his hobby.

Emily and Ralph had married and now have a baby boy, almost a year old, called Timothy. They still lived at the farm as Wilf had built them a house in the grounds.

Beth still followed Alex everywhere when he was home from school. She, like her mother Liza and grandmother, was an excellent horse woman and did extremely well in the local gymkhana. Wilf encouraged her, he could see her potential. She missed her riding during the week as she and Susan were both at school. Beth lived in the stable or was out riding and jumping in the paddock at the weekends. Susan rode too but not with the same intensity, she was no match for Beth so did not try to be.

Susan came into her own with her painting and drawing, she had a natural gift for perspectives. I also noticed that she played her guitar frequently and was becoming quite proficient. She sang quietly as she strummed and the sound was very pleasant to listen to. Not like the usual learner. Michael and Alex had taken their guitars to school, where they could have lessons.

Chapter 14 New Year 1980

Stephen asked me to marry him on New Year's Eve. We had all been to a party in the village hall; danced, done the Hokey Kokey and finally sung Auld Lang Syne. Everybody kissed everybody and wished them a Happy New Year 1980.

Stephen and I went outside the hall for a breath of fresh air. He asked me if I would become Mrs. Stephen Brand

I simply said, 'yes please' and we kissed.

The time seemed right now; he had wanted to divorce Mary many years ago but I did not feel right about that. Selfish maybe, but I also knew I did not want to give up my freedom as I felt being married meant living in the city with Stephen. That is where his work is and I needed to be at the farm as well as the city. Now, wanting to be with him, the place, took second place.

When we all arrived back at the farm, Stephen said he wanted to make the first announcement of 1980. 'Maggie has agreed to marry me.'

Wilf rushed out to get some champagne for a toast. Glasses appeared, corks popped.

'Here's to Maggie and Stephen; every happiness.'

'Every happiness,' they all repeated.

'Speech, speech,' someone called, indicating me.

'Let's make my birthday an extra special day shall we?' I turned to Stephen for agreement.

'Wonderful idea,' he said. 'To Maggie's birthday,' they lifted their glasses to toast the day.

'What a wonderful way to end one year and start another,' Wilf whispered to me. 'I wish you every happiness dear daughter.'

And I replied, 'thank you for the happiness you have given me, I thought my life was over in 1966, instead it was just beginning.'

There was a lot of planning to be done, as I had only given myself six weeks to organise the wedding in time for my birthday.

Being summer, we could have a marquee on the lawn; people could wander in and out of the house, so it did not matter how many guests we had. On my side there would be all the people from the local area plus the ones from town. Stephen had no close family, only two cousins who lived in Australia and he didn't keep in contact with them other than a Christmas card. However, we both had many friends at work and also people from the batch and I knew we would find beds for them all somewhere. I could rely on friends for that.

The wedding would be at the village church and Susan and Beth wanted to be bridesmaids. I was almost certain that Diane would want to be my flower girl so I asked Kathleen to ask her.

'I don't want anything fussy,' I kept saying. 'I have been married before remember.'

Wilf would give me away.

'I never thought I would have such a pleasure as taking my daughter down the aisle,' he told me.

'Ah! Now I know why you told me that Stephen likes me, you were planning far ahead, weren't you?' I teased him.

The days flew past, everyone helped; suits were ordered, dresses chosen. Jonesy and Emily wanted to do the catering but I said I preferred them to enjoy the day, not be working. We compromised; they would do the baking and make the cake but we would get people in on the day to do the work. Every time I went into the kitchen there were cook books on the table and wonderful aromas coming from the stove. Hymns were chosen and flowers ordered. Beth and Susan wanted to be in charge of decorating the church.

Stephen called me every day. We had decided to tour around the South Island for our honeymoon. It was too soon after our trip to Europe to be going again and as I said. I had not even been to the South Island but had heard how beautiful it was.

Stephen was delighted to be showing me more of New Zealand. I was just opening my post, after having a cup of coffee with Barney the postman, when the telephone rang. It was Stephen.

'You are very early,' I said.

'Yes, I know, but I have just heard from Bangkok that they have a problem, which I must sort out before we go away. I'm flying over there this evening so will be away for two days.'

'Running out on me are you, going to find a Thai girl instead,' I teased him.

'You are the only girl for me but I promise to bring you back a silk dress. What colour would you like?'

'I'll leave that up to you,' I replied.

'Alright my love, look after yourself while I'm away. I'll call you on Thursday night. I should be back around 10 o'clock.

'I'll wait up for your call, take care, I love you.'

'I love you too,' he sent me a kiss down the phone.

I sent one back and the phone clicked off.

My alarm woke me at 7 o'clock wanting an early start as I had a lot of work to do before I went away. I made myself a cup of coffee in my room first then set to. The morning sun streamed through the window of my sitting room and I chided myself for not painting at this hour every morning. It was perfect. I worked happily with no break. As I put the finishing touches to my work I started to feel hungry and realised that I had not had any breakfast. I put down my brushes and stood back to view my efforts. It was finished so I could go away with a clear conscience. I went along to the kitchen.

'Wondered where you were,' commented Jonesy.

'I got carried away with my work. I had to finish it before I go away,' I told her.

I poured coffee and popped two slices of bread into the toaster. The radio was playing a favourite tune and I hummed along with it. The toast popped up and I reached for it just as the music stopped. I was spreading butter on my toast as a voice said there was an announcement. I had a premonition, my skin tightened, I felt sick. The plane had gone down approaching Bangkok, there were no survivors.

I ran to my bedroom and climbed into bed. I wanted to die too. I knew I should think of Michael and Alex and Wilf but I wanted to die. I could not take it again. Wilf would look after the boys. I wanted to die. I could not face it anymore. I curled into a ball, closed my eyes tightly and covered my ears to shut everything out.

I came to consciousness to the sound of sobbing by my side. Wilf's head was buried into the bedclothes. His shoulders heaved with each sob. I put out my arms to comfort him and he put his arms around me and we sobbed together.

I remember very little of the next few weeks. Other people took over. The wedding arrangements were cancelled by someone. There were investigations made into the crash and explosion that caused it. I was taken to a Memorial service, but I was in another world.

I understood Mary, Stephen's wife and how she shut herself off. I refused to belong to the human earth; to feel anything, as I floated through time.

Someone must have put food into my mouth and poured fluid down my throat; I went thin but I did not die.

I don't remember when I started waking in the early hours of the morning to find myself by my easel, painting strange pictures; ethereal, spiritual paintings. They seemed to ease my mind and very slowly I seemed to come back down to earth.

I started to notice the quietness about the house, no children's voices, no plop, plop of the tennis ball, no splashing in the swimming pool. Everyone must have died with me I thought. I went through into the kitchen and Emily quietened the radio. I realised how it must be for everyone living in the house, weeks and weeks of mourning.

I leaned over and turned up the radio, music filled the room.

'That's better,' I said as I smiled at Emily. She burst into tears and mumbled into her handkerchief. I could hardly hear what she was saying. I think it was a prayer. Jonesy came to see what the noise was and I smiled at her.

'Oh, thank God,' she said and threw her arms around me. I laughed at them both; a little giggle to start with then a real laugh. They laughed with me and it broke the silence of the house. I was back. The whole house became alive again and the people in it.

Stephen had left a will; everything he had was left to me, his future wife. Wilf and the solicitors had dealt with everything they could. Stephen's business partner, Paul Stone had been very helpful and the business had carried on. Jonesy had remembered I had said my work was finished so Paul collected it.

I liked Paul and his wife, Marie. Stephen and I had spent many happy hours with them at their home and they were looking forward to the wedding. Marie had sorted out Stephen's apartment, emptying the fridge, freezer and cupboards; also attending to his mail. Stephen also had a half share in an art gallery in the city. He had helped a friend, years earlier when the other partner had wanted their money out of the business, and Stephen had become a sort of sleeping partner, so did not have anything to do with the running of the gallery.

He also had another apartment, where his mother used to live, but he rented this out as an income.

There was a lot for me to think about and I had to take it slowly.

'One day at a time,' Wilf kept reminding me.

Alex and Michael were wonderful; they were delighted that I had "come back to them," as they put it. I had missed Alex's birthday completely, so must make up for it.

'How would you like to go on a holiday to Fiji with me?' I asked them.

'Oh yes,' said Alex. 'Dusky maidens on the beach,' and he swayed from side to side in demonstration. 'We could have a week at the next school break.'

'I have a doubles tournament booked for then,' said Michael. 'I can't let the team down, but you and Alex go; it is for his birthday anyway.'

'What do you think Alex?' I asked.

'Sounds great to me,' he answered.

'Right I'll book it,' I said.

I asked Wilf if he would join us but he said it would be good for me to have some time on my own with Alex. Get to know him better.

I felt the need for physical exercise. I had lost a lot of weight and my muscles were weak through lack of use. I swam every day, even though the weather was cooler, and took to riding again. The horse enjoyed a good gallop on the beach and the dogs came along too. It was good to feel the sea breeze on my face. I released my thoughts as I was beginning to allow myself to feel again.

The time on holiday with Alex benefitted us both. I had taken my paints and spent hours absorbing the views onto canvas. My perspective of colours, the sea and sky had developed in a new way.

I had said I would not do any more children's book work. It had been enjoyable for many years and the last series had been extremely fulfilling but as I had emerged from my quiet time, I had started to paint in a different way. A free flowing interpretation. I liked the way I was not restricted and showed more expression. As I painted in the holiday atmosphere, I felt a new anticipation of the picture I was painting, developing as it went along. Like turning the pages of a good book as the story develops. I even persuaded Alex to have a go and we sat happily chatting as we painted.

Alex knew what he wanted to do with his life; work on the farm as he had always said. He was not looking forward to Agricultural College. He knew it was good to have a degree but, as he saw it, he was not going to be employed by anyone else so did not see the need in his case. There was already a job for him and he would rather get on with the practical side of farming. He could do everything already and Wilf could show him whatever else he needed to know.

I pointed out that there were many other aspects he would learn, such as land analysis for example and new techniques.

'That's what I mean,' he added, 'I don't want to do that. If I was going to specialise in that field, OK, but those are the people that farmers employ for their knowledge on a short term basis and technology is changing all the time. We read about that in books and magazines.'

I could see his point. 'Let's see what happens. You have a few years to go before you can leave school anyway,' I said.

He told me that he enjoyed his guitar lessons and would like to belong to the school band but the guitar to have was an electric one. I guess he was giving me a hint.

'Do you sing as well?' I asked.

'Sometimes, if I can remember the words,' he replied

'Why don't you have a go at writing your own music and words, then you will not forget them?' I suggested laughing but his face was quite serious when he said, 'That's a good idea.'

Alex met up with a nice group of young people, so spent much of his time around the pool and in the evenings after dinner there was always some sort of entertainment going on.

Chapter 15 The Gallery

When we returned home everyone said how good we looked with our new sun tans.

I drove Alex back to school intending to see the solicitor and visit Stephen's apartment. I had to deal with it sometime, so the sooner it was done the better.

I could not face going into the office, so telephoned Paul Stone and he was at the apartment when I arrived.

'Have you decided what you are going to do with it?' he asked.

'Yes, I am going to keep it. I know I will spend time here. Tell me what you know about the gallery will you.'

'I don't know very much. Stephen helped Tony Davis in a financial capacity. Tony is an artist, as you know. However, he sells other people's work, on a commission basis, as well as his own, so there is a lot of variety of crafts on display. Haven't you been there yet?'

'I once went with Stephen when I first came to Wellington to work. I wonder why Stephen never mentioned his involvement.'

'I don't think he thought of himself in the art field, so did not consider himself involved. It was just a business venture that did not bring in a big return.'

'I will go along there tomorrow. I hope Tony doesn't mind having a woman partner; I am more interested than Stephen appeared to be.'

'I'm sure he will welcome your interest; you can enter some of your own paintings as well. Are you staying here at the apartment? You know you are welcome to stay with us. Marie would love to have you.'

'Thank you, but I want to stay here. I have to face it sometime. I just did not want to come here on my own first, so thank you for being here. It must be upsetting for you too.'

'Well, you know where we are if you need us. Don't hesitate to telephone or call in any time, will you. I had better get back to the office now and do come there whenever you want to - promise?'

I thanked him for his kindness and being there for me. I gave him a bouquet of flowers to give to Marie.

'I may get around to decorating the place one day, perhaps Marie could help me choose the papers and fabrics,' I told Paul.

'I'm sure she would enjoy that. I'll tell her.' Paul left and I was alone.

I stood by the window, looking out at the view, not really seeing it as it is now, but as I remembered it when I was here with Stephen. I felt he was here with me and expected him to put his hands on my shoulders and ask me what I would like to drink. I ventured into the bedroom, desperately holding back the tears. I opened the wardrobe door and there were his clothes. I took out his favourite jacket and held it close to me, trying to recapture the feel of him. The tears ran down my cheeks silently, I lay on the bed and drifted away into blankness.

When I woke it was getting dark; I drew the curtains and made a pot of tea and sat before the television, not really seeing the pictures. After about an hour I started to feel sleepy so went back to the empty bed and slept through the night.

Another empty day I thought, as I climbed out of bed and pulled back the curtains. A jogger was going past the building. What a good idea; I put on my trainers and track suit and set off down the hill. By the Marina, I stopped for a coffee and croissant, bought a newspaper, then walked back up the hill.

It was about 11 o'clock when I eventually got to the gallery and I was very impressed with the layout. Tony was pleased to see me. I had telephoned him earlier to say that I would be coming and he had a pot of coffee ready. We walked about the gallery, hot mugs in our hands and he told me about the people who did the variety of work; potters, woodcarvers, and glass blowers. The colours and textures amazed me and the many aspects of painting made me aware of my limited knowledge. I really had been in my own little world. Now something was making me step out of that safe harbour and see a much broader scene. I felt quite excited and told Tony so. He said he was delighted and hoped I would take an active interest.

'Oh, I will,' I said, 'I am glad you feel that way.'

'Actually,' he said, 'I do have a problem. I have to go into hospital for an operation; only for three days, it is not serious, but I could do with some help in here. Would there be any chance you could be here?'

'I am so sorry you have to have an operation and of course I will help you. When is it you need me?'

'In two weeks' time. I have a woman, Andrea, who works part-time and she will do some extra hours but she has a little girl, so only works during school times.'

'I understand,' I told him and we discussed the dates and times and arranged for me to come in before that, to get the hang of things. In fact I started straight away with Tony taking me through into the office to, "learn the ropes."

'No time like the present,' he said.

We talked about painting, his and mine. I told him how I was developing a new technique, after years of constructed book illustration work and was enjoying the free flowing movement.

'Bring some in,' he told me, 'a new face on the wall is always attractive. You may become famous, you never know, everyone has to start somewhere.'

I invited him out to lunch and we talked easily as we sat overlooking the waterfront. I told him a little of my background; coming from England and so on. He had been over to Europe in his younger days, toured about working his way around from country to country for two years, after leaving Art College.

He had stayed in the north of England for over six months, working in the textile industry. The countryside reminded him of New Zealand; sheep country of course and the summer had been lovely but, as the winter approached, he decided to come home to New Zealand.

I guess he would be around my age and he never mentioned a family and I did not ask.

'How long has the gallery been open, Tony?'

'This will be our thirteenth year; I had a friend who did interior design and we started it together. Things did not work out between us and he left to set up on his own, that's when Stephen bought his share and I went along the way of selling other artists designs. There is scope to develop the interior design side again, if you are interested in that.'

'I feel quite excited as it is; you cannot imagine how wonderful it feels to be doing something again after weeks and weeks of despair. All I could see in the future was a big black hole and now all this.'

'Yes, there is light at the end of the tunnel.'

'You are so right Tony, and I thank you for your help.'

219

I went back to the farm and told Wilf all the news. He was delighted. I asked him to go down with me, when I returned. I felt sure it would do him good and I wanted him to see the gallery. He agreed to come with me, to enjoy our being alone together as we had been when I first came to New Zealand in 1966.

'Do you remember sitting on One Tree Hill when I told you about your mother and me?'

'I did not know I was pregnant at the time and now Alex is thirteen years old,' I added, 'and I discovered my lovely father too.'

'And I found my lovely daughter,' he laughed. 'Here we go again, the mutual admiration society,' we both laughed together.

The time at the gallery was enjoyable but I realised how low my energy was. I tired very quickly. Sometimes there were hours when no one came in, then the door would open and there would be a rush.

'That's how it is,' Tony told me.

One day a man and woman came in. I could tell by their accents that they were from America. They admired so many paintings and objects as they wondered around, I thought they were just sight-seers passing through as were many of our customers. I offered my assistance but they preferred to wander on their own, so I listened from the far end of the room until they needed me.

When they had finished looking they came to me with a list of things they wanted. I couldn't believe how much they wanted to buy.

'We have a gallery back home in New York and we just love all this,' he told me as his arm swept around indicating our display. 'Can you supply us with more on a regular basis?'

I assured him we could; hoping I was doing the right thing.

They were on a cruise ship in the harbour and would be back in New York in three weeks' time. They asked if we could ship their order over.

'We certainly could,' I said and added that we would send details and photographs of various pieces that could be made but were not on display in the gallery at the moment.

I was doubly pleased as they had chosen two of my paintings. I had heard her comment,

'Those are just beautiful Jim, I must have them.' They asked about the people involved and I explained that I had only recently come into the business as a partner.

'Do you display anything?' she asked. I told her about my paintings and she went into raptures; I felt quite embarrassed.

When I told Tony that we were in the export business, he laughed and hugged me.

'I knew you would be lucky for us. It's time you took a trip around our suppliers, don't you think? Tell them the good news. Your idea to send photographs is brilliant and perhaps we could get a catalogue made up as you are in the publishing business.'

'So I am; I had not thought of it in that way, so much has happened to me,' I replied.

After we closed the gallery Tony took Wilf and me to see his Potter friends, Frank and Nora. They were a lovely couple who were wrapped up in their work and each other. They lived in a large old house and the basement was taken over as their workshop. We were shown around and I had a go on the potter's wheel, my hands guiding the clay as I had been shown. It felt quite good, then my timing went wrong and wobble-wobble, my clay became a lump of nothingness. We all laughed and I decided to stick to painting, it is easier.

Tony told them about the American order, the idea for photographs and eventually a catalogue.

'This deserves a celebration,' said Frank as he went off to get a bottle of something. We sat around the table and toasted the gallery and our futures. 'Success to everyone,' we agreed.

Word soon got around to the other people involved in the gallery and we were invited to visit them.

Wilf and I took a break over to the South Island; I had not been there before but it was where Stephen and I were going to spend our honeymoon. Now, I was going with Wilf. I could choose no better companion, in the circumstances.

We flew down to Queenstown and Fiordland; the scenery was magnificent with snow-capped mountains and deep lakes. Being out of the main tourist season it was very quiet compared with the summer, Wilf told me. We had dinner on board the steamer as we cruised the lake. What a romantic place, I thought.

We visited our glass suppliers and had a fantastic day in the workshop watching them work; as with the potters, I decided I would stick to painting.

The next day we hired a car and made our way slowly up the island back towards Christchurch, the largest city in the South Island. We spent the night at a place called Akeroa, originally a French settlement. Wilf's friends had a hotel there and they were delighted to see us.

The house was magnificent; two storeys with balconies running along the front and sides at ground and first floor levels. The bedroom windows opened onto the balcony to a view out across the bay. Boats of all sizes were on the water, and sails in many colours dotted the scene.

Everything was in the style of the old house; the china, silver, crystal and furniture being of the period it was built. When we went in to dinner, a real log fire was burning in the dining room grate and candles on the table gave an atmosphere of the nineteenth century. The flames reflected in the crystal goblets and the beautiful paintings in ornate gold frames decorating the walls looked down on us. I felt I ought to be dressed in a long gown with an off the shoulder neckline and my hair up on the top of my head, garlanded with flowers.

The next day we went into Christchurch. The city is built on a flat plain with hills around it and many of the buildings are like back in Britain. In fact Christchurch is said to be like Cambridge with the river running through it and punting a favourite past time.

We visited friends of Tony who supplied the gallery with wood carvings. It was a father and son business, the son being disabled and working from his wheelchair. They also carved in bone in the traditional Maori designs of the fish hook and birds.

It was very delicate work and Wilf bought one for me to hang around my neck. We spent the night in Christchurch and before dinner we strolled along the riverbank and around the beautiful gardens. It was like spring in England.

In the morning I could not resist going around the shops. I was glad I had Beth and Susan to buy for, as there were such wonderful things. I stocked up towards my Christmas reserves or any other time I needed a present. Sometimes, just out of the blue as a kind of saying thank you.

We had flown from the North Island but returned on the sea ferry. The crossing was calm and interesting. I took photographs to remind me of the rugged coastline and the long narrow entry into Wellington harbour, which was a vista from every angle.

I was so pleased I had seen some of the South Island, even if it was only a very small part. When Wilf had first suggested it my reaction was to say another time, but something told me that the time was now. It had proved to be the right decision.

Wilf looked well. He had enjoyed showing me around, it was his first visit for over twenty years.

We called in at the gallery on our return and Tony was delighted to see us. I remarked how fit and healthy he was looking. He told us that he had been organising the exports to America and everything was working out so well. He also explained what we needed from Paul Stone and there would be no problem. They worked well together.

When Wilf and I returned to the farm, I felt an urgent need to paint. To express all my pent up feelings onto canvas. I had seen so many wonderful things and places and felt deep emotions, which were bursting to get out.

I had found that, although it was peaceful at the apartment, I could not paint the same as I did at the farm. I needed the seclusion of my old room. My time became split between the gallery and the farm.

In no time it was Christmas again and I was thankful I had shopped in Christchurch a couple of months earlier. It made decisions what to buy much easier. At least I had made a start, I thought.

For Michael's birthday I had given him some money and a tennis racquet. One could never go wrong there, but for Christmas I was stumped for both of my boys. I know they both enjoy having the money to spend themselves but I liked to have gifts to open on Christmas morning. It was a tradition I was not going to let go of, as I enjoyed it myself.

I came up with the idea, really for Michael as he was going away to University. He had applied to a London University to do a Law Degree. I bought them a set of luggage each; three cases per set, one fitting into the other. Then, I filled the small one with bits and pieces such as records, socks, chocolate, and tapes all wrapped separately. I am the child, I thought, I love watching people opening presents, even when I know what is inside. I wanted to arrange as much as possible in early December as my memories of last year could spoil my planning if I left it too late; I needed time to cope.

The gallery was going to take a lot of my time too. I did not know it even existed last Christmas, I thought as I wrapped presents, and all these people I had never met. What a strange year again.

Christmas and New Year came and went. There was a sadness over it although everyone tried to be jolly, we were aware of the missing person.

I somehow managed to paint a few pictures and took them down to the gallery.

As I was carrying them in from my car and propping them against the counter, a woman was looking at them.

'Have you painted these?' she asked.

'Yes, do you like them?'

'I certainly do, I wish I could paint. Could you teach me?'

I was taken aback by the question. 'Have you ever painted?' I asked her.

'Only at school but I have the time now and would like to learn.'

'There are many art groups in the city,' I told her.

'I just like the idea of an artist whose paintings I admire,' she said.

'Everyone has their own style, so even if I showed you how I paint it doesn't mean yours will turn out the same, do you see what I mean?'

'Perhaps you will think about it. I also have a friend who wants to learn.'

That's how I started giving lessons in the lunch break; people coming out of offices with their sandwiches to eat as they went along. We worked in the bright light of the front window and this created a lot of interest for passer-by's and the gallery became a focal point to visit.

'Another good idea,' said Tony.

'I had not realised it would boost sales in the shop,' I replied.

Chapter 16 Cancer

It was a few weeks later as I showered one morning that I noticed the lump in my breast. A very tiny lump like a pea. A swollen gland I told myself, it will go away. Maybe the time of the month and my hormones are playing up. It was still there a week later and was I imagining it or was it bigger? I had to find out sometime so I made an appointment to see the doctor in the city.

At last the waiting for results was over. It was cancer. What do I do now?

I told Wilf.

'Oh dear, no!' he cried as he swept me into his arms in a bear hug. I burst into tears.

'I can't take any more stress, I feel so weak already,' I sobbed.

Wilf held my shoulders and looked me straight in the eyes. 'We'll not be beaten, we will win through. I'll help you and so will everyone else, remember that you are not alone my love.'

I went for the operation, not really expecting to come through. I was not angry or sad. I just accepted it must be meant to be. I felt I had had my time with the boys and Wilf and it was now time for me to go. So, I was surprised when I came to and found myself still in this world.

Everything had gone well, I was told, but I needed some therapy to make sure.

Wilf stayed with me at the apartment and took me for treatment. This seemed to go on for months with check-up after check-up. I lost track of time and wished I had spent more time with Michael before he left for England. He was upset at leaving me but I assured him I was on the mend and in good hands.

'Just go and do your best,' I told him. 'I am proud of you and you will come back here as a Solicitor. Anyway, I may come over to see what you are getting up to.'

'I love you Mum, you are the best mother any man could ask for.' I would remember those words.

When my treatment became less frequent we went back to the farm. I painted in the mornings, I painted in the afternoons, and I painted in the evenings. Painting became my salvation and the pictures were selling too. I seemed to have acquired a regular market, especially in America.

Two years passed with no return of the cancer anywhere and I dared to hope I was free of it.

Alex was playing up about staying on at school to do his two higher years. He wanted to leave and come back to the farm. Wilf did not want to seem harsh but preferred him to stay until he was eighteen, even if he did not go on to Agricultural College. This seemed to appease Alex and he agreed to do the two years.

'We will face the rest later,' Wilf told me. 'I don't want you worrying about him. Leave it to me. What are grandfather's for anyway?'

The next two years were quiet ones. I needed recovery time, I told myself. I went back to the gallery again; Tony had employed more staff and he gave lessons to small groups as I had done. I did not want to take that on again yet, so was pleased he was keeping the interest going.

I sat in the apartment one day and recalled what someone had said years earlier. "Everything we do is for a reason." I reflected this and with age and time I could now see the sense the words made. Every lesson is to help yourself and others in the next experience.

I thought of all the children I had taught to paint in the Home. That's where the words were spoken, I remembered. I wondered what has happened to all those children and what they were doing now.

I had enjoyed my first teaching experience; such a very basic exercise. I should write it all down I thought. I could publish a book for children, "How to Paint at Home." I could do one for adult beginners too. There must be a dozen books like that my mind ran on, but I'll check it out the next time I go into a book store. That's how I started my book. I seemed to work well on it in the apartment and my painting back at the farm. I kept the two separate. I felt fitter than I had for a long time, my mind fully occupied.

One of the highlights was a visit from Alan, Kathleen and their daughter, Diane. She was a lovely happy child. I saw a lot more of the north

Island as Wilf and I took them on a tour. First we went to meet them off the plane at Auckland, which brought back happy memories for Wilf and me. Then we went up through the Bay of Islands to the very northern tip.

We laughed a lot and did many silly things like chasing seagulls on the sand and running in and out of the sea like children. Anyone watching would think we were in our second childhood and I think we were. Everything went well. The weather was marvellous, food and accommodation excellent.

Even stupid things like running out of petrol, we laughed about; singing as we strode along the road to find a garage. I think the sun had gone to our heads.

We headed south and across to Rotorua to see the steaming geysers shooting up into the sky. We relaxed in the hot pools after hectic days of sightseeing. We ate well and slept well too and I felt fitter than I had ever imagined possible.

We made our way back to the farm to recover. Kathleen and Alan both loved the house and I looked at it again through newcomer's eyes. Long and rambling with trailing plants covering the veranda roof and down the porch. The rockery covered with colour, leading down to the lawn and tennis court. The swimming pool surrounded on three sides with trellises to catch the sun and flowers everywhere.

It really is a picture, I thought. I must paint it; why had I not thought of it before. I'll paint a picture for Wilf's birthday. What a good idea.

Alan, Kathleen and little Diane left us, making us promise that we would visit them. They had had a wonderful time and so had we. They were now going back to Auckland to stay with Alan's sister Sandra her husband and two boys.

I received a letter from Alex's housemaster asking me to call to see him as he was not happy with Alex's efforts. Wilf was annoyed when I showed it to him as he did not want me stressed. We agreed to go together the following week.

It appeared that Alex was more interested in playing the guitar. Not the one I had bought him but an electric model he must have bought with his Christmas money. The housemaster wanted me to know so that I could speak to Alex myself.

'There is a drug problem these days,' he told us, 'I hope Alex is not involved.'

I felt a shock of fear go through me.

Wilf must have seen my reaction as he turned to me quickly. 'He had better not be on drugs,' he said, in the heaviest voice I had ever heard from him.

We took Alex for lunch and Wilf promised me that he would not get angry.

'Let's hear what Alex has to say first,' I said.

Alex was full of beans, telling us everything was fine. He asked how I was and about my check-ups.

Wilf asked him why he thought the housemaster had written to me.

'Part of his job,' he replied. 'My marks haven't been too good in some subjects, that all.'

'And why haven't they been too good?' Wilf asked.

'I just can't get on with some of this advanced stuff. I'm wasting my time here. I bet he did not mention my electronics project. I have top marks in that. He's not interested in electronics, so he does not grade them as important, but that is where the future is.'

I remembered Alex's room at the farm; piles of equipment to repair; tape recorders or record players. In fact Alex had run the village disco last Christmas; making some of the equipment himself. He had always been happiest when in the farm workshop and later with his head under a car bonnet. He was a very practical person.

I heard Wilf ask Alex about the 'pop group' he belonged to.

'Oh, that's great, you should hear us,' he answered.

'What about drugs?' I faced him with it.

'What do you mean? I am not on drugs, if that's what's worrying you. Give me credit for more sense than that.' He looked at me and I felt disloyal towards him. I knew he intended me to feel that way. He was disappointed in me.

'I'm sorry Alex, but it is so easy to get involved in these things and I know you always have to have a go at everything.'

'Trust me mother; I may have my hair long, it is the fashion, it goes with the times but drugs, no, not for me. I've seen the results and I like being in charge of myself. Does that make sense?'

He sounded so sensible and adult. I was annoyed that the housemaster had upset me so, but I appreciated his position, now my mind was easier. The question would have come up one day, no doubt, so better now and have it over with. I believed Wilf seemed impressed with Alex's attitude also. Later he told me that he was glad he had approached Alex gently.

It was very apparent that Alex would not be going to agricultural college next year so it would be better for him to come back to the farm, as he had always wanted.

Letters arrived regularly from Michael, he was enjoying University. He had made some good friends; one from America, another from Canada and others who live in Britain. He didn't specify whether they were male or female, but went on at great length about his visit to Wimbledon for the tennis and his enjoyment of walking in the countryside with a rambling club.

In the meantime, I developed my books. One was a simple instruction, in story form to teach children how to paint and draw. To develop how they look at and see things with a simple form of perspective. The other one was for adult beginners so more complicated in the variety of instruction. I

235

enjoyed putting them both together and felt pleased with myself when Paul Stone liked them and he set about producing them.

At that time the building next to the gallery became vacant. I thought it was an opportunity not to be wasted. I suggested to Tony that we extend into it; selling art books, picture frames and other equipment needed in the art world. We had been suggesting places where people could buy their needs, so why not supply them ourselves. Tony was quite enthusiastic about it so we took the lease and enjoyed planning how to arrange the new shop. Ideas flowed between us as we worked so well together.

We arranged the opening to coincide with the release of my new books. It was quite a grand affair, extremely well organised by a local public relations firm. A television crew were there to record Tony and myself cutting the ribbon fixed across the doorway. Wine and nibbles were passed around and I signed my book for people; there was a party atmosphere and I felt I was on a film set.

We were on the television news that evening; watching it on the portable set in the gallery office, we all laughed at ourselves on the screen, but seriously it went down well. We were all very pleased after the hard work we had put into it and, had we not had so much to drink earlier in the afternoon, we would have opened another bottle to celebrate further but we all agreed that a cup of tea was what was needed the most.

I slept very well that night and the next morning at breakfast Wilf said he had too. He had enjoyed being involved in developing the shop project but was ready for a rest back at the farm. I realised that he would soon be sixty-six years old. I must get the picture of the house finished before then, I reminded myself.

We returned to the farm, happy to be home in the peace of the countryside; well, for me it was but for Wilf, who was still very involved in running the farm, it meant work.

Liza did a wonderful job in the office along with Rosemary, who did most of the typing, but it would be good, I thought for Alex to relieve Wilf of some of his work, although I know Alex is not an administrative person. Time will sort it out, I comforted my troubled mind.

As I worked on the picture of the house that afternoon there was a knock on my sitting room door. It was Liza and Emily who wanted a word with me. They came in and sat down and I made some tea.

'This is cosy,' I said as I poured the tea, 'we should do it more often. We always seem to congregate around the kitchen table.'

'It's Beth and Susan,' Liza began, 'they are leaving school at the end of term and they want to go to Secretarial College in Wellington. She looked across at Emily, we're worried about them and wondered if you could suggest anywhere they could stay. We don't want them sharing a house with other students, you don't know what things lead to these days, with drugs and sex.'

'Well, let me think,' I took a sip of tea. 'My other apartment is on a long term lease so they can't move in there unfortunately.

Yes, I know, I cannot promise yet but Tony moved into the rooms above the new shop so there is his old apartment behind the gallery. There is a door at the back of the building so it is private. How does that sound?'

'Terrific, I hope Tony agrees,' said Emily and Liza.

'Oh, I think he will; he seems to think I have some good ideas, and another thing, there is always room for a few hours part-time work too, if they want to earn some pocket money; keep them out of mischief.'

Liza stood up. 'That's a relief,' she said as she walked over to look out of the window. 'What a lovely view from this end of the house,' she turned and saw my painting of the house. 'Oh, that is beautiful,' her voice filled with admiration.

Emily joined her, 'Oh yes,' she agreed.

'I am doing it for Wilf's birthday. I hope he likes it.'

'No doubt about that, let's give him a surprise party. It would be fun.'

We conspired like school girls. We had to let Jonesy in on it, we couldn't do otherwise. I felt sad that the boys would not be here.

It was decided, with Wilf's birthday falling on a Sunday, that a lunch time party would be the best. Someone suggested the first barbeque of the year, but it has been known to rain heavily other years, so playing safe, it was better to be inside and weather permitting, sit outside as suits us. We could always get the barbeque going for a few steaks and chops when we saw what the weather was like that morning but keep all the salads and other goodies on the dining room table.

Many ideas were given as to how to get Wilf out of the house early on a Sunday morning. It was decided to ask his friend to suggest a round of golf and bring Wilf back in time for lunch and his surprise. Everyone rose to the occasion.

The freezer filled up with pre-cooked goodies and lists of food to be prepared were kept off the kitchen table and in a safe place, away from Wilf's eyes.

I finished the painting and put it into a frame I had selected from the gallery shop. I stood back from it and admired the choice of frame now it was finished. Yes, I thought, it did look good. The house made a beautiful subject; I had enjoyed my project, more so now, as it was for Wilf. I felt excited in anticipation of his reaction when he opened the wrapping and saw it.

Luckily the day was fine and sunny. I had watched the long term weather forecast, realising that if it was to rain then there would be an excuse not to play golf. Wilf was a fair weather golfer, not an, 'any weather' addict as some men are.

As soon as he left the house for the golf club, we all set to. Cloths on the tables, china out of the cupboards, glasses shining, napkins folded and flowers arranged. Peter sorted out the unused barbeque ready for use. We all helped in the kitchen; defrosting things in the microwave, washing salad, decorating trifles and cakes, buttering French sticks for garlic bread and scrubbing potatoes to put in the oven. Quiches appeared on the table with piles of steaks, chops and sausages for the barbeque. Wilf had no idea of the hive of industry involved in his surprise party as he enjoyed a leisurely game of golf.

People started to arrive and as previously directed they parked their cars in the field behind the house. Someone kept watch on the drive to announce Wilf's arrival. Len had telephoned from the golf club to say they were leaving so we had time to get organised before they came. There was an air of excitement about the place as we anticipated Wilf's surprise.

When they arrived, Jonesy was working in the kitchen and Emily stood barring the kitchen door as she pretended to be talking to Jonesy.

'Margaret is in there waiting for you.' Emily guided him away. Wilf headed for the sitting room, you could have heard a pin drop it was so quiet. He opened the door and "Happy Birthday" chorused loudly from inside the room. He took a step back in surprise, then went forward again for hugs and kisses. Everyone was laughing at their own cleverness, pulling off the surprise. It was obvious, from Wilf's reaction, he had no idea what had been planned.

The barbeque was lit, drinks poured, nibbles passed around and presents given. He had never had so much fuss, he said, as he happily unwrapped his gifts. 'Christmas all to myself,' he joked as he let me help him with the paper.

'What did we do before sticky tape?' Wilf asked, as someone had been overly zealous with it. 'I need scissors to get into this one.'

A car pulled up at the side door and Alex got out of the passenger side, a girl from the other.

'I cadged a lift. Couldn't miss this day could I?' He hugged me and introduced his companion, Barbara, then went over to Wilf. 'Thought you would do this without me did you?' He hugged Wilf then gave him a present. I thought that Wilf was going to cry.

Wilf eventually got around to my gift which stood up on the table at the back of the pile. He unwrapped it carefully, it was obviously a picture. He looked at it then looked up at me and gave one big sob; his handkerchief appeared from his pocket and he wiped his eyes and blew his nose.

'Oh Margaret, it is beautiful. Why didn't I think of a picture of the house before?' We had more hugs and kisses.

We could all tell the barbeque was ready; the smells making our mouths water so we collected our plates and filled them with delicious food. The chattering subsided as we occupied ourselves with eating.

I heard the telephone ring inside and someone answered it. It was for Wilf; Michael calling from London to wish him happy birthday. I had a quick word too.

'I can hear the voices,' he said.

'A pity you can't smell the food,' I returned.

'I have a good imagination. Love you all, and I will write.' Click, he was gone. I felt sad he wasn't with us but was happy for the success of the day. What a strange thing emotion is, up and down so quickly, all mixed up.

Chapter 17 New Zealand 1985

In no time it would be Christmas again and after Michael's telephone call I missed him so much that I decided to call him back. I suggested he come home for Christmas; let it be a surprise for everyone. He thought it a great idea and I would arrange everything from this end.

'Just let me know the dates you can travel.' I was getting good at this surprise thing. I patted myself on the back.

Knowing that Michael was coming, spurred me on to plan Christmas. He could fly down to Wellington; I could meet him, show him the gallery and introduce him to everyone. He had told me in a letter that he had seen my books in the shops in London. He wanted to stand in the shop and point to the books and say, 'My mother wrote that.' He felt so proud of me.

Beth and Susan were so pleased that Tony had agreed to their staying at the gallery apartment. I told them I was going to the city the week before Christmas for three days and as they would have finished school, if they wished to come with me, they could stay with me and see the apartment. Just to be sure they liked it. They were thrilled with the plan, as they could do their Christmas shopping. I liked the plan too and would give them a good time in the city.

Now, what about presents; what ideas can I come up with this year. I put my mind into action.

I started by being practical for Beth and Susan. I would get them large holdalls to match the suitcases I had bought previously and fill them with sleeping bags and other things for camping and sleeping away from home. It crossed my mind that they may be used for extra people sleeping at the apartment but pushed it out of my mind; they are only young once, I chided myself.

My plans for Emily, Jonesy and Liza were already made when I painted the house for Wilf. I decided to paint portraits of each of their pet animals; Emily's collie, Jonesy's cat and Liza's horse. I had managed to take good photographs; nobody took any notice of me taking photographs anymore as I took so many. Sometimes, just to be able to catch a scene or a certain light.

Thankfully, I was painting these pictures when I spent time in the city apartment otherwise I could have been rumbled when Emily and Liza came to see me. Animals were not my forte but I enjoyed the new subjects and they turned out quite well, for an amateur portrait painter. This had set me thinking that I could do portraits of Wilf, Michael and Alex; maybe sometime in the future, the scope was limitless.

We eventually got to the apartment, Beth, Susan and myself, after a breakdown on the way when we had to be towed into a garage for repairs. We enjoyed looking around the small town and having lunch while the work was done on the car. Beth and Susan kept calling me Aunty Maggie, as they had done since they could first talk but it seemed out of place now, so I asked them to drop the Aunty bit.

'There are two reasons,' I told them. 'One being that you are adults now and the other is that I don't feel "auntyish." In fact I feel quite young when I am with you two.' They laughed at that.

'OK Aunty Ma . . . I mean Maggie' Beth said.

It was later than we intended when we arrived in the city, so we left our things still packed and went straight to the shops. It was late night opening so we spent a happy hour, before the shops closed, and then went for dinner.

I chose a restaurant on the waterfront, quite a trendy place; a bit noisy for me but right for young people. It's the new fashion to have bare floor boards, table tops and windows. In fact nothing to absorb the noise of people scraping chairs and talking, then there is background music trying to compete with all of this but it was lively and that is what we needed. The Christmas atmosphere was with us.

The next morning we went to the gallery; Beth and Susan were very impressed.

'What beautiful things, look at this. Oh, I like that. What marvellous colours,' they went on enthusing about what they saw.

I introduced them to everyone in The Gallery, then went through into the art shop. Someone produced coffee and Tony and I talked about what was selling and what was not. The girls wandered about looking around the shelves at everything.

'Do you want to see the apartment?' I asked.

'Yes please,' they agreed.

'It's better we go in at the back, which is your main door, come on.'

I took them around the back of the building and unlocked the door. The entrance opened onto a staircase, which lead straight up to the first floor. There was another door on the landing which opened onto a large airy living room where big windows let in bright sunlight.

'Oh, it's lovely,' Susan said.

We went through into a passageway that led to a kitchen which was large enough to have a small table and chairs. Across the passageway were two bedrooms of similar size to each other.

'Just a few of your own things about the place and you will feel quite at home,' I said.

'It is perfect for us. Will you come for dinner when we get settled in?'

'That's a date,' I replied.

Beth kissed me. 'Thank you Maggie, it is just perfect.'

I told them they could move the furniture about as they wished. I sat on the settee while they had another look around the place, opening doors and drawers and deciding who should have which room by tossing a coin. They seemed very happy with the result.

We left the gallery and went back to the shops. I left them to do their shopping and arranged to meet them at 5 o'clock.

'I'm taking you for a surprise,' I told them.

'I like surprises,' Beth said laughing.

'You will like this one, but we will have to go back to the apartment to get changed as we are eating out again.'

As arranged I picked them up. They had been busy; their arms were full of parcels.

'Spent all of your money?' I asked.

'And more,' said Susan, 'wait until you see what we have bought. Isn't it exciting?' she giggled in the back of the car.

I made a pot of tea while the girls displayed their purchases; then they had a quick shower, made up their faces, combed their hair and emerged from the bedroom looking young but much older at the same time. They are going to break some hearts I thought. I told them how pretty they looked and added 'older.' They were both happy about the adage.

'Really,' Beth said and seemed to grow another two inches taller.

We drove around the waterfront, going through little hamlets on the water side. When we arrived at the airport I just said I had to pick someone up before we went to dinner and did they mind. They both replied,' Of course not.'

The plane was on time. I had checked with the airport earlier. It seemed forever; the waiting.

'Let's have a coffee or something stronger,' I said. The girls looked at me questioningly. I had forgotten their ages. I bought two coffees and a gin and tonic which I needed badly. I was so excited and trying not to show it. I sat so that I could see the information board; the plane had landed so he was probably waiting for his luggage. Oh hurry up I thought.

'I must go to the toilet,' I said. 'I won't be a minute.' I hurried to the ladies room, knowing that I had plenty of time but afraid to think I might miss him.

The girls had finished their coffees and I emptied my glass then guided them to the arrivals barrier. People started to come through with their trolleys, waving to greet each other. I waved and shot along the rail. The girls following me, not knowing what I was up to. Michael saw me and we flew into each other's arms. Susan and Beth stood mouths open, transfixed. I let go of Michael and he hugged them both at once, an arm around each.

'What a wonderful surprise Maggie.'

As we trundled out to the car park, laughing. I turned to Michael, 'I hope you are not too tired, we haven't eaten yet. I know you eat often on the plane so can you bear with us going to a restaurant?'

'No problem, as long as I am dressed ok?'

'You are fine,' I assured him.

Our timing was perfect. We entered the restaurant and I gave my name. We were lead to a booth and just about to order drinks and look at the menu when someone came up behind the waiter. It was Alex, right on time.

'Hello brother,' he said.

Michael looked up from the menu and a grin spread across his face. He stood up and leaning over the table grasped Alex's hand.

The girls giggled, 'Another surprise,' Susan said clapping her hands together. Beth just sat and looked at Alex.

We eventually settled down and chose from the menu. Orders out of the way, questions started to flow.

'Which way did you come? How many hours? How long are you here for?'

Michael answered their questions and told them he was over for three weeks, three wonderful weeks. Alex had finished at school so we were all travelling back to the farm together.

The girls were really into this surprise business by now and could not wait to get home. Susan gave instructions to Michael.

'You will have to keep your head down in the car when we go up the drive, then you can pop up in the kitchen. I'll go and get Uncle Wilf into the kitchen first and make sure everyone is there.

We did just that, parking so that no one could see into the car from the kitchen window. I went in with Alex and greeted Jonesy and Emily. Beth went into the office to fetch her mother and Susan headed for the sitting room where Jonesy said Wilf was reading the paper.

Wilf came through into the kitchen and hugged me and Alex; Beth and I came in with Liza and everyone was chatting away as Jonesy put on the jug; her answer to every occasion.

There was a knock at the door.

'Answer it will you Wilf,' I asked.

He opened the door and there stood Michael.

'Surprise, surprise,' chorused Beth and Susan, jumping up and down.

Michael's arms went around Wilf. I think Wilf couldn't believe his eyes, he seemed rooted to the spot. Then Jonesy was mopping at her eyes with her apron and mumbling something as she stood in Michael's arms, her face in his chest. This must be a Happy Christmas, I thought. At least it has got off to a good start.

We all sat around the kitchen table. Emily and Jonesy had produced piles of sandwiches and a homemade cake. Everyone was full of ideas.

'We must get a tree cut and the decorations out of the loft', said Alex.

'We can do that this afternoon,' added Michael.

'I'll make some rum truffles,' said Susan, I know the recipe.

'I'll help Alex decorate the tree,' said Beth.

'All this energy,' I said to Wilf, 'I feel quite worn out listening to them.'

'Come and have a ride with me this afternoon let the young ones do the work. You've done quite enough these past few days from what I can gather.'

'That sounds a lovely idea. I'll just go and change.'

Wilf had the horses ready when I went into the yard. We ambled along the back road, down to the beach, our favourite route. The horses knew their way, they needed no guidance. It all seemed so effortless and I felt my whole body relaxing with the gentle rhythm.

It was so good to be back at the farm, the soft sea breeze and sound of the waves, easing my mind. The city was alright in small doses.

We walked the horses along the edge of the water.

'Ready for a gallop?' Wilf called to me.

'I'll race you,' I called back.

It was exhilarating, pounding along on a big strong horse. We reached the gully and turned up onto the hillside, where we dismounted to give the horses a rest. Wilf and I sat on the grass while the horses grazed leisurely. My pounding heart calmed after the strenuous gallop.

'I could stay in this spot forever,' I said.

'I know what you mean, Maggie, but there would be some worried people if we did; come on, I'll help you up.'

We mounted the horses and rode back to the farm.

'I really enjoyed that, thank you for the suggestion.'

'Me too,' Wilf said.

Preparations for Christmas went on. The tree was brought in and decorated. We had the ceremony of turning on the fairy lights. Close all the curtains, all lights out, ready.

'Oh how lovely,' hands clapped. 'It's beautiful' and 'Good job there' were comments that flew about the room as we sat in the light of the Christmas tree. drinking glasses of sherry.

We were all going down to the village restaurant for dinner, including Jonesy, Emily, Liza and their husbands; no cooking tonight. There were fourteen of us which made the small restaurant full but it had been booked for weeks now. On the way home we sang carols loudly.

'Shhh, you will wake everybody,' someone said.

'No, impossible, we are all hear,' was the reply. And the singing continued with more force than before.

The boys went off visiting friends the next day. Michael had a lot of catching up to do after being away so long.

We had been invited out to dinner that night so there was no meal to prepare again.

Christmas Eve came around and some went off to the midnight service at the church. I stayed at home with Wilf; it was peaceful and cosy.

'I hope you like your present tomorrow,' Wilf said.

'Tell me about it. Is it big or small?' I questioned, knowing he was teasing me.

'Let me think,' he paused. 'I would say middle size.'

'Is it heavy or light,' I asked him.

'Just medium,' he teased me.

I got up from my chair and tickled him in the ribs.

'I won't make you any hot chocolate for that,' I said.

The next day came and I did find out what was 'middle size and medium weight.'

It was a portrait, painted by Tony, of me by my easel. The likeness and stance were remarkable. I didn't know how he had done it. I like Tony's style; it is a little contemporary and he must have watched me for hours to get it so life like. I was thrilled.

'I love it Wilf, but where are we going to put it?'

'I have just the place for it,' he already had a hook in the wall. My animal portraits went down very well; again I don't know why I had not thought of it before.

Everyone loved their presents. Dinner was marvellous and the weather wonderful. The tennis court and swimming pool were in full swing.

I closed my eyes as I sat relaxing on the veranda. The plop plop of the tennis balls and happy voices giving me a secure feeling of belonging.

I did eventually get some time alone with Michael. He told me how he felt about his studies. It was hard work but he saw it as a challenge and knew he had to put in a lot of effort, in order to reap the rewards in the future.

'What do you think of London, now you have been there so long?' I was wondering if he would choose to stay and work there after he qualified or come home to New Zealand.

'I just love it. There is so much to do and not necessarily needing a lot of money either; just being with people at the pub, talking, discussing different things. So many people, so many cultures; it fascinates me. I have always been interested in politics and world affairs. I would like to be more involved along those lines in the future.'

It sounded like Wilf speaking to me. I flashed back in my mind to remember the days when Michael would sit with Wilf, watching the news together. At the time, I thought it unusual for a young boy to like the news programmes but Michael was always full of questions of why, when and wherefore. Wilf told Michael about the news and world affairs. I remember one summer, I was painting in my room with the windows open. Michael and Wilf were on the veranda and Wilf was explaining about the political situation and how politics and parliament works.

"Running a country is like running a large business,' he said, 'it is important to have the right man or woman for the job, and these people are working for the people of the country. That's why we have elections to choose the person we want to represent us and the party. If the job is not being done properly then the people elect another person and party."

I was fascinated listening to the conversation and the questions Michael was putting to Wilf.

I asked Michael what he thought of Scotland and the north of England and my home town. I told him that I had heard in a letter from Mary that he had visited her. He was only there a couple of hours and spent that time with Mary while his friends looked around the town before moving on. They were staying at Youth Hostels and some of the places were magnificent old houses that used to belong to the gentry.

'Buildings meant to last not like some of the modern architecture but "no place like home," he said. He liked the wooden houses, even though they could be a problem, needing to paint them every so often.

I interjected with, 'What about the coloured roofs.' I then went on to tell him about my first visit to Auckland and One Tree Hill with Wilf and my fascination with the many roof colours.

'No place like home,' Michael repeated.

'Are you coming back then, when you finish University?'

'Oh yes,' he said

I sighed with relief.

Michael continued telling me his plans. 'I want to travel in the future, but I intend to live in New Zealand. I've been away long enough to satisfy me for some time. The Continent was great and I saw some wonderful places in the long summer breaks but this time next year I will be home and hopefully working in the city, earning my own living. I can't go on forever being a kept man can I?' He leaned over and planted a kiss on my cheek.

'Thanks for everything Maggie, I do appreciate all you have done for me; best Mum in the world.'

I told him not to be silly. I was proud of him.

I told Michael how Alex didn't want to go to college, but seemed more interested in his "pop group" and 'what about drugs?' I added.

Michael told me not to worry, Alex is not worse than most young people who all have a go at things but don't have to become addicted.

'You mean you tried drugs?' I asked.

'Tried is the word. There is no way I am on drugs or Alex. It is around us, but we don't need it. It is not our style. Believe me; you have no need to worry.'

'I see such terrible things on the television.'

'I know, Mum, but just for instance; we don't smoke do we, right. You don't smoke, right but you were surrounded by smokers in your younger days. Just as much as now, and drinking too for that matter but are you an addict? No. Well it is the same for me and Alex; just because it's around us we don't have to partake of it.'

'I understand when you put it like that,' I told him. 'I apologise for not giving you credit where it is due; do you forgive me?'

'Of course I do. How about a cup of tea? I'll make it,' he said getting up.

Oh how lucky I am to have so much sense around me. The boys are now men and I must remember that fact. They have their own lives to live and in these modern times it can't be easy for young people, I thought.

Michael brought in the tea and biscuits.

'Have you met any nice girls?' I asked as I poured the tea.

He laughed. 'Of course I have, but no one special. No one I am going to bring home to meet you.'

'I had visions of you meeting some foreign girl and never coming back to live here,' I told him.

'Unless that happens between now and next August, I'll be back,' he teased me. 'In fact I want to make some enquiries about jobs before I go back. Are you planning to go to the city? If so I would like to go with you.'

'I'll go whenever you wish. I would like you to see the gallery. If we get off straight after New Year, that should give us time.'

'Better make it on the 2nd January, there may be some sore heads about,' Michael laughed.

'Ours included,' I laughed.

Alex and Beth came onto the tennis court and we watched them play.

'She has a crush on him,' I told Michael.

'She's young and so is he. Time will sort it out,' he replied.

'Come and play,' Alex called to us.

'Do you want to?' Michael asked me.

'I'm not very good,' I replied.

He pulled me out of the chair. 'Come on, we can beat them.'

Time passed quickly; New Year came and went, sore heads and all. Michael and I had a super time in the city; Michael thought the gallery was, quote, "way ahead of its time."

He was very impressed. 'Rome, London and New York have nothing like it,' he said

'Ah! Ha!' I answered, thinking he was joking.

'No I mean it, it's great.'

He made some enquiries about future employment. Wilf had given him the name of someone he knew in a legal firm and he came away smiling.

'There is a chance there. It depends on my results of course, but if they're ok then I could be in.' He picked me up and swung me around in a circle. 'Whoopee,' he cried. No one was in the car park, thank goodness. They would think we were mad.

'Let's go on the water, I fancy a sail. What do you think?' he asked

'Sounds good to me.'

We took the harbour cruise and enjoyed the fresh sea breeze.

'I love this country,' Michael said. 'I'm happy to work and live here forever; take a few holidays of course but I want to be a real part of the running of this place to see it grow important in the world. It has so much to offer; more and more people are going to come here. The world is getting smaller with flights becoming shorter and speed faster. Tourism is going to grow and grow.'

I felt happy about the future, seeing it through the eyes of someone so young and enthusiastic. Michael, Alex and all young ones like them are the future.

It was very sad, Michael leaving, but knowing he would be back in a few months made it bearable.

Alex's and my birthday came around and I asked him what he would like. He wanted money as everything is so expensive, he told me. I knew what he meant; costs were going up and he had to have money for some social life, although what sort of social life did worry me.

I talked to Wilf about it.

'Different in my days at school' he said, 'but then so is everything else; he doesn't have long to go now, then he will be back here at the farm doing some physical work, that is what I think he needs. To get into some real work that satisfies him.' That was Wilf's opinion. I agreed but had a niggling doubt. We were soon to find out.

Alex left school as soon as he was eighteen and went with the pop group to play at a club in Auckland.

His answer to my question, 'why?' was.

'It is a chance of a life time and the band couldn't afford to miss it.' He was happy he was not coming home and, if I cared about him, I would understand and not worry.

Wilf made some enquiries and it did all seem legitimate. What could we do but keep our fingers crossed that everything was alright? A few months went by and Alex telephoned to say he was off to Europe; gigs in Glasgow, Manchester, Birmingham then over to Germany.

I did not know what to make of it, never having been involved in the music industry, but all these bands had to start somewhere. I wrote to Michael, giving him all the details, asking him to go to see Alex, as soon as he arrived in Britain, and let me know how he was.

A reply from Michael told me not to worry; he would go and see Alex. The band was being advertised on the same billing as some quite famous groups, so it was all above board, he wrote.

My imagination ran riot. I watched television for similar bands, and listened to the kind of music on the radio station that seemed to be for that age group. Michael and Alex had always played their own radios and records in the house but it had not seemed as extreme as the music now. It must be a new era I have not noticed coming on, I thought, but where do they get their names from I wondered.

I also noticed a change in the kitchen. The radio had always been tuned into the music chat shows but now it was the "top pop" programme.

Emily's little boy enjoyed it and showed us how much with the latest dance movements. We all had a go and agreed it was the exercise we all needed.

'Shakes up the liver,' Jonesy said.

I busied myself painting. No sooner had I taken some pictures to the gallery than they were gone. I was becoming quite "popular" myself.

Wilf had to take things easier, as he had had a few pains in his chest.

"Warnings," the doctor told him, "no need to worry if you do as you are told and that means stop working as though you are thirty years younger than you are."

I think Wilf had been looking forward to Alex coming back to the farm and taking over some of the responsibilities and regretted suggesting Agricultural College. Maybe he blamed himself a little for Alex going off and felt he could have handled it all better. Wilf was really disappointed in himself more than Alex.

Wilf came with me to the gallery for a few days. He always enjoyed himself there and everyone was pleased to see him. I suggested he get some ideas on wood carving and he could do it at the farm. He only needed a few tools. We talked to Tony about it.

'I have just what you need' and he went upstairs to his apartment and came down with the tools.

'This must be meant to be,' I smiled at Wilf, as he examined the tools and asked Tony about them.

'I used to do a bit of carving myself,' Tony explained, 'but not anymore, you are welcome to them, Wilf. Why not go into the shop, I'm sure there will be a book on wood carving there.'

'If there is,' I said, heading for the shop holding Wilf's arm, 'then I'll treat you to it.'

'Promise to send your masterpieces to The Gallery, we need the commission,' laughed Tony, as we disappeared in to the shop.

Wilf spent the next two days absorbed in the book.

'The more I read the more I like the idea,' he told me as I interrupted to hand him a drink.

'I hadn't realised just what is involved, even though I watched it done; so many types of wood, even driftwood. I have often looked at the shapes on the beach and thought how interesting they are.' Wilf was full of enthusiasm.

'Well, we're going back home tomorrow, so you can collect all you need.'

'I think I should take you out tonight for such a good idea, and say thank you for the book.'

'I'm not saying no to that one, where shall we go?' I asked.

'Let's go on the waterfront, I like it there and there is so much to see,' suggested Wilf.

'Would you mind greatly if I asked Beth and Susan to join us. I intended to take them out to dinner before I left but I have been so busy I haven't had the time to talk to them. They have made the apartment look lovely and I had promised to eat with them the next time I came down.'

'Call them up, see if they can make it,' said Wilf. 'I can manage to take out three women. I'll be the envy of all the men in the restaurant,' his eyes twinkled with laughter.

When we got home there had been a telephone call from Michael. What's wrong I thought, so I called back straight away.

'Were you in bed?' I asked when Michael answered.

'Just going,' he replied. 'I only wanted you to know I saw Alex today, he's fine, no problems.'

'Oh good, I thought there was something wrong,' I said.

'Oh Mum,' his voice chided me. 'I wouldn't have rung had I known you were away, but I thought it better to let you know now than in a week's time in a letter.'

'Yes, thank you Michael. I do appreciate it.'

'How is Wilf,' he asked. I explained about the wood carving.

'Maybe another genius in the family,' his voice sounded happy.

'Are you alright?' I asked.

'Yes, but better next week when I get my results. It's agony, this waiting.'

'Let me know how you get on. Promise you will phone and not leave me waiting for a letter. If I am not at home I won't worry as I will know what it is about.'

263

'Ok. Love you all,' his voice went and the phone clicked as he replaced the receiver.

Wilf came back from the beach with a sack full of bits and pieces of driftwood.

'What do you think of that Margaret?' he held up a piece, turning it from side to side.

'I don't know. I'll leave it to your imagination. I remember deciding to stick to painting long ago,' I told him.

In no time the call came from Michael about his results. He had done very well and was happy with his achievements after all the years of work.

'Does that mean you will get the position you were interested in?' I asked him.

'I hope so,' he replied. He would be coming home in two weeks and wanted some time to celebrate and unwind.

I received a letter from Alex, he was alright, he wrote, but, as I reread the letter, I got the feeling that he was not as wrapped up in his new life as he had been. Perhaps he was just a bit homesick. It was certainly a lot different from the life he was used to.

There were a few anxious moments with Emily's little boy. He was knocked down by a car in the village. He had been going for an ice-cream and didn't look before he crossed the road to the shop. He must have thought he was safe, when a car came around the corner on the wrong side of the road. It was an American driving. He was in a terrible state with no other cars on the road to remind him he had wandered over to the right hand side as they drove in America. Timothy had no broken bones but he was kept in hospital overnight just to be sure there was no concussion.

Michael came home complaining of the cold, leaving summer in England to come back to winter and it was a cold winter; the coldest for some years. I said a thank you for my electric blanket every night as I climbed into a warm bed.

He wasn't with us for long, eager to get off to his new appointment in the city, he would be staying at my apartment. When I suggested it, he said yes but only until he could get something himself. He wanted to be independent after all these years and to pay his own way. I asked him to call on Beth and Susan and keep in touch. It was lovely to have him back in the country again; permanently I hoped.

It was into the New Year when Wilf said he wanted to talk to me about his will.

'Are you ill?' was my first reaction.

'No, I just want to get it straight. I have to do this sometime with taxes and such to sort out.'

He wanted to know how I felt about his leaving his shares in the Company to the boys and not me.

'Yes, do that,' I told him, 'I have enough security and they will all go to Michael and Alex too, except for a few bequests of course.'

I think reading between the lines, Wilf hoped that if anything happened to him then Alex would come back and run the farm. I hoped Alex would come back too, but before anything happened to Wilf.

'You'll live forever.' I could not bear to think of Wilf gone. 'As long as you don't overdo anything, a creaking gate goes on and on, as the saying goes. Don't you dare leave me, I won't stand for it,' I hugged him.

The telephone rang and I jumped at the noise breaking the quietness.

'Hello Mum.' It was Alex.

'Where are you?' I asked as he sounded clear and close.

'I'm in Auckland,' he replied. In this country! My heart pounded.

'Are you alright?'

'Yes, fine,' he answered as I fired questions at him.

'Are you coming home?' I asked.

'Not yet, I have things to do, but in a couple of weeks. Is everybody ok?'

'Yes but better for seeing you. It's good to hear you so near.'

'Right, I'll let you know when I am coming. It's good to be back. See you soon.'

'Bless you Alex,' I said emotionally. The phone clicked.

One minute we were talking about wills and death, then, the next, just through a telephone call, I was jumping for joy. 'He's coming home.' I pulled Wilf out of his chair and danced him around the room. I must tell Jonesy, I raced through into the kitchen. Then I called Michael to tell him the news.

When Alex arrived he looked fit and healthy; much better than I expected him to look after my impression of pop group life in dark smoky places.

He told us that although he had enjoyed the experience, he could not see himself doing it forever. It was not active enough, so he was joining a Special Force.

'What's that,' I wanted to know.

'Well it is not the police force as you know it.'

'Is it the Army?' I asked, imagining seeing him at war somewhere.

'No, it's not,' he said and I breathed a sigh of relief but I gathered that this Special Force was a rather active life, and he was going away for training.

'What sort of training?' I wanted to know.

'Oh, getting fit, shooting, climbing, psychology,' he said.

'Psychology, I interjected, what's that for?'

'To understand people and know how they will act,' he told me. He seemed very enthusiastic about it all. I did not know what to think but I was pleased he was doing it in this country, that was enough.

I saw Wilf's face drop as Alex told us of his plans. I know he was hoping that Alex was coming home to work on the farm.

Weeks went by and I spent more time at the gallery; it was a pleasure being in the city, now that Michael was there. He had found himself an apartment and so had his independence but we always had a few dinners together, catching up on what was happening to us all.

Susan asked me to dinner, there was a young man there too. She introduced me to James with a flush on her cheeks. The meal was excellent; her catering course proving to be successful.

Apparently, James was doing a Hotel Management course, so many of their lectures combined. His parents had a hotel and they wanted James to qualify and bring the latest methods into the, hopefully, expanding business. Susan told me that she had seen James in lectures but it was not until he kept appearing in the gallery shop when she was working there, that she really noticed him.

He would come in every day for just a pencil or a rubber; until one day he asked her if she enjoyed films and that was it; their first date. I asked where Beth was.

Susan told me that Beth was away for the weekend. 'She's "potty" about Keith, a young man who is a horse rider, show jumper, whatever. He's training for the Olympic Games.

I told Susan how nice the apartment looked. It was obvious that a lot of planning had gone into making it look casually homely. Susan was proud of their combined efforts, pointing out how she had bought the lovely flowing curtains, in the church charity shop, for a song. They were so long that she had been able to cut some of the material off the bottom and make some cushions which looked good on the plain coloured suite. As Susan talked, her face was animated with happiness. She's a real home maker I thought and James will be a very lucky man.

Time passed smoothly for a while. Wilf was enjoying his wood carving and being successful at selling some pieces boosted his ego and proved to him that people liked his work.

Alex said he too was enjoying his job but did not tell us much about it. I now watched the news for drug snatches, terrorists and such instead of pop bands. He is certainly having a varied life, I thought, and the main thing is, he is happy.

Michael was doing well also and getting a good name for his achievements. There was also a girl on the scene but he didn't want to talk about it. He did not say as much but I felt he didn't want to bring her home yet; so it could not be serious.

A letter came for me to the gallery. It was from America, the Snyder's; the people who had a gallery in New York, that we had been supplying now for years.

They were extending their gallery and wanted me to go over there. They were displaying so much of my work and people were asking about me and if they could meet me. Did I think it possible, all expenses would be paid, of course.

Tony said I should go; it would be good for the gallery, good publicity.

I answered that I considered it an honour and thanked them for asking me.

The whole trip was a wonderment for me. I was treated like royalty, wined and dined in the very best of places. When they do anything, in New York, they do it very well. No expense had been spared with their gallery and I gasped with pleasure at the way the paintings were displayed. No wonder they sold so many, I thought, but what prices they were asking; how do people afford so much money. I wished Tony was with me to see all of this.

I took advantage of being in America to go and see Mary Ann and Des Donaldson in Denver. As with New York, the memories were painful, but I knew I had to do this, as part of the growing period, to be able to carry on living without Stephen.

They were delighted to see me and made me very welcome. It was arranged that I go with them to visit their son and his family in Mexico. It was wonderful and a real tonic to me as I listened to the lively music and dancing.

The weather was hot and dry and I sunbathed then swam in the pool and dried off in the sun again. I rode for miles and miles out into the desert in the most silent silence imaginable. I wished Wilf was with me to enjoy the interesting culture and variety of things to see. I sent dozens of postcards back home instructing everyone not to throw them away.

When I eventually returned, I had been away for three months. I had bought so many interesting objects that I had to have them all shipped back in a crate.

There was an invitation waiting for me. Susan was getting married to James. Their courses were over and Susan had come back to the farm for a while which had made their hearts grow fonder; they wanted to be together. James's parents were delighted and Susan would fit perfectly into the hotel life with her training.

Emily was happy and upset at the same time, knowing that Susan would have left the farm anyway, to be able to get a job in the field she had chosen. She liked James she told me, as we sat having a cup of coffee just after my return.

'I think it is the realisation that my little girl is so grown up that makes me want to cry,' she said. 'I do so hope she will be happy. I suppose it's because of the mess her father and I made of our lives.'

I pointed out how happy and successful her relationship was with Ralph and let us hope that Susan and James make it so with their first attempt. We ended up laughing together and, treating ourselves to a huge chunk of cake, we discussed plans for the wedding.

The reception would be at the village hall; there were a lot of people to invite, everyone for miles around plus James's family and their joint friends of course. I did suggest to Emily that they have a marquee on the lawn. She said thank you but there would be so many people and I understood what she meant.

It was a beautiful day in every way. Susan looked a picture in her high necked Victorian dress which she had designed and made herself, from a picture of her great grandmother. Beth was her bridesmaid and she too wore a dress of the same period, once more designed and made by Susan.

The village church was full to overflowing and as I stood watching the photographer arrange his groups for the photographs on the steps after the lovely ceremony, I wondered about Beth and Keith. Would this urge them on; although I gathered their relationship was "fiery" at times.

Emily cried most of the time in the church. 'I never knew I could be so happy,' she said, as we walked back down the aisle.

Alex came, looking remarkably handsome, brimming with health and a glorious tan. Beth was making overtures to him, which I am sure was to make Keith jealous. Michael looked elegant, tall and slim. He came on his own I noticed.

A disco had been arranged for the evening and everyone for miles around came and the music went on until the early hours of the morning. As before, there was no one to disturb as they were all there at the party.

All these lives moving on I thought, changing and growing; where does time go!

Twenty two years since Martin died and I was their age.

Chapter 18 New Zealand 1988

Michael's twenty-fifth birthday came. I was in the city at the time and I gave him his present as we had dinner together. I also told him that he had an inheritance from his grandparents.

It was really the money from Jenny and Mark, which they had inherited from their parents, and the Solicitor had put into a trust all those years ago. To be released when he became twenty-five years of age. All he had to do was sign the papers and it was his. I told him approximately how much it was.

'Gosh,' he said, 'what a surprise; I had no idea.'

'You could buy your own apartment now,' I suggested.

I almost told him how I had adopted him but, when he hugged me and told me I was the best mother in the world, I couldn't shatter it; selfish or not, it's not as though his parents are still alive, I consoled myself.

I had set up a similar account for Alex to inherit, when he reached the same age; starting it with my parent's money and then adding to it.

It was two years later that we had another wedding; this time for Beth. Yes! She and Keith tied the knot, as the saying goes. They had parted not long after Susan's wedding and each to go their own ways.

After that, Beth gave Liza a lot of sleepless nights as she worried about the company Beth was keeping. She did not come to the farm very often but when she did, there was a need to worry at the sight of her unkempt appearance. Her hair looked as though it needed a good wash and so did her clothes. She was not staying in the apartment above the gallery anymore; the girls gave it up when they finished college and Susan came back to the farm. Beth was sharing some rooms with some other young people and I dared not to think what the conditions were, going by Beth's appearance.

Keith had gone away to Europe. After being in the Olympics, he wanted to see more of the world and he did not ask Beth to go with him. This was when she started to act in a wild, uncaring fashion. Keith eventually came back home and said he had missed her; would she forgive him and she did.

Liz and Beth wanted the marriage service and reception at home. It was becoming quite a popular way to get married, as was done in America. They would have a marquee on the lawn. We knew the score, having arranged it all before for my own intended marriage.

It was very good for me to have the girl's weddings to enjoy and be involved with. Michael and Alex would eventually marry but I assumed their future wives would be marrying from their own parent's homes.

It was a perfect day; Beth looked radiant, with her dark hair contrasting with the white veil and long satin gown. She shone in the sunlight as they gave their vows; both speaking with clear strong voices. Keith has an eastern European look about him. I must ask where his family originates from, I thought, as I watched the service. I looked across at his parents; it must be on his father's side the same colouring and features. I felt totally relaxed and happy as I sat by Wilf's side, enjoying being a guest and having no responsibilities to think about; just absorbing the happy feelings being created by this wonderful occasion. There was a dance floor laid outside the marquee and everyone danced the night away under the stars.

It was not long after the wedding that my life seemed to fall apart again. Wilf took the telephone call. I heard Wilf say, SHOT, in a shocked voice. I knew it was Alex he was referring to. Oh no! My heart dropped to my feet, or so it felt, then blood pounded to my head. Wilf turned to me and saw my face.

'He's alright,' he said. He came off the telephone, putting his hand on my shoulder to sit me down while he explained.

There had been a helicopter raid on a farm at the far north of the Island. Cannabis was being grown; it was big business and had been under surveillance for a long time. Some men were pinned down in a hut and wouldn't give up. They made a break for it, firing guns as they went. Alex was shot in the leg. That did not seem so bad, in comparison to my imagination, at the time. However it did have further repercussions.

His knee had been badly damaged and he would not be considered fit enough to continue in the job. Even with good treatment and healing the knee could let him down again, in extreme circumstances and that was not good enough. Every member of the team had to be in top class condition or it could jeopardise other men's lives.

Alex was offered a desk job but he said no. If he couldn't be part of the active team then he wanted out.

He had all the necessary physical treatment and his knee healed very well. He had to do exercises regularly. He eventually came home, looking a shadow of his former self. Although he was fit and healthy, he seemed to have shrunk in stature and was a very depressed young man who didn't have any enthusiasm to do anything.

We tried to encourage him to be interested in various things but he would just walk away and go off to brood. I became more and more worried about his attitude.

I had to go to the gallery and Michael met me for dinner that evening. We talked mostly about Alex and my concern for him. I told Michael how Alex walked about like a zombie or stayed in bed all day.

'There is nothing we can do, just be there for him until he's ready to talk. He's full of anger but time will help,' Michael advised

Michael also told me that he had had a letter from a girl called Janet Prince who he had met years ago in England when he had been youth hostelling.

Their first meeting had been in Scotland, near Edinburgh; they had been at the same hostel and had shared the washing up duties after breakfast. The second time, they had met in similar circumstances but on the West coast of Scotland. They had laughed when they met again and said, "We must stop meeting like this."

"We'll get talked about," she had joked. They had enjoyed each other's company and she seemed much older than her sixteen years. He had given her his home address and there had been the occasional letter. Janet told him that she was at University in Newcastle and hoped, when she was finished, to take a year out to travel through Asia, Australia and America. Michael had said not to miss him out if she got this far. Janet and her friend Laura had been in Australia for some time and would be in New Zealand in May.

'Can't we put them off?' I asked Michael. 'It's awkward with Alex being this way; they can come here to the apartment instead

'I've been thinking about it,' Michael told me. It would be good for Alex, he'll maybe make an effort and will not be rude to them, I'm sure. I'll warn them first so they will know what to expect; anyway, Laura is a nurse. I am positive, the more I think about it, it will be ok.'

'I hope you are going to be there some of the time,' I said.

'I'll take some leave to show the girls around and try to get Alex to make up a foursome. It will be alright Mum, we may even get him to play tennis and ride again. It will all work out, you'll see.'

How I wanted him to be right.

Michael met the girls at the airport and drove them to the farm by way of a round about route, to take in some of the sights. Alex knew they were coming but he did not seem interested. When they arrived, he kept out of the way. I showed them to their rooms and suggested they join us in the sitting room, when they were ready; no hurry, everything is easy here.

I sat with Wilf and Michael until they came in; no sign of Alex. Michael introduced them to Wilf and offered them a drink. Wilf asked about their travels; where they had been, what they had liked and so forth.

They were both very pretty girls. Janet had long straight silky brown hair and fair skin, she was quite tall and slim with lovely long legs. Laura was shorter and her hair was quite auburn with pale skin; she had freckles from the sunshine.

We went into dinner and I went to Alex's room to see if he was going to join us. I was amazed to see him changed out of his track suit, which he seemed to live in. He was quiet but came with me to the dining room. I introduced Janet and

Laura to him. Wilf poured the wine and we toasted them a happy holiday in New Zealand.

Wilf started to tell of his time in Yorkshire in the war. Janet said she loved the Yorkshire moors and Whitby. Wilf spoke about the Abbey and all the steps to be climbed up to it.

Michael mentioned Dracula. 'Perhaps he came over here with Captain Cook or at least one of his ancestors.'

'Do you have vampires in New Zealand?' asked Laura.

We all laughed, the wine and good food having its effect on the company.

Laura asked Wilf where he was in Yorkshire and he told her and added that is where Margaret is from too, of course.

'I don't go there much now, but my grandmother is from that town,' said Laura.

'What is her name, perhaps I remember her?' I said.

'She's called Bridget Downey; my mother was Elizabeth Downey until she changed her name to Ellis when she married my father. My mother would be older than you.'

I told her that my grandmother's and grandfather's names were Edith and Adam Mathews and he was the local bank manager. My mother's name was Sarah.

'I do have a faint recollection of an Elizabeth Downey at school; it is funny how we remember people older than ourselves, rather than the younger ones. She had very dark hair, if I remember correctly.'

'Yes, she had very dark hair,' Laura said, 'how strange. It's a small world.'

'You said your mother had dark hair,' I questioned Laura.

'Yes,' she replied, 'she died three years ago. My father remarried last year.'

'Where do you live now?' I asked her.

'Still in the Midlands; Janet and I were at school together, until she went to Newcastle University, while I did nursing in Birmingham.'

I noticed Alex becoming more interested as she talked about her family and the connection with my home town.

'I did a gig in Birmingham,' he said.

'Really?' Laura said and asked questions about the group and when he was there.

'I was there,' Laura said. 'It was great. Where else did you go?'

Alex started to talk about the other venues and about Germany. I learnt more about that time in his life in those few minutes than I ever could just talking to him myself. We all sat enrapt with the conversation between Laura and Alex.

Wilf looked across the table at me. 'More wine?' he asked smiling.

'Yes please,' I held my glass over to him. He winked at me as he poured the wine into my glass.

It was many, many months since I had heard Alex so animated, as though he had come out of a dark state. Michael was right in bringing the girls here. I looked across at Michael and smiled. He knew what I was thinking.

We all went out onto the veranda after dinner. It was a bright clear night and we looked at the stars, pointing out to Janet and Laura the Southern Cross. I breathed in the crisp fresh air and felt a shiver of relaxation go from my head down to the ends of my toes. I was letting go months of worry and tension. Alex would be alright now, I just knew it. I raised my eyes upwards once more and said, 'thank you.'

The next morning at breakfast, Alex asked Janet and Laura if they could ride. Neither of them could.

'Would you like to try?' he ventured.

Looking at each other first, then with nods of their heads, they indicated they would like to have a go.

'I don't think I can get up there,' Laura said as she stood looking up at Bluey, 'he's very big.'

'Not really. Watch and I'll show you.' Alex demonstrated how to mount, getting on and off the horse a few times. 'Now your turn,' he turned to Laura.

With a little help she went up into the saddle: her face a picture of disbelief that she had done it and was up there.

'Now you Janet, up on Snowy,' Alex said. She too looked amazed at her accomplishment. Alex lead Bluey and Michael lead Snowy, gently following each other around the yard; both men giving words of encouragement to the girls.

'That's enough for one day,' Alex said and both girls dismounted. Thrilled with their efforts, they chatted happily.

'What about a ride to the beach?' Michael suggested. 'We can all go on Bluey and Snowy, then you will get the feel of the horses.'

With a bit of effort on all parts, Alex and Laura mounted Bluey and Janet and Michael on Snowy.

'I must have a photograph of this,' I said, 'Just wait a minute until I get my camera.'

They all posed for their photograph, the girls waving to me.

'Say cheese,' I called.

The horses ambled off down the road to the beach and happy voices drifted back to me.

It was later at lunch that the next part of the miracle with Alex happened. We were sitting around the kitchen table, the girls were telling Wilf, Emily and Jonesy about their riding experience. Laura began to ask questions about the farm. Before Wilf could answer her, Alex started talking about the sheep, cattle and crops; he went on and on at great length.

'You obviously enjoy working on the farm,' Laura said.

Alex was silent for a few moments then he answered, 'Yes I do.' He looked up at Wilf. Wilf's grin was from ear to ear.

I had been watching Wilf's face as Alex was talking. He couldn't believe his own ears, he thought they were playing tricks on him, so he told me later as we enjoyed a few moments together on the veranda. Janet and Michael were playing tennis; Laura and Alex were watching them. I saw Alex extend his leg and Laura put her hand on his knee; he was telling her about his accident. The ball went plop, plop; music to my ears. I closed my eyes and dozed.

There was no need for me to think about dinner; that had been arranged. We were having a barbeque and the girls were in the kitchen helping with the salads; washing lettuce, cutting tomatoes, cucumber and so on. The men were preparing the steaks and chops.

'Look at the size of those steaks,' I heard Laura's voice as it drifted through the window.

'I'll never manage one of those,' Janet added.

You will, you'll see,' I heard Michael reply. 'After all this fresh air and exercise, you'll soon put one of those away.'

It was getting quite chilly now, in the evenings, so after the meal we quickly went inside for coffee. Thick sweaters were discarded and we settled down in the sitting room. Alex brought out the guitars and after a bit of tuning the strings, he and Michael strummed happily, singing well known folk songs. We all joined in with the words. Janet and Laura sat on the floor, clapping their hands to the rhythm.

Wilf and I left them to it and went to bed. I couldn't sleep straight away, I was too happy and wanted to savour this happening; not lose it in sleep. I stood by my easel, picked up a brush and started to paint.

The next day Wilf told me that Alex had come to his room. He wanted to work on the farm. Wilf had told him how delighted he was, and how it had always been his dream for Alex. They had come to some decision, but would really sort it out later. First, Alex should enjoy a few days with Laura, Janet and Michael; show them some real New Zealand hospitality.

When I saw these changes in Alex, I realised how it had been for every one when I was ill after Stephen's death and my eventual return to the living. That's what it was; a return to the living and I would be grateful to Laura and Janet forever.

As the days went by, it was obvious there was something special between Laura and Alex; they had a need to touch each other at the slightest provocation. Their eyes were constantly searching for one another, across a room or just over the table. Body language said it all.

Michael and Janet were getting on well together too but with much more reserve. Michael has a more courteous manner than Alex, and Janet has a quieter, shyer disposition, more so than Laura.

I had made a pot of tea and cut slices of a homemade cake when the door opened and they all trooped in. It was lovely to see the smiling, laughing young faces and I felt happy basking in all the merriment. They were discussing where to go next, and what to show the girls. I suggested they may like to go to the batch. Alex and Michael jumped at the idea. I explained to Janet and Laura that a batch is the name for a holiday cottage and in the South Island they used the word "crib." I also added that I did not want them to think I wanted them to leave.

'You will need some warm sweaters there,' I told the girls when it was decided. 'Come and see what I have, there must be something you like.' We trooped through into my bedroom and ransacked my wardrobe. We had great fun as Laura and Janet tried on different clothes. They were soon kitted out for winter.

'It is a great pity you missed our summer,' I told them, 'You must come back again.'

Janet said that every season has its own beauty and Laura agreed with her. 'Anyway,' said Janet, 'we have been in such hot climates in Asia and Northern Australia that it is refreshing to be cooler.'

'Yes, I had not thought of it that way; if you stay long enough here, you can go skiing. It's lovely at The Chateau, a hotel in the mountains. What are your plans?' I asked.

'The idea is to go to the South Island for a couple of weeks, then we fly to Honolulu, for three weeks, on our way to America.'

'I love it in America,' I told them and we shared our experiences, chatting about our likes and dislikes in the places we had been.

I was looking for Wilf later in the day and found him in his workshop. Janet was with him. I stood in the doorway; they didn't see me straight away, they were both occupied with their carving; talking easily to each other.

'You look as though you have done that before,' I said, as I wandered over to Janet and examined her work.

'Yes, I have. My father's hobby is wood carving, but he calls it whittling.'

'Does your mother do it too?' I asked.

'Her hobby was embroidery, she was very clever. She died five years ago and my father remarried last year.'

'You and Laura have a lot in common, don't you?'

'Yes, we have helped each other through many a crises,' she replied.

I had forgotten what I had come to the workshop for.

Chapter 19 Laura and Janet

The next morning the car was packed and they were ready for the off. They would not starve, not with the amount of food supplied by Emily and Jonesy. We all waved goodbye.

'Have a great time,' I called. 'Take some photographs.' The car stopped and reversed back; Michael's arm appeared out of the window. I put the camera into his hand, 'Bye now,' we chorused. They stayed at the batch for a week; fishing, walking and sailing.

Two days after they returned to the farm, Michael had to go back to work. It had been a wonderful time for all of them and Alex was ready to start work with a vengeance. Michael took Janet and Laura with him to the city. They were to stay in my apartment for a few days to be able to look around Wellington, our capital city, then go over on the ferry to the South Island.

Alex was up and working the morning after they left but I noticed he telephoned my apartment that night. This became a regular occurrence each evening after dinner; then, sometimes he would go out onto the veranda with his guitar and play soft romantic songs.

He is in love with Laura, I thought. I hope she feels the same way about him. I had a vision of him back in his shell, feeling rejected.

When the girls left for the South Island; he was the one receiving the calls. 9 pm on the dot, the telephone would ring. It was no use anyone else answering it, we knew who it would be for. It seemed that Laura was missing Alex as much as he was missing her.

They would be coming back to the farm for a week, before leaving for Honolulu. What is going to happen, I thought? Wilf asked me a similar question. We decided that all we could do was wait and see how the events would unfold.

I had to go into the local town one day; Alex gave me a lift, as he was going in for some farm supplies. The conversation was Laura, Laura and more Laura.

'Do you like her? Do you think she likes me? Do you think she would like to live in New Zealand?' The questions went on and on. I told him that I liked Laura very much, and I was sure she liked him and talking about living in New Zealand sounded very serious to me.

'I am in love with her,' Alex told me.

'I can tell you are,' I replied, 'but you hardly know her. I don't want you with a broken heart after a holiday romance; just give it some time.'

'There isn't much time though, is there? That's the point.' Alex sounded very anxious.

'See what happens when she comes back here, you will have a week to see each other,' I tried to comfort him.

He settled for that; we arrived in town and went about our separate business.

On the way back home we talked about Michael and Janet.

'They really like each other.' He explained that Janet had told Laura that she really liked Michael but was a bit in awe of his important job. "He's so clever," she had said

'Well, Janet is an intelligent girl,' I said. 'Perhaps she has an inferiority complex and under estimates herself. She's certainly an attractive girl and they look so good together.'

'Do Laura and I look good together?' Alex asked.

'Yes, you look very good together, an ideal couple.'

His face shone with happiness. I put up a prayer that it would all work out as he wanted it to. He needed a good break to help him sort out his life and he needed a good woman to join him. I hoped it would be Laura as I feared the alternative.

The girls came back, Laura spending all of her time with Alex, even going to work with him. She drove the tractor, moved sheep, mended fences and they both came home to dinner each evening looking healthy and radiant.

Janet spent time with me. We painted together and I saw she had a natural gift for colours. She saw the painting I was finishing. It was the one I had started the night Alex came alive again, that's all I can call it. It was sunrise over the sea, the pinks and golds over the water, the silhouette of flax growing in the foreground, and a tiny bird taking nectar from flowers in the morning dew.

Janet told me that Michael had forewarned them, Laura and her, regarding Alex being depressed about his knee accident and having to leave the Force, although he seemed fine and full of life now.

'That's the effect of you two coming here,' I told her.

'You mean Laura, don't you?' We looked at each other and laughed.

'Are you happy about them?' I asked her.

'Yes, they seem made for each other, my only worry is, is it a holiday romance?'

'I admit that I have thought that too,' I agreed. 'Did you enjoy Wellington?'

'Yes, I loved it, especially being on the water. Birmingham is in the middle of England, as you know, and I feel the need to go to see the sea every few months.'

'Perhaps you were a sailor in a past life,' I told her and we laughed together. I put on the jug to boil. 'What about some tea or do you prefer coffee?'

'Tea would be lovely,' she answered, 'Michael has a very important job, hasn't he?'

I remembered my conversation with Alex and was aware that Janet was nervous about Michael's position.

'Yes,' I replied, 'but nothing he can't handle. He is trained for it you know, just as you are trained in your career. It always seems more complicated to someone else but ask him to do your work and he would be lost. He probably thinks you have a very important career ahead of you, which you have of course. It wouldn't do for us all to do the same thing, would it? We are all equal, just contributing in our individual ways towards life.'

Very quietly she said, 'Yes, no one can be entirely alone, we all need each other to survive.'

I wondered what she had gone through in her childhood. Perhaps, with the death of her mother; she felt alone when her father remarried. I would have asked her more but Laura came in then to see what we were doing.

'Have you had a good day?' she directed at both of us.

We both said we had, and I asked what she had been up to.

'I have never walked so much in my life. It wouldn't be too bad on the flat but it's all hills around here.' We laughed at her.

It must be time for another cup of tea if you are back from work. I hope Alex is paying you for all this help,' I added.

'Gosh, living here is more than enough. We can never repay your kindness to us.

The time drew closer for them to leave and I could feel the anxiety in Alex; he had had a lot of time to talk to Laura.

He came to my room and we sat quietly as he related how he had told Laura his feelings for her and wanted her to stay. She returned his feelings but she had to go back home, then she would return.

She couldn't just leave Janet to go on her own. They had to finish the trip together, as planned. Alex could understand that, couldn't he? He did understand but wished it could be otherwise. Would she become engaged to him, until she could return to get married? She said she would.

Alex panicked because there was no time to buy a ring, so I loaned them one of mine, until they could get the real thing.

We booked dinner at the village restaurant for their last evening and toasted the happy but sad couple.

'Everything worthwhile is worth waiting for,' said Wilf as he gave the toast and we all raised our glasses to that.

Alex took the time off work to drive the girls to the airport. He wanted every last minute with Laura. At least he had something to keep going for now. They were spending two weeks in Hawaii, a month touring America, then England and home.

'I'll be back in October,' Laura promised Alex. They would have a Christmas wedding.

Alex arrived back from the airport with an enormous bouquet of flowers and a big box of chocolates from Janet and Laura to say thank you to everybody for being so kind to them.

It was two weeks later that Laura telephoned Alex to say she was coming back. She missed Alex too much and Janet said it was fine by her as she might get a job in Hawaii; she liked the islands very much. Both girls felt there was no need to return home as, although they knew their father's loved them, they were happy with their new wives. It would mean finding somewhere to live and work anyway.

Laura returned; it was still going to be a Christmas wedding, and Janet would come over from Hawaii to be the bridesmaid. Laura and I made plans for the wedding; a wedding I had never thought to plan, having two sons. I was going to make the most of it, and enjoy every minute of the preparation.

Laura asked Wilf if he would give her away. She liked the idea of a marriage service in the open air at the house. 'On the veranda; we could make it beautiful. Will it be legal, done like this?' she asked.

We assured her that it would be quite legal, she would be Mrs. Powell.

'Laura Powell, Laura Powell, I like the sound of that. Mrs. Alex Powell. I like that too.' We laughed with her.

Wilf was happy to have Alex on the farm He realised that his time away had made him appreciate the farm more. He had sown his wild oats and valued home ground, as well as being more responsible, now he was becoming a married man.

Michael would be Alex's best man. I wondered how he felt about Janet, but he kept his feelings to himself. I knew they wrote to each other, but they had been doing that for years, which had led to all of this happening in the first place.

It was Michael who told me that Janet had found a job, a year's contract, in Hawaii with an American Public Relations firm which specialised in tourism.

It was in October that I received a letter from Mary, my friend in England; it was bad news. She had discovered a lump in her breast. Those words made my heart beat faster; knowing from my own experience how she had felt.

The operation had been successful and now time and therapy would tell. I prayed that she would be as lucky as me and have no recurrent symptoms.

I sat down and answered her letter straight away. As I wrote the date 10th October, 1991, I felt a shock of recognition on two counts. One being the dreadful day in 1966 when I arrived in Australia to find my sister Jenny murdered by her husband and the other, my realisation that I had known Mary for forty years since we met when we started primary school in 1951.

The next piece of unhappiness came a couple of weeks later, when Jonesy's husband, Bob, died. He had not taken care when he had warnings, and kept on doing things he shouldn't have done. He had only been retired for a few years.

Jonesy knew she could keep on living in the same house. She still liked to come into the kitchen and potter about, feeling useful. She went to stay with her sister after the funeral for a week. I thought she may come back and tell us she had decided to go and live with her, but no. We had been her family and she was part of ours. A mother to me from the first time I had heard her soft voice when I arrived here at the farm.

We did get some good news not long after this. Emily brought it; her daughter, Susan, had a baby boy and they were calling him Stewart. Emily and Peter were so happy and invited us over for a drink to celebrate. She couldn't wait to go to see the baby and her daughter.

'Go as soon as you want to,' Wilf and I told her. 'We can manage the house while you are away.'

'Yes, we can manage,' added Jonesy.

It would be good for Jonesy to be back feeling in charge for a short while; keep her mind off her loss, as long as she didn't overdo it.

One day Laura and Alex asked Wilf and me if they could talk to us; they had a brilliant idea and wanted to know our opinion of it. We sat together in the sitting room and Alex explained.

Laura had been walking in the garden one day and, looking up at the house, noticed the window at the end of the gable in the roof. She asked Alex what it was for. He had taken her up into the roof space where, as children he and Michael used to play in the winter.

'This could be made beautiful,' Laura said.

'It would need more light,' added Alex.

'What about dormer windows. Would it be possible Alex?'

They had come down the stairs and looked at the front of the house and decided; yes, it would lend itself to three dormer windows.

So now the question was. 'What did Wilf and I think?'

'Let's go and look,' I suggested.

We all went out onto the veranda and down the steps onto the lawn, turning to look back at the house.

'It would look beautiful from the outside, but is there enough roof space height to justify all the work?' Wilf asked.

'Come and look,' Laura cried excitedly; aware that we were not opposed to their idea.

The space was very large. I had not noticed it before as there was no need to. It was just somewhere for the children to play safely and store unused pieces of furniture, trunks and things.

An architect came and measured up, he drew up the plans. Because the building was long across the front and had a wing going back from each end; it could be made into a substantial apartment. It would make an ideal home for Laura and Alex and I could keep my sitting room and spare bedroom, which I had intended giving over to them.

In no time the work was under way. Laura asked me if I would help her to choose furnishings and fittings. We had a great time in the shops looking at curtain fabrics, wall papers, kitchen and bathroom fittings; bringing home piles of samples and brochures for Alex and Wilf to see. The dining room almost became an office with the table spread with plans and the samples. We ate in the kitchen, most days, as it was impossible to keep on top of all the dust throughout the whole house.

Chapter 20 Relationships

I had to go to the gallery the following week, as there was a lot to be done on the approach to Christmas. Tony needed as much help as he could muster. He knew I had a wedding coming up but he appreciated a week of my time and I was sorry I could not give him more.

I collected many of the things, which had been ordered when Laura and I did our shopping, and headed back to the farm, anticipating Laura's reaction to the new curtains, lamps, sheets and bedcovers. She was delighted as she opened the parcels and showed them to everyone who was around. However, I felt a restraint in her; she was not the bright bubbly girl I had left behind. What has gone wrong? I wondered.

I asked Wilf if he had noticed anything; had Alex and Laura had a row or something. Is the work upstairs alright? There had to be a reason for such an obvious change.

'There is nothing wrong that I know of,' Wilf told me. 'Although, I have not seen much of Laura all week, come to think of it.'

The next morning I made a point of seeing Laura alone. I asked if she had heard anything about the job she had applied for.

'No not yet, the Hospital Authority will write when they know something,' she told me, 'The position could become available next year; maybe in February,'

'That sounds very hopeful; it will give you a chance to settle in after your honeymoon.'

Suddenly she burst into tears. She sobbed and sobbed. 'We shall not be getting married,' she cried.

I put my arms around her until she calmed down then holding her hands I asked, 'What do you mean?'

'Look at this,' she handed me a letter from her pocket.

'It's from my grandmother,' she said.

I took the letter, noticing the postmark from England. The address at the start of the letter was from my old home town. I read on. It was saying that Laura and Alex had the same grandfather. "The children you have could be daft." I smiled to myself at the northern expression "daft."

'Could that happen?' Laura asked me. 'I know it was not allowed at one time for first cousins to marry.'

I put my arm around her shoulders as I thought about it. 'Just let me think for a minute,' I told her, then continued. 'Now, your grandmother is Bridget Downey and she thinks that my father, Alex's grandfather is Ted Davies,' I started to laugh, then explained to the sad faced Laura. 'My father is Wilf, but no one in England knows that except my friend Mary.' I told her the story of Sarah and Wilf and the war years.

She was fascinated by the story. 'Oh, isn't it sad, they could not be together.'

'What I am wondering is what are we going to tell your grandmother.'

Later that evening I told Wilf about Laura's letter. He recalled Sarah's suspicions of her husband, Ted, before he went away in the war. I wonder if she would have felt she should stay with him if she had known he had another child and been unfaithful.

'It's all ifs,' he said sadly.

The day of the wedding drew near, and everyone was in a flurry of excitement. There had never been so much continuous movement about the place. Workmen finishing off the upstairs apartment, curtains being fitted, carpets laid and furniture being delivered. The number of times Laura called me up stairs to ask me how I like this or that; does it look better here or there as she carried pictures around the room to find the best position before making holes in the walls. She would place a lamp on a table in a corner then step back to view it from every angle of the room. It was lovely to see her so happy again, her mind at rest about her future family not being "daft."

Seeing all the new furniture and sparkling clean paint made me notice how shabby my sitting room was. I decided to have the decorators do something about it.

I called Laura to come down from the apartment to turn the tables on her and ask her opinion of colours for my room. Wilf came looking for me and asked what we were doing now. I explained and he looked around the room He did not say anything but, later that day, he asked me if he should do something with the rest of the house before the wedding. It was becoming catching.

By the actual wedding day, everything was beautiful. The decorating was finished and the apartment liveable. The weather favoured us with a bright sunny day. Michael had met Janet at the airport and they had travelled to the farm together. The marquee was in place, the dance floor put down and caterers swarmed everywhere. What seemed chaos, suddenly fell into place and tranquillity reigned.

The guests all sat facing the house in anticipation. Alex stood on the veranda with Michael at his side. The music changed and everyone hushed. Laura came through the door at the far end of the veranda on Wilf's arm, Janet behind her. The contours of the white silk showed off Laura's lovely figure and her hair shone through the light veil. She carried a bouquet of peach coloured roses and her satin shoes were a perfect match to them.

Janet's dress was the colour of Laura's bouquet. The colour enhanced the creaminess of her beautiful skin and contrasted with her dark hair, which was decorated with small white flowers and she carried a posy to match.

I watched Alex as he looked at Laura coming towards him; there was no doubt he loved her; no second thoughts about getting married. He was positive in his action and it showed as Laura approached him.

I noticed that Michael's eyes went straight to Janet and I wondered what his thoughts and feelings were.

The service started and, as I listened, I reflected on the number of times I had heard those same words. I prayed that they would be happy. They did not even know each other existed at this time last year. Please let the future be good to them.

In no time at all, everyone was drinking and enjoying the wonderful selection of food on the buffet.

I told Wilf how calm and proud he had looked as he walked along the veranda with Laura. He said how nervous he had been, having never done it before, but how happy he was to have experienced the moment he never expected to know.

'I should have been there for you,' he told me wistfully.

I held his hand as I told him that he would have been there for me the second time, had not Stephen died and I would have been so proud.

'I love you, Wilf Franklin,' I said as I hugged him.

'And I love you too, my darling daughter,' he kissed me.

The speeches over, the music began and Alex took Laura onto the dance floor. They swept around the floor as though they had been doing it for years; two bodies in perfect tune with each other. More couples joined them and the photographer moved around with his video camera, capturing the movements of the dancing couples.

The sun went down and the dancing continued; the music changing to a popular disco theme. People sat on the veranda watching the scene; some reflecting on the past and how things used to be, others on the future and how it will be.

Laura and Alex had looked radiant when they started the dancing, a perfect pair. They had been joined by Michael and Janet, who also looked so right together. I did hope it would work out for them and I was amused as I watched them; they had no idea how other people saw them, with eyes for no one but each other. I wondered what their problem was. Perhaps it will dissolve with this experience. I hoped so. Time can be so short, as I had found out.

Michael had to go back to his office on the Monday and Janet would go back with him, although, she had another two days before her return to Hawaii. So, they would have some time alone together.

I had noticed a change in her since her return; she was more confident and self-assured. Working suited her and gave her a maturity that comes with independence.

The honeymooners came home; they had loved Tasmania. It had been Laura's choice of place to go. There had not been time when she and Janet were in Australia. It's such a big country. Alex would have gone anywhere, as long as Laura was with him. Married life suited them both as they brimmed with health and happiness.

I went down to the gallery a few weeks after the wedding. Tony went on at great length about how wonderful the wedding had been and what a lovely place the farm was. He wished he had accepted my previous invitations as it was so peaceful in the country. I laughed as I reminded him of the noise over the last few months.

'More peaceful here in the city,' I said.

Michael had dinner with me one evening and, of course, the conversation was of and around Janet.

'She seems much more self-assured,' I ventured. 'Do you think it is because she is working?'

'Oh yes, definitely, she really enjoys it. She seems to have dropped into the right line of work straight away, and she can do that kind of work anywhere,' he added.

'Does she ask you about your work? Why I ask is that she seems in awe of what you do,' I told him what Laura had said.

'I don't think it is what I do but I think she doubts her own abilities, having never earned her own living, but now she is working, well, you have noticed the difference in her yourself.'

He had explained to Janet how the legal system worked and talked about the type of cases he handled. He told her of Legal Aide for people who couldn't afford to pay the fees and how he liked to work on these cases.

They had so much in common, like music, books, films and even politics. She was very interested to know what is happening in this country politically and they talked about world affairs too.

He told me how he was missing Janet and how her coming back for the wedding had proved it not to be a holiday infatuation.

'I wish I could be more impulsive like Alex and Laura.'

'But you are different sorts of people. It wouldn't do for us to be the same. There is nothing wrong with being cautious and making sure. That is yours and Janet's natures. What about her coming back here to work?' I asked.

'She has a year's contract and will not break it.'

'That is good. It shows she is a reliable and responsible person.'

The next time I saw Michael was my birthday. He came to the farm for the weekend. He was very excited about something and wanted my opinion. It appeared that a Member of Parliament was hinting at retiring and it had been suggested that Michael might like to try for the seat when the time came.

I said that anything that could make him sound so happy must be good and he had always been involved in politics since he had returned from England anyway.

'It's just that I had not thought in that direction,' he said.

When he told Wilf, he was delighted and thought it a great idea. 'You are just the right sort of person we need in government; wish there were more like you,' Wilf said as he shook Michael's hand.

It was also Alex's birthday, and being twenty-five years old meant he could have his inheritance. He was astounded and had no idea there was anything from his grandparents.

'Why didn't you tell me?' he asked.

'It would not have been a lovely surprise then, would it? 'I replied as I too enjoyed seeing his smiling face.

Laura had been successful in getting the job she had been hoping for. A woman who had left to have a baby had not returned to the job so Laura had been offered it. She travelled each day by car to the hospital in town.

'If children can go on a bus each day, then I can go by car' is what she said when Alex pointed out the distance. She loved the work and as with Janet I noticed a new confidence about her.

Summer passed and the chill of autumn came. It was in July that Michael told me he was taking his holidays and going to Hawaii to see Janet. I wondered if he would bring her back with him. He did more than that!

I received a telephone call from Michael to say that they had just been married in a chapel by the sea. They were very happy and hoped we were at their news. They would be back in New Zealand in two weeks.

I told him how happy I was, what lovely news and could I speak to Janet.

Janet's voice was very emotional as I told her how happy I was for them and she apologised for not having the wedding at the farm with everyone. It had obviously bothered her.

'Perhaps we can have a blessing when you return,' I said.

'That's a good idea,' she replied, with relief in her voice.

'Bless you both,' I said, 'See you soon.'

When they returned, they looked radiant. We sat at the kitchen table looking at their wedding photographs. Janet was wearing a simple white dress with flowers in her hair. They were barefoot in the sand, with garlands around their necks.

Janet gave me a present. It was a model carousel. The horses were painted white with gold flowers twisting down the poles. It was delightful and as I turned it, music played.

As the carousel went round so did my memory; back with the familiar tune, our tune, Martin's and mine. Back to the dance the evening when we became engaged and I floated on air once more.

'Are you alright Maggie?'

I came back to the present time. 'Yes, yes, I was just in a daydream. I'm fine.

Michael told me that he had missed Janet so much; writing letters had made it worse, not better, so he had decided to do something about it. He had told her about the retiring Member of Parliament and his name being put forward. Well, it was now definite and he wanted her to come back to New Zealand and share his life with him; to go into this from the beginning, together.

Janet had told him that she had never felt so alone as when they were away from each other; it was as though a large part of her was missing. The past year working in Hawaii had been a wonderful experience and had opened a gateway to her future; changing her from a student into a woman.

It was a very busy time for them as they campaigned for votes. If they can survive this they can survive anything was one of my many thoughts as I heard what they had to do.

Michael was very popular in the city in so many ways. He was known to support charities and physically get involved in raising money. Both Michael and Janet had done parachute and bungee jumps, which had scared me to death, but voting day was near and we were all with fingers crossed that Michael would be successful.

Chapter 21 New Zealand 1993

As I stood in my sitting room, looking out at the view over the hills, I heard Wilf's car. It brought me back from the past and into the present time. I went out to meet him and gave him a hug and kiss.

'It's so good to have you back,' I said.

I don't know whether it was the tone of my voice or what, but Wilf asked me what was wrong. I could hardly speak from pent up emotion, so took a couple of deep breaths and told him about the letters.

He asked to see them and I gave them to him to read. I made a pot of tea while he looked at them, then joined him in the sitting room and we discussed them, each voicing our opinions.

It was so good to have him to talk to. Wilf told me that Michael knew he was adopted and explained to me the circumstances but he did not think Michael knew about the happenings in Australia.

'Will you leave this to me now, Margaret? I promise to sort it all out. I don't want you to worry anymore. If I could get my hands on whoever did this, I would strangle them on the spot.'

We had a quiet dinner together, Wilf opened a bottle of wine and we sat and watched the television for a while. The relief of having Wilf home and to talk to made me relax for the first time in days and I quickly felt weary. We both had an early night.

The next day I wandered about, filling my time, waiting for 6.30pm to come round. Wilf had said he would take the call. He knew what he was going to say. Just a pity he couldn't get his hands down the telephone. Just before 6.30pm Wilf asked me to sit in front of the television with him. I was becoming more and more agitated as the time approached. Wilf had said, "Trust me," and I did, implicitly. He had turned on the television but the sound was mute, we sat together waiting, as the seconds went by. When the phone rang I jumped in surprise, although I had been expecting it.

Wilf calmly rose, or at least he looked calm to me. He picked up the receiver and listened a while then said, 'I know who you are and I advise you to watch channel one, right now.'

He put down the phone, walked to the table, poured two glasses of wine and handed one to me. He sat by my side on the settee and pressed the control of the television. The sound came up.

The regular nightly interview, by well known presenter was just starting. Michael was being introduced to the audience.

'We wish to welcome our new Member of Parliament,' and so on, and so forth. 'I would like to congratulate you on your appointment. I also understand that we have something more to celebrate; your birthday!'

A tray with a bottle of wine and two glasses were brought on by an attractive hostess. Wine was poured, glasses touched, happy birthday and thank-yous were said.

'Now Sir, may I ask, have you any 'pet' projects up your sleeve that you want to work on?'

Michael smiled; the content had obviously been chosen carefully.

'Yes, as a matter of fact I do.' Michael's face became serious.

'I am greatly concerned by the increasing number of battered women and their children; their need for help. In many cases help could be given before it gets to such a serious stage of looking for a sheltered home. You see, I too am a child of such a situation.

As Michael told the background of his early life, a mental picture came back to me of Jenny sprawled on the bed, covered in red lipstick and 'SLUT' scrawled on the wall above her head.

The autopsy had shown many breaks in her bones. Mark must have thrown her about like a rag doll. Her mouth showed she had been gagged for some time, her tongue was swollen and there was semen in her throat. There was severe bruising to her stomach, and a rupture many days old; she must have been in agony for days.

Mark's autopsy had shown he had died of a gunshot wound to the head. However, he also had a massive tumour on his brain.

I was brought back to the present by Wilf squeezing my hand. Michael was saying that his mother's sister, Maggie, had become his mother and he felt proud to call her that. She had not only been a mother but a very good friend too, he told the reporter.

He went on to explain that he had been lucky, so wanted to help those less fortunate.

'I would like to propose a toast to her,' Michael said. They lifted their glasses, looking towards the camera, as though straight at me. 'To Maggie,' Michael said

'To Maggie,' the interviewer repeated.

Wilf poured another glass of wine and we touched glasses.

'Here's to Maggie, my wonderful daughter,' he said.

'Here's to Wilf, my wonderful father,' I said.

'Sounds as if we're back in the mutual admiration society again,' said Wilf.

We both laughed; a laugh of relief.

The interviewer was thanking Michael and wishing him luck. It was over, with everything out in the open. There was nothing to fear. Who it was sending those letters remained a mystery. I hoped and prayed that be true but I reckoned Michael was not the kind of man to tolerate blackmail and so . . .

After the television interview, Michael and Janet came to the farm for the weekend to celebrate his birthday with us. We had planned it many weeks before and I was so glad of that, as over the past week I had been useless at making decisions on anything.

The letters had taken over my mind completely. I wanted desperately to talk to Michael, to ask him questions and explain so many things and most of all to thank him for his understanding. There is no wonder he is in the position he is, in government; he has a maturity that is very rare in a young man, and others must have recognised it.

The party was wonderful in every way, the food was marvellous and the atmosphere was joyous and peaceful. I realised my happiness was many fold. I had let go of so many years of restraining aspects, keeping secrets that no long needed to be kept. The relief was tremendous. I had not realised how much strain I had been carrying until I was able to let it go. I felt so light as if a great weight had been lifted from my shoulders. A weight that I had carried willingly but now gladly let go.

When I did get some private time with Michael he explained that when I was ill, with my cancer, he had needed his birth certificate for his passport. He had not wanted to bother me in hospital, so had looked in the drawer where he knew I kept all my papers. At first he could not find it although he came across Alex's so he delved further thinking it must be at the bottom of everything. He eventually found it.

He became interested in the certificate, looking at the names and dates and comparing it with Alex's. He talked to Wilf about the past although he knew that I only knew Wilf was my father when Alex was born because I had told him the story about the war years. The boys had loved to hear these stories and of the times when I was a girl at school. I had told them of my sister and how she and her husband were killed in a car crash, as had been my parents and the death of Martin, their father and how brave he had been.

Wilf had sat quietly with Michael and told him something very important had happened when he was a baby and that his real mother was my sister who had died and Margaret had brought him to New Zealand, as her son, along with Alex. She had always intended to tell him, but the time never seemed appropriate. She did not want to stir up past memories that could upset him; the doctor had advised her on this. It had seemed better to let things be and the years passed.

'"When Margaret is well again you could ask her about it," Wilf had suggested to Michael, "but I don't want to rake up the past for her, not when she is under enough strain as it is. Let's pray that she gets through this operation. I don't know how I will cope if anything happens to Margaret. I've had her in my life for such a few years, I know I am being selfish but please don't upset her in any way. Wait until she's really well before you go delving into the past."

'Don't worry; as far as I am concerned Maggie is my mother and if my real mother was her sister, then it's all the same family anyway. Not like a complete stranger.'

This knowledge had satisfied Michael for many years, while he was away at University in England having a busy life. He did say that he had wondered about his father, although he knew that Mark and Martin were brothers and there, again the same family.

It was not until he returned to New Zealand to work for a law firm and I gave him his inheritance that he once more became curious. He contacted the solicitors involved and asked for more details and so eventually learned the whole story.

I asked him why he never told me he knew.

He said it was about the time of Alex's depression and we all had enough concern, without bringing up the death of my sister and the horror of it. He also realised my reasoning to do what I did, in not wanting to stir up memories for him. He understood my decision and how difficult it must have been to adapt to it, so why upset anything. He thought I had been very brave and had I not been there for him he could have been in a children's home or fostered by complete strangers.

I said I could not have done it without Wilf to help me.

'He's a good man,' Michael said. I was his mother, as far as he was concerned, Alex was his brother and Wilf his grandfather.

When Wilf had told him about the blackmail letters he was sorry for the agony I had been through and the best way to deal with it was to speak out on television, to be completely open and let everyone listening know how he felt about his past.

'I just wish I had told you I knew sooner then we could have sorted it out without you getting upset.' Michael said, 'I just wish I knew who did this to you. I would not like to be in their shoes, if I find out.

'I would like the letters, if you don't mind,' he said, 'I may be able to find out something. Obviously a sick mind, but it's best to know who my enemies are then I will know how to deal with them.'

Some very good news came from Janet, she was having a baby. It would be born around the New Year.

So, the weeks passed, I had an exhibition to get on with, a lot of work to catch up on. After my mind being occupied, as it had been, the relief was enormous and my energy returned. I had a new lease of life and a new perspective to apply to my painting.

I was in the city at the gallery when Michael called. He wanted me to have lunch with him. We went to our favourite little restaurant, overlooking the fountain. How handsome he is I thought as he came towards me, how proud I was of him and my heart swelled with love. Can a child ever realise it is given this kind of love? Only when they have children of their own, I thought. I wished Michael and Janet that knowledge in the near future with their child.

We ordered our meal and Michael started to tell me a story. After the blackmail episode, he had made many enquiries, talked to friends of his in the police department, off the record. There had not seemed much he could do until yesterday. Apparently, a woman had been caught going through the customs in Australia, carrying a parcel of drugs. She was very sick and had been taken to hospital.

'She has given doctor's your name as she wants to see you to tell you something,' Michael told me. 'She will not speak to anyone else. The police had thought it a gimmick but decided to contact the police in Wellington, and I was informed.

'I must go,' I told him. I knew I had to. Michael was concerned as he could not accompany me at this time. No matter, I would call Alan, and would stay with him.

Chapter 22 Asha

Australia 1993

I flew out the next morning. Alan met me at the airport. It was so good to see him after so long. We hugged each other then he held me at arm's length.

'It's wonderful to see you, Maggie, you are looking so good.' His eyes twinkled with merriment, obviously happy to see me.

I basked in his praise. I felt good.

'I'm sorry I could not get to Alex's wedding, you know how it was.'

'Yes,' I said, 'I am so sorry about Kathleen but she's out of pain now isn't she. How are you getting along without her?'

'As you know she was ill for so long, I'm used to being on my own. She was in the nursing home for over two years before she died.

'I've just seen Diane off to England, she wants to get as much experience as she can and has a chance to work at a gallery in London.

'She always took notice of you, Maggie, and greatly admires your work.'

'Well, Alan, I will always be happy to support her if she comes back to New Zealand.' I have a gallery there as you know.'

I looked at him as he carried my case and put it into the car. He was still such a handsome man. I flipped back in my mind to the first time I had seen him, coming out of Jenny's house, and how he had become such a dear friend. Perhaps had circumstances been different and I had just been Jenny's sister visiting them for a holiday, then, maybe, we would have become more involved but it was too soon after Martin. My concern, at the time, was to get Michael away as the Psychiatrist had suggested.

They were sad times, and I was very confused also realising I was pregnant by my dead husband. I had thought my periods had stopped through shock and stress over Martin, but no, I was over three months pregnant.

I came out of the past when Alan opened the car door. He took me straight to the hospital. I said I would tell him all later. He kissed my cheek and said to call him when I wanted him to come and collect me.

I entered the hospital in trepidation of what was to come and was directed to a small room, where I met my half-sister for the first time. I realised that finding out that Wilf was my real father makes her no relation really. However, she was Jenny's half-sister and I decided not to make Asha any wiser. She was dying, she knew that. How she had lived so long was a mystery to her.

She told me that she did not remember our father. I let her believe Ted was my father too. Her grandfather had told her how Ted came to be with them in the war. How her mother had found him on the beach and thought him to be dead but she had felt a faint breath and pulled him away from the water. They all thought he would die from the infection to his severed arm but Siwa persevered, using special leaves and bark to bind his wounds and making mixtures for him to drink. He started to recover. It was dangerous for them to stay in the village on the beach because of the Japanese soldiers so they moved into the jungle. Siwa made a bed that could be pulled along and that's how they moved Ted with them. Some of the people objected to him going, saying he would be another person to feed and what could a man with one arm do? Siwa said she would feed him and she would grow crops and work.

As Ted recovered he used his engineering skills to set up new ways of doing things that the people did not know. He brought water to the crops and living area by constructing a type of aqueduct and gained the respect of all the people in many ways and was accepted amongst them.

Ted and Siwa lived together and she became pregnant and had Asha; a perfect little girl. Life had gone on and years passed until the Japanese attacked and many people were slaughtered. Ted was knocked unconscious but when he came round and searched for Siwa he found her at the edge of the clearing, dead. She had curled her body around Asha to protect her. His little girl was alive. He became more and more one of the people and had not someone else told the American soldiers when they arrived, at the end of the war in Japan to liberate the Islands that Ted was British, he would never have left the village.

Her grandfather told her that, after a year, money started to come from England; money to be used to keep and educate Asha, when she became old enough to attend school. Grandfather opened a bank account; the money came from solicitors in England with a funny name, Banks, Banks and Brady. The three Bs grandfather had said. He told Asha to be sure to remember this.

She enjoyed learning about the world and would look at the atlas, at the map of Great Britain and pick out the name, Newcastle, where grandfather said Banks, Banks and Brady were. Her father must be near there too. She used to think and plan in her mind to go and see him one day. Only in her faintest dreams did she imagine him coming to the school to see her. She saw him as tall, dark and handsome, arriving at the school and her running towards him to be lifted off the ground and swung around like grandfather had done when she was a little girl.

I could see Asha's eyes starting to close and I thought she was going to sleep. I did not want to tire her too much, so sat quietly by her side and I too felt my eyes drooping. I must have slept only a few seconds but was awakened by Asha touching my arm. She continued as though she had never stopped, so may have been in a day dream.

She said, 'One day I was called to the principal's office and told that my grandfather had died. I ran upstairs and flung myself down on the bed and wept and wept; who would look after me now? How I prayed for my father to come. Maybe, when he heard that grandfather had died, he would come and take me back to England with him. I would look after him just like my mother had done all those years ago.

'Weeks passed and I was called to the principal's office again. My heart leapt at the thought of my hopes and prayers being answered. I opened the door and a man turned to me as I entered. It was my Uncle. My heart dropped as I had met him only once before at my grandfather's funeral. I had not liked the way he looked at me and, when he spoke to me, he had a creepy voice.'

'I am going to look after you now. There is no more money for fancy schools and you will have to earn your living. I followed him from the school, carrying my belongings in one case. It was my birthday, I was fourteen years old.'

I thought, she is two years older than me.

Asha continued, 'I was taken to a house in the city where there were other girls. Not girls like at school. No uniforms here. These girls wore silky garments and shiny high heeled shoes, lipstick and make-up on their faces. I thought they were quite beautiful.

I was taken to a room, quite a small room with only one bed. In school I shared with six girls so to have a room to myself was wonderful. The view from the small window looked down into a court yard filled with dustbins and rubbish. It smelt nasty. I was shown around the house and told I could help in the kitchen, preparing the food. After a few days I was allowed into the office. My uncle said, why waste all that education and that I could do some paperwork for him. Add up figures in the books.

Through the glass window in the office I watched many men come and go, up and down the stairs. I was peeping through the window one day when the man I was watching saw me and came and looked through the window. A few days later I heard this same man talking to my Uncle.

'"Are you keeping that one for yourself?" he asked Uncle. "I will pay double for that."

'The next evening after I had had dinner, I was taken to my room by one of the girls. She gave me a silky dress to wear and put lipstick and eye shadow on my face. My hair was combed into a fashionable older style, then, I was told to look in the mirror. The person looking back at me looked like a woman. I saw that through the silky dress my breasts looked larger as they swelled under the material and my nipples stood out. As I turned the silk swayed and showed how my hips rounded from my waist. Hands clapping behind me made me turn to the door; my Uncle stood there.

'"I am going to teach you how to really earn your living," he said.

He signalled for the other girl to leave then quietly closed the door. He came towards me and put his hands on my shoulders, my skin crept with fear and revulsion.

'"First, I want a smile on your face and you keep it there, whatever happens to you. Do you understand? You must look as though you are enjoying yourself and are happy. You know what the other girls do in their rooms don't you."

'I did know and had tried to imagine doing it myself but felt horror at the thought of those fat ugly men sharing my bed.

'"I am going to teach you how to please me and every man you meet' and he started to remove my dress.

'He sat on a chair and made me kneel down in front of him, undid his zip and pulled my head forward. I closed my mind and did everything as Uncle directed me to do. What else is there for me now? I felt total despair. My father will not want to know me now, not now.'

Asha told me she planned her escape, as the years went by.

'I will get to England, to my father. I will not tell him about this life here. I still did the books in the office and Uncle made me sort out the money into piles before it was put into the safe. I never made mistakes as I was clever. I devised a plan.

'I did not record some of the men's visits, especially when Uncle was away. I had to be very careful which visits I did not record or he would think those girls were not working well and they would be in trouble. I kept the very small amounts in a safe place in my room. I was also very careful with my tips. The girls were allowed to keep their tips to buy their bits and pieces of what they fancied. If we were good with our clients then sometimes the man would leave his small change on the table by the bed for the girl to keep. It was always best to do everything the man wanted then, he might leave a big tip.

'One day I realised that something was out of place in my room. I closed the door and looked in my special place. My money was there and my heart stopped pounding with the relief of seeing the money intact but who had been in my room searching. I thought of each person in the house and it came to me that Uncle had been very peculiar about the books recently. He was always in the office these days, checking things. Does he suspect I thought; what should I do? Should I leave now? Have I enough money? I will have to make some concrete plans to move on.

'I read the papers and decided on a district to go to on the other side of the city. I would hide there and write to England to the solicitors. A few days later, Uncle said he was going to be away on business for a few days. Now is my chance I thought. I bundled up my few belongings, taking nothing that I could be accused of stealing, except the money of course but no one knew about that. I left the house saying that I was going to the market; nothing wrong with that. Perhaps when I do not return they will think I have been murdered or something. Nobody will worry about me; just another girl that disappeared. Oh how good that would be but I will not know if that is what they think. Uncle might come looking for me. I had hidden my things out in the yard at the back of the building, so I left the kitchen with only a small bag. I crept around the back making sure no one was there and retrieved my bundle from the hiding place. I walked away, wanting to run but not wanting to attract attention to myself. I walked and walked further and further and came to the park area.

There were tourists about, mostly dressed in European clothes. I knew I was near the centre of the city. Now I had to get to the other side. As far away from Uncle as I could get. By the time night fell I was exhausted, and crawled into the doorway of a shop and fell asleep. I was awakened by someone tugging at my arm; a small boy stood over me.'

'"Who are you?" he said.

'"Go away, I want to sleep," I replied.

'"You'll get caught," he said as he ran away.

'I looked around the corner of the shop entrance and a policeman was coming along the pavement. I ran too; the boy whistled from across the street and I ran across to join him as he disappeared down an alleyway. He waved from a doorway then bobbed back out of sight. I crept towards the doorway.

'"Boo," he called, laughing as I peered into the darkness. My heart jumped. His face was all smiles at my reaction.

'"My name is Tony, what's yours?" he asked.

'"I am Asha," I told him.

'"What do you want here?" he asked.

'"I am looking for a job,"' I replied.

331

"'If you can sew, I can get you a job," Tony said.

"'I can sew. Where is the job?"

"'Here," he said, pointing into the doorway. I looked at the sign on the side of the entrance. It said it was a Garment Manufacturers.

"'I know the big boss," Tony was saying, 'come on.' He pushed open the door and led me up a steep stairway, as we went up the stairs and through another door the noise of people's voices became more distinct. There was a large room with big tables and many girls sat sewing by hand.

Through a door at the far end of the room I could see another room through the glass panes and when this door was pushed open I could hear the sound of sewing machines. In the corner was a glassed off section. The office I thought. A man came out of this area when he saw Tony and me.

"'I've got a good worker her Mr. Mac," said Tony, indicating me.

"'Is that so Tony, and how would you know what I need."

"'Mr. Mac is from Glasgow in Scotland," said Tony ignoring Mr Mac's question.

"'I need a job Mr. Mac," I said. 'I am a very good sewer and I can use a machine or sew by hand.'

"'Well now it must be your lucky day, as one of the girls is off sick and I have a special order to get out." He turned to face the room, which I realised had gone quiet. All the girls were listening to our conversation; still doing their work but their ears wide open.

'"Now then girls, looks as if Tony has turned up trumps for us. Do you think he deserves a medal?" The faces turned towards him and looked blank. They did not know what he was talking about, but someone said yes and they all agreed. Yes, yes went around the room.

'Tony looked pleased. "Have you any deliveries for me today, Mr. Mac?"

'"Later lad, later," said Mr. Mac, "let's get this girl to work. Now I wonder what you can do. Let's try you over here." He indicated a table and a girl came forward.

'"Get her going on the blue blouses," he told her.

I settled myself where I was told, so that I could watch how to do the work. I could not believe my luck, a job!

'A whistle blew and everyone put down their work and left the room.

'"This way," my instructor indicated with her finger. It was time for a break.

'We sat outside in a yard at the back of the building, the girls eating their food. I took something to eat out of my bag.

'"Do you have anywhere to sleep," a girl asked.

'"No, not yet," I replied.

'"My name is Li, you can sleep at the hostel. I sleep there too."

'The whistle blew again, back to work. I was very interested in the work and happy to have found a job so quickly but by the time we were allowed to finish my back was aching. I went with Li and most of the girls up another flight of narrow stairs into another large room.

'There were mattresses around the walls, some were already spread on the floor and girls curled up on them fast asleep. Li lead me to a corner of the room, she said something to an older woman and another mattress was produced from a large cupboard. There was a lot of chatting now they were free from work and some girls started disappearing through a door and reappearing through another door further down the room carrying plates of food.

'I followed Li, we picked up a plate and joined the queue. A woman was serving food; a spoonful of rice and a spoonful of a brown mixture. It must be meat of some sort I thought. We sat down to eat our food, I felt very weary, so much had happened to me since I had left Uncles to pretend to go to market. What a long day. I curled up on my mattress, my arm though the handle of my bag. Li will awaken me when it is time to get up I thought and I fell asleep.

'I worked for weeks and weeks, never leaving the building; it was a secure feeling. We did not get paid very much and our food and board were taken out of it. There was very little left but I did not need very much. I was happy in the work and the routine, the girls were good company and there were no men making their demands on me. I was very content.

'I had written a letter to the solicitors, Banks, Banks and Brady and the day I received a reply I couldn't wait to be on my own to read it. My excitement became despair as I read my father had died in a car crash in February 1964. I knew that Uncle had been taking my money from when my grandfather had died and keeping it for himself, making me believe I had to work for him.

'The money my father had been sending must have stopped around the time I had noticed a change in my Uncle, perhaps he was searching my room to see if I knew anything. My mind ran about in all directions looking for answers and I felt better at having taken money from Uncle as he had been taking mine for years. Much, much more than I took.

'What happened to my father?' Asha asked me. I took hold of her frail hand and told her about the crash on the night that Martin and I became engaged. I told her of the lovely dinner we had together before they drove home leaving us to join our friends at a dance. I told her about my marriage to Martin and his death while saving a child's life two years later. I asked what had happened to her so she continued her story.

'The months passed and I was transferred to another section. It was promotion as Mr. Mac was pleased with my work. There was a man who distributed the work to the girls. His name was Shi. He seemed to like me and the girls teased me about it. I liked him too. He was very nice, quite good looking but much older than me. He gave me more and more important work, special beading on expensive garments made of beautiful silks. These garments were a pleasure to work on but a strain on the nerves in case anything went wrong but I received more money for such work.

'Many years went by, and then I started to be sick. I bought medicine but it was very expensive and my savings dwindled quickly. This went on a long time and eventually I could not go to work. I was not allowed to live in the hostel if I was not working. I did not know what to do. I had never thought of this happening to me. I lay in the hostel one day too ill to go to work when Shi came to see me. We had become very good friends.'

'"I am sorry Asha but you must leave the hostel if you don't work. It is the rule. Other girls need to be employed and have somewhere to live."

'"What can I do?" I asked him.

'"You can come and live with me, I have my own room," he said proudly.

'"You live on your own?"

'"Yes and you are welcome," he replied

'I had no option and he was very kind. I moved in to share Shi's room. He was a very considerate man and told me that he had always liked me but was shy and thought that a young girl like me would not be interested in an old man like him.

'"You are not an old man," I told him. "Why did you never marry?"

'"As I said I am very shy and I looked after my mother after my father died. I always seemed to be at work with no time or money to spend on girls but now my mother is gone. She died last year, I am free."

'With the caring from Shi and not having to worry about working, I soon recovered. I would always be weak but well enough to work. Shi had become used to me being at home when he returned from work. I always had a hot meal ready for him and made his homecoming very pleasant. He did not want me to go back to the workshop, so being in charge of work distribution he arranged for me to do work from home.

'Mr. Mac had said that was ok and to look after your little lady. Mr. Mac knew what a good worker Shi was. It would have been hard to find and train someone who knew the girls and their work as well as Shi did.

'There was a little yard where we lived, just enough room for a bench to sit on and a few pots of plants to make it pretty. I used to spend a lot of my time out there. Shi used to bring work home for me to do, making sure it was special work and I got well paid. Without my hostel and food to pay for, I was well able to contribute to our expenses.

'Life took on a secure feeling. It was like I imagined what being married would be like. Shi never mentioned marriage and I did not want to upset him. We slept in the same bed and sometimes we would make love, but not like with

Uncle and the other men. It was very gentle. Shi was a very considerate man.

'One day I got a terrible fright when I was in the market place. I turned around to see a man looking at me. My heart pounded and my temperature rose. It was Uncle. No, it wasn't, he was too young to be Uncle. The man looked as Uncle had looked when I left his house and I realised how much time had passed. How many years had gone by since then and how old Uncle would be now. He may be dead I thought but I am not going to find out. How lucky I have been. It was a fortunate day for me when I moved in with Shi.

'Many contented years passed; Tony had become quite important in the factory. Shi told me that Tony might take over from Mr. Mac. The whole business had grown so big. Over the years, Tony used to pop in to see me and call in for a chat between doing his deliveries. We would talk about the past and I would call him my saviour. Had I not met him in the doorway those many years ago, what would have become of me? Tony said I was his favourite, like a sister. He would sometimes come for a meal in the evenings after work and as we sat eating I felt as though I had a real family.

'This all had to change. Tony came to see me one day with a very sad face. He told me that there had been an accident, Shi had been knocked down by a car and taken to the hospital but had died of a wound to his head. The car had never stopped. My days became so black I had had twenty beautiful safe years with Shi; years without worry and with a wonderful man. I was thankful for those years. I knew I had to keep working and Tony arranged this for me. My work was very important, special orders that had to be kept secret for the Fashion Houses in Europe Tony had told me. It was getting harder on my eyes but if I worked outside in the sunlight, I could manage. It became difficult to pay all the bills on one wage.

'One day, as I was passing a bar, I noticed an older man looking at me. He was indicating I join him at his table. I walked over to the table and sat down wondering if I was imagining it but he asked me to have a drink and we talked. He made a suggestion which at first I declined but then thought about the money and the bills to be paid. We went back to my room and this became a regular weekly occurrence and it helped with the rent.

'Over the months I built up a regular cliental of nice men, then one day a man called to see me. He said I needed someone to look after me, to protect me from being beaten up by someone. My heart froze as I knew he meant he would beat me up if I did not pay up. I told him I was too old for business, couldn't he see. Just look at me I told him, trying to make him see he was wasting his time; he should be looking after some younger girls.

'"Yes, you are right," he sneered as he hit me across the face and thumped me in the stomach, "Bloody old," he said and walked out.

'I had fallen on the floor hitting my head against the dresser. I eventually crept over to my bed and curled up in a ball holding my stomach against the pain.

'Because I had not put anything on my face to stop the bruising the next day I did not go out of the house. I was frightened to let any of my clients come near in case I was being watched by the man. My sewing was delivered and I worked through the day. The pain in my stomach did not go away and I had to get more medicine; medicine costs money. How I wished that Shi was with me but I must be strong, I must manage.

'The years went on and I became more ill, my eye sight getting worse; I was given sewing to do but not the special kind anymore. Tony did all he could. He worked at a new factory now way out of town. He was also married and had a family of his own to look after. He came to see me sometimes. I always tried to be cheerful when he came and thanked him for his kindnesses.'

Asha's eyes started to close again and she drifted off to sleep. I sat quietly by her side while she rested.

When Asha awoke, I asked her how she knew about me and she continued her tale.

'I was in a bar one evening having a quiet drink, a couple were dancing and as the music stopped I heard the young man ask the girl if she would like a drink. My attention was drawn by his English accent. The girl agreed and they sat down in the next booth to me. The young man signalled to a waitress and ordered the drinks. The girl asked his name.'

'He replied, "My name is John."'

'I was half listening; the other half of my mind was remembering the days when young men wanted to buy me drinks. Now, I was lucky when the lights are dim or a man has bad eyesight.

The young man asked her name and she replied that it was "Susu".

'"That's a very pretty name," he said. Their drinks were delivered, then I heard her ask where he came from and he said England.'

'"Yes, I know that from your voice," said Susu, but where in England?'

'"From the north," he said.

'"Do you live in a big city?"

'"Yes, a city called Newcastle."

' Newcastle! What I heard made my heart pound. I had to have another look at this young man; any connection with that place was a connection with my father. "Remember the three B's," my grandfather had said.

'Even though it was years ago and I knew my father was dead, I wanted to look. Perhaps, my father had been like this young man at this age. I sat until they were leaving and followed them. They went to her place and I waited. Eventually, he left and went to where he lived.

'I did not know what possessed me to behave like that but I had to know more. I found out where he worked and followed him whenever I could. I watched him come out of the offices for lunch and join other people. I watched him after work, sometimes going home, other times going into a bar or for something to eat. I had to talk to him. It became an obsession with me.

'The opportunity came in the same bar where I had first seen him with the girl Susu. He was sitting alone at the bar, probably waiting for somebody. I sat next to him and ordered my drink. I looked at him and said, "You are from England aren't you?" He seemed deep in thought but answered "Yes" in an uninterested manner. I tried again and told him the town the solicitors said my father came from.

'His head turned, "where did you say?"

'I repeated the name.

'"I know that place," he said with more interest. "I know people who live there. What is your name?"

'I told him and my father's name and how I was born during the war.

'"Shall we go and sit in a booth to talk; it's quieter over there than here at the bar," He said. "Let me get you a drink." I could not believe my luck.

'John asked me questions and I answered all I knew. I told him about the solicitors, Banks, Banks and Brady in Newcastle and the letter from them telling me my father had died in a car crash in February 1964 and how the money he had been sending had stopped at that date. I did not tell him about my time with Uncle.

'John asked to see the letter which I always kept with me. I took it from my handbag and gave it to him. He read it and was quiet for a long time, obviously thinking deeply. I did not dare disturb him, although, I wanted to know so much. He looked up at me. It was a look as though he was seeing me for the first time; a searching look.

'"You have two sisters," he said.

'My body froze inside as though I had stopped breathing.

'"One of them died."

'I felt sick. "The other one?" I asked.

'"Oh, she's alive alright."

'I felt relief. "Please tell me all about them," I begged.

'"The older one died as I said, the younger one is called Margaret. Not young now though."

'"Tell me about her," I asked. His voice started to change as he spoke about Margaret.

'"She lives in a big house, has a new car whenever she wants to, flips around the world as suits her, thinks she's the Queen she does, the bitch is rich and famous."

'"How has she become rich and famous?" I asked.

'"Painting, she's an artist; used your money to go to New Zealand to live."

'"What do you mean?"

'"Don't be stupid woman; you should have had your share when your father died."

'I thought of my life, the horror and wasted years. The fear I had of each tomorrow. John ordered more drinks. He was getting drunk and me with him. I didn't have to think of tomorrow yet. Just another drink made it seem further away.

'Yes John was right. I had been done out of my inheritance; first, by my uncle, then by my own sisters. I asked John if he would help me to go and see my sister in New Zealand.

'"Don't be stupid woman; she wouldn't want to know you."

'I felt hurt by his words but he had been around here long enough to know who and what I was and he was right. Who would want to know me, especially someone rich and famous?

'Now I started to feel angry too and bitter like John sounded. "Why do you dislike her?" I asked him.

'"Dislike her, I don't dislike her, I hate her and I hate her son more." He spat out the words. "You should hate her too. I will get back at him though."

'"What has he done to you?"

'"He took my girl, the rotten bastard, the rotten bastard; I'll get him though."

'We had another drink and John said, "I'm going back to the UK next week. Give me your letter and I will find out anything I can. Who knows what news I might bring back?"

'I handed him my precious piece of paper. The only contact I had with my past.

'Three weeks went past, three weeks of tormented anticipation. I had dreams and nightmares, dreams of how it could have been.

Dreams of meeting my sisters, coming towards each other with open arms of greeting, hugging each other.

'Oh, the feelings in dreams are so real. Then the nightmares, back with Uncle and the terror of escaping from him and hiding from him, until I would awake with the realisation and the feeling of the thump- thump of my heart as if it was going to burst.

'The night arrived when we had arranged to meet again in the same place as before. I was there very early and sat where we had sat the last time we met. It seemed as if time had stopped. I looked around the bar, people were doing the usual things but in slow motion. I wanted to hurry them up. I wanted the clock above the bar to move on. Then, there he was, walking towards the bar. I wanted to attract his attention but did not want to leave the table. I might lose it to someone else. Damn that my glass was empty; if I get up it will look as though I am leaving the table for good. It was too noisy for me to call to him. I felt desperate; he turned, drink in hand and looked about him. I stood up and waved my arm as high as I could. He saw me. Oh, the relief. I felt on a high and that's without drugs; on just real anticipation. Please let him have some good news for me. He seemed to saunter across the room. He stopped to talk to someone for a few minutes then continued towards me.

'"Hi there, how's things?" He asked.

'"Ok, did you have a good time?" I dared not say, have you anything good to tell me. I had to wait; aware, even in the short time I had known him, of his volatile temper. Like a spoilt child who has to have his own way.

'"Yes, I had a good time, if that's possible in that bloody cold weather. It's supposed to be spring, more like the middle of winter."

'"Did you go to Newcastle?"

"Oh yes, I went to check out my flat there. I rent it out to a friend of mine, so stayed there for a couple of days; nothing broken, everything in order."

'I waited.

'"I went to see your solicitor, showed him the letter; it was his father who had dealt with it years ago but he was interested in the story, so he looked out the file on the case. Apparently his father had been instructed to send on money which he received at three monthly intervals for your grandfather who had opened an account for your education. It continued like that until the accident in which Ted Davies died. There was no further instruction about inheritance; that was the end."

'"It only tells me what I already know. My uncle was keeping my money for himself until it stopped arriving; how easy for some people to steal and break the law; people who know how. Perhaps my sister Margaret will help me, if she knows the story. You say she is rich, she could afford something."

'"I told you before she wouldn't want to know you; not because of the money but think of the scandal; her father's bastard daughter. I bet her mother did not know either. In those days it was different, another country and culture to what you know. Everybody worried about what everyone else thought; the neighbours, friends. It did not matter about the person involved but how it looked to anyone else; scandal; hide it away as though it never happened. No, I have a better idea, you can get your inheritance and I'll get my revenge."

'John put his hand into his jacket pocket and brought out two envelops. One he handed to me which I recognised as the one I had given to him containing my solicitor's letter. The other he put onto the table and tapped it with his finger.

'"This is how," he sneered. "I need a drink. What about you?"

'Did I need a drink I thought? Yes I need a big one.

'We both knew what we meant. It was the start of something between us. Let's start it well. He signalled to the waitress then went back to the envelope on the table.

'"I want to show you something." He opened the envelope and took out two pieces of paper. Handing me one of the pieces, he asked, "What do you think of that?"

'I took the folded paper and unfolded it as though it was a hot brick. It was a newspaper cutting of a wedding photograph. I looked at the people and tried to read the printing underneath. "I cannot see properly in this light. Tell me what it says."

'His finger pointed to each person. "The bride and groom in the centre are Michael and Janet Powell, on one side is Alex and Laura Powell, the groom's brother and sister-in-law and on the other side is the groom's mother, Mrs. Margaret Powell and Mr. Wilfred Franklin."

"My sister Margaret." I wished my eyesight was better. I took the cutting back from him and held it up towards the dim light on the wall above our table. "I must go to the Ladies room to see this. The light is better there."

'Making my way across the bar to the Ladies room, my throat felt tight. I had to see Margaret and her family. I stood under the bare light bulb and searched the photograph. How I wished it was in colour. I went into a cubicle and sat down to think in peace; the words underneath said it was a "Blessing of a Marriage" which had taken place in Hawaii.

'I tried to imagine the colour of the clothes they were wearing. Margaret's hat was quite small, whereas the younger woman was wearing a large picture hat. The bride's dress was ankle length, not full but hung as though made of some soft flowing material and she too wore a picture hat. I dreamed that I was there outside the church on the steps where the photograph had been taken.

'I was brought back from my dream by someone banging on the door of the cubicle. How long had I been here, I wondered. Perhaps John had left. I hurried back to the table, relieved to see him still there. A woman was leaning over him, her dress hung open at the front; trying to sell her wares I thought. Oh please, don't let him be interested in her. He looked up as I approached and the girl stood back. I sat down at the table, the girl looking from me to him and back. Obviously wondering what his interest was in me. She was young and beautiful with a firm slim body.

'"Later" I heard him say to her waving her away with his hand.

'She turned slowly, hands on her hips in a provocative way, pacified for the moment.

'"Thought you had left; you were a long time."

I' ignored the remark and asked him to tell me about the wedding.

'"You know as much as I do about that but that's my girl not his."

'"Tell me about her then. Any information would be welcome to me."

'"I have loved her for years. Watched over her and protected her. When she was at university I used to sit behind her in some of the lectures and let the other men know she was mine and to keep away from her. I know she liked me as she used to turn and look at me sometimes. She dropped her books once, I helped her pick them up and I touched her hand as I gave her back her books. She was shaking; her hand trembled as it touched mine. I knew then that she had strong feelings for me.

"'When she went into the coffee bar with her friends, I used to sit in the corner, just to look at her. She sometimes sat with her back to me but I knew it was so that she could see me in the reflection of the window. I knew that she would grow to love me the more we saw each other. In the university holidays I used to go to where she lived but she only spent a short time there. She worked with a girlfriend in a hotel in Devon. I went there too but did not let her see me. I watched them on the beach and swimming in the sea. I will marry you one day I vowed.

"'You will be mine. I knew I had to have a good job to be able to get married and I had an interview with an oil company. Its good money on the oil rigs; two years of that and I could buy us a house and she too would be finished at university by then. I liked being older than her, in charge of things. At the end of her last year at University I heard that she planned with a friend to take a year off before working.

"'They were going to see the world; Asia, Australia, America touring and working their way around the globe. She would be ready to settle down when she came back but she met him Michael ruddy Powell. He must have rushed her into marriage before she knew what she wanted.

"'You asked why I hate him, now you know. He has ruined my life. There is no girl in the world like Janet. The only girl for me, but I'll make him sorry, I'll make him pay. With their high, fancy ideas, thinks money counts for everything they do.

He will know what it's like to have everything taken from him, and to have to grovel to other people. Everyone will know who he really is and the lies they live with."

'He stopped ranting and reached for the other piece of paper in the envelope, this time he opened it himself very carefully and handed the paper to me. It was much older than the first cutting, the date at the top said 11th October, 1966. It was part of a page from a newspaper, one part of it being outlined in green ink.

'"What is it?" I asked.

'He remembered that I could not see in the dim light.

'"It's about your sister. She was beaten up by her husband and murdered then he shot himself."

'I felt shocked as he read the newspaper report, very sad and upset. This was not just anybody he was speaking about but my sister; the sister I had never known; we shared the same father, her blood and mine were the same. I had been beaten and abused over the years, never knowing that my sister was being treated in the same way. I did not think that could happen in England. I had never thought about the possibility before, in my mind it was a country where everything must be perfect; people were always trying to get permission to go there.

'"I know they had a baby before they left England. I also know that the baby must be thirty years old now. While I was in England I checked the date of birth; just guess Michael's birthday.

Yes, they are the same dates. Michael is the one Margaret calls her son; mother of the groom, it said in the wedding photograph."

'"I wonder if Michael knows he is adopted," I said.

'"More important," John said, "does he know his real father murdered his mother then shot himself? I know he does not know, I know he has no idea about any of it."

'"How do you know that?" I asked.

'He touched his nose, indicating I was being too nosey. "That's my business. I wonder how much it would be worth to Margaret to keep it hidden away where it has been for twenty seven years. That's where you can get your inheritance from. How much do you want?"

'"That's blackmail," I answered. "I can't do that to my own sister."

'"Ok" and he started to fold up the paper cutting. "No skin off my nose, suit yourself."

'From the corner of my eye I saw the young girl sidling towards him.

'"Tell me more," I said quickly, "what do you have in mind?" Once more I had his attention.

'"Way I see it, even if Michael did know he is adopted, he does not know about his past. In which case, Margaret has something to hide." John was talking out loud as though to himself. "Whichever way it is, the public do not know who he is, it could ruin his future. He's in a very important position in New Zealand. A position of trust and could become a Member of Parliament very soon, according to the reports in the newspapers.

'"He seems to have an unblemished record, a real goody, goody; too good to be true. The papers would love a story like this one, especially the opposition party. Find one weak link in the chain and the rest will fall apart, they say. One lie and they look for more and soon people start to mistrust, not reliable anymore, they would say. Can't trust him; it's human nature to doubt."

'The voice went on and on, revelling in the downfall of this man. This innocent man, the son of my sister whichever one, they were both my sisters, so Michael is my nephew. How could I be party to this; I did have a choice as had been pointed out to me but what was in it for him? If Margaret paid up to keep everything hidden, how would John get anything out of it? I asked him that question.

'"Stupid," I cringed at his words and tone. "When she's paid up I would still let the papers know. That would be my sweet revenge, reading the headlines in the newspaper; Government Minister Resigns." His eyes had a glazed faraway look, a stiff smile on his thin lips.

'"Why would you do this for me?" I asked.

'"Ah well, that's another story. You get your inheritance and you do something for me in return."

'"Do something for you," I was thinking, "what could I do for you?"

353

"I have a little job for you. I have a package I want delivering. If you deliver the package for me, I'll sort out your sister and get you fifty thousand US dollars."

"What I cried, fifty thousand US dollars. I can't believe that." The thought of that amount of money knocked me back in my seat.

"Quiet," he said touching my arm. From the corner of my eye I once more saw the young girl watching us. He turned and waved his hand to tell her to go away. "I am going to the New Zealand office next month, I will check everything out and bring back your money, trust me."

"She won't pay that much money, will she?"

"It's peanuts to her, peanuts to keep her lies and secrets out of the papers to protect her wonderful son. She will pay up alright by the time I have finished with her she will be a wreck and glad to get it over with. So you see, I get my package delivered, you get your money and I get my sweet revenge and we all live happily ever after, as the fairy tale goes."

'How could I do this to good people? I was thinking as he spoke, then I thought of my squalid little room, my age, what I now see when I look in the mirror, how am I going to even earn my living and I need to go to the doctors. I am not well, but it all costs money, a lot of money. Margaret has enough to spare, peanuts is what he called it. I could live the rest of my life in comfort. Perhaps travel to some of the places I have seen in magazines. With some new clothes, no one would know what I am, maybe, I could even go to New Zealand to see Margaret, she would not know me of course but I could look at her, maybe, even speak to her. Oh dreams, they all take money; I realised I was being given a chance, not a very nice chance but the only one to get out of this life.

'Oh that it could have come sooner, years ago but the fact that it has come at all must mean that it is meant to be. I knew that the package to be delivered must be drugs. I knew what could happen to me if I was caught. I read about it in the papers all the time. There was always a catch to anything. I had learnt this as a lesson many years ago, so it was not unexpected. What were my alternatives; stay as I am or risk everything, deliver the package and wait for the money. Risk everything, I said to myself. What is there to risk? I had the answer. "I'll do it," I told John.

'So, a partnership was formed; one for money, the other for revenge.'

Asha was becoming much weaker, her eyes starting to close. I asked her one more question.

'Tell me Asha, who is this John, what is his other name?'

Faintly, she replied, 'John, you know him as Jonathan . . .'her eyes closed.

'Jonathan,' I repeated but she was asleep.

The only Jonathan I know is Mary and Ian's son, one of the twins. I felt sick as I thought about it. I am Jonathan's godmother; I have not done a good job. In fact, I have not done a job at all.

Somehow, leaving England and living in New Zealand seemed to take me away from that responsibility. He had two parents to look after him and guide him, two people I greatly admired for their wisdom but it answered a lot of questions as to where he got his information; my letters to Mary all those years ago.

I thought of Mary and how ill she is; she has not been as lucky as I was, her cancer had broken out in other parts of her body and Ian's devastation at what is happening to her. In her letters to me she wrote of Matthew and how well he is doing as a partner in his firm of accountants but more proudly of Jonathan and his job abroad. How little she knew her son and she would be made no wiser by me, not in the last few weeks of her life.

I thought of Asha being duped by him and not getting her money and conned into taking another or more packages through customs and getting caught.

Oh, had I known I would have given her the money and stupid Jonathan; I would have paid him to let me know I had a sister but he was not really interested in the money. As he had said to Asha, he wanted the downfall of Michael. There was so much I did not know.

I returned from my reverie and looked at Asha, her eyes were still closed. I squeezed her hand gently, she looked at peace, she had passed on; no more worries about tomorrow for her.

I telephoned Michael to tell him of Asha's death. I did not tell him about Jonathan, I would tell him later when we were alone.

I called Alan, 'Can you fetch me home now?'

'I certainly can,' he replied.

There was a calendar on the wall above the telephone; someone had ringed today in bright red marker pen. Was it a birthday? For me it was another fateful day. It was the 10th OCTOBER 1993.

I sat a while in thought; going back over the years.

10th October 1966

Remembering Jenny and Mark and my time at the Children's Home and my first sight of Alan with his magnificent tan and Kathy, his lovely wife for so many years and now gone.

I heard the door open and looked up to see Alan walking towards me. As I stood up he held his arms open and I walked into them; he held me close and whispered my name. I had the feeling once more that I had come home and a great peace spread over me.

THE END

About The Author

Beryl was born in the north of England. Over the years she spent a lot of time in Australia, New Zealand and America. She is now retired to live and write in Cyprus and is an active member of The Paphos Writers Group.

This is her first novel and is now working on the second part of this trilogy.

If you enjoyed my story watch out for "Suzies Secret" coming soon.

Beryl Lowe